PERFECT

Other Books by Harry Kraus, M.D.

Could I Have This Dance?
For the Rest of My Life
All I'll Ever Need

PerFecT

Harry Kraus, MD

ZONDERVAN®

ZONDERVAN.com/
AUTHORTRACKER
follow your favorite authors

Perfect
Copyright © 2008 by Harry Kraus

Requests for information should be addressed to:

Zondervan, *Grand Rapids, Michigan 49530*

Library of Congress Cataloging-in-Publication Data

Kraus, Harry Lee, 1960–
    Perfect / by Harry Kraus.
       p. cm.
    ISBN 978-0-310-27284-7 (softcover)
    1. Traffic accident investigation—Fiction. I. Title.
PS3561.R2875P47 2008
813'.54—dc22

                                            2007039350

Interior design by Michelle Espinoza

Printed in the United States of America

08 09 10 11 12 13 • 22 21 20 19 18 17 16 15 14 13 12 11 10 9 8 7 6 5 4 3 2 1

For the only perfect one.
Hebrews 5:9

PERFECT

CHAPTER 1

I peered over a box of Special K at my husband and smiled because today I was going to run away with another man. The back of the cereal box was emblazoned with a doleful woman being pampered by four men. "Win a Cosmopolitan makeover." I crunched the healthy flakes thinking about my plans to change my safe life. Today is the start of a new me. I reached for my husband's Cocoa Krispies and sprinkled the sugar-laden morsels onto the top of the reliable whole wheat. That was me. Healthy. Doing the right thing. Drowning in a well of good intentions. My husband's eyebrows rose—a nearly imperceptible gesture, but I caught it before he refocused on the *Wall Street Journal*. I slid the sweet over my tongue and chewed my revenge, crushing every calorie and refusing to feel an ounce of guilt. I was done with that. At least for now. Down with fiber. Up with chocolate and other sins.

I was the daughter of a Christian minister. That alone was enough to keep me from divorcing Henry. Every denomination has its top ten list of evils. Of course divorce wasn't as high on the list as homosexuality, but it certainly made the top three. So I had never given it serious thought. Murder, I'd contemplated. Divorce, never. I was a good Christian.

Until today.

I was sure the church would be quick to raise their eyebrows in judgment. I'd been doing it myself, and it had stopped me from acting out my dream a thousand times. But I'd been riding a dizzying pendulum from comfort to desolation for months, and I'd decided to escape.

I was married. But I was alone.

I'd sat in church. But I felt abandoned by the faithful.

I was anxious over my plan. But terrified of the inertia that had anchored my life in sameness. Sameness could be good if your skin reflected your heart. For me, I'd lived a lie, and knew I'd die if I kept smiling in front of my pain.

Henry reached for a knife and dissected an English muffin. It threatened to split unevenly, but he paused and teased the rebellious bread into even halves. Exacting work, performed with flawless dexterity. He was a surgeon, a dreadfully good one, and I was part of his perfect world.

"What time's your flight?"

I'd told him three times. "Eleven." He still thought I was going to a business convention. *I am*, I told myself. *I'm in the business of rescuing my life.*

"I should go with you."

My gut tightened, but I remained outwardly cool. With all the smiling I'd done in church, I should get an Olympic medal for divorcing my face from my feelings. "You have a paper to write?"

He sulked. "Funny."

The last time I had taken Henry to a convention relating to my work, he had spent a week locked in a hotel suite ordering room service and writing a paper on outcome predictors in patients with multi-system organ failure or some such folly of life-and-death importance.

We lived on a wooded knoll just north of Charlottesville, he the prodigious surgeon, and I his adoring wife. Our house and yard were *Southern Living*-perfect. We vacationed in Europe, dined at the Boarshead Inn, and worshiped at First Baptist. Of course, I'd known for years that Henry only worshiped himself, but he didn't seem sick of the hypocrisy of spending an hour in the Lord's house marveling at his own greatness. Well, I for one was ill of pushing under the surface the reality that boiled beneath the calm.

We drove his and her's Mercedes, both sedans, even though I had wanted the convertible. We had a diversified investment portfolio, season tickets to see the Virginia Cavaliers play football, regular seats at the Washington Opera, and sex three times a week, all managed with surgical efficiency. I had heard Henry brag that he'd removed a gallbladder from a patient in nineteen minutes once. "Skin to skin in under twenty minutes," he beamed, in the surgical lingo for time from opening the skin to closing the skin.

That's fifteen minutes longer than he spent with me last night, I thought. *Skin to skin in less than four minutes.*

I'd spent my professional life reading subtle clues, the whys and hows of motor vehicle accidents. Skid marks, velocities, folded fenders. These were the things that whispered their secrets to me. It linked me to Henry in a weird sort of way. I figured out what happened at crash scenes. He took over from there and did the neat life-saving stuff. That was Henry. Captivated by the inner workings of anatomy and physiology, but blind to the cause-and-effect of the road we'd traveled together.

This month Henry and I would have been married for six years, happily for six months. Once I stopped worshiping him, he seemed content to purchase my affections. It worked for a while. But it was going to end today.

I'd clawed to a position of respect as an accident reconstructionist. As a consultant, I was valued by law enforcement and insurance companies alike. As a professional witness, I was feared. But my hard-earned identity ended when I left my occupation bubble. Everywhere else, I was defined by the men who loved me. I was the pastor's daughter. Dr. Henry Stratford's wife.

I didn't hate him. It's hard to hate someone who won't fight back. I'd tried endlessly to get him to hear me. And not with subtlety. I bared my soul, then my fangs. He walked away, silently slinking back to the hospital and the operating arena where he was king and lord. Henry J. Stratford, Jr., M.D., Ph.D., F.A.C.S., F.R.C.S. So many letters that they had to use two lines on his office door at the University of Virginia.

I was young. A trophy wife. Blonde from a bottle only because he wanted me blonde. I'd been arm candy at so many cocktail parties where I'd listened to the boys of surgery that I thought I could fake my way into the club. Just name an organ and attach *-ectomy* or *-otomy* to the end, rant about long room turnover times, reference Billroth, Halstead, or DeBakey every fifteen minutes, and complain about low reimbursements and Medicaid.

I'd spent the last five years smiling when potbellied men talked about blood, pus, feces, urine, or worse — as if secretions and their quantity should interest anyone but the ones who charted them for fun and profit. If Henry was the prototype, I thought, surgeons should be quarantined from the public, unleashed only to yield the blade to heal, and then herded back to their own boorish brood.

The sweet brown milk in the bottom of my cereal bowl called for more. I shook out the last of the Cocoa Krispies and avoided my husband's eyes.

"Back on Sunday night?"

I smiled again and turned my cheek to accept his goodbye kiss. Functional. To the point. Predictable as the way he double-checked his fly before leaving the house. "I've told you six times, Henry."

He looked past me at his briefcase. On to the next subject. The next patient. The next case. "I'm giving Grand Rounds this morning."

"Mmm." I gave him the dutiful answer he deserved. It was all the encouragement he needed to continue while I stared at the last floating piece of puffed rice. I chased it around the bowl with singular determination. It bobbed and weaved before I gave up and lifted the bowl to my lips. It's the new me. Down with etiquette. Up with savoring immediate pleasures like milk saturated with syrupy chocolate.

"Our data shows that prehospital IV resuscitation of the penetrating trauma patient actually worsens outcomes over the—" He stopped midsentence and watched as I backhanded the milk about to drip from my chin.

I smiled demurely, set down the bowl and intertwined my fingers on the table. I tilted my head to let him know he had my undivided attention and loyalty. It was a body-language lie, further evidence of the heart-face disconnect game I played.

He arrested the drop of his chin and, with a slight shake of his head to show his shock at my behavior, continued, "— the scoop-and-run approach where the paramedics avoid the time delays of field resuscitation."

"Mmmmmm." This answer was intentionally longer than the first to show my growing interest in the bull that issued from his pontifications.

He paused on our tiled foyer and studied himself in the full-length mirror. Our friends thought it was for me to check my designer dresses. That's a gas. Spend one morning with Henry and you'll see why we have a mirror there. It was seven feet high and framed in oak, gold-leafed and antiqued with little dents. Stress-patterned to look old. Appearances can be deceiving. The hall table was behind him with a bouquet of fresh-cut daffodils offset so that they would appear to his right when he admired his reflection.

He touched the edge of his graying temple. The hair was just above his ears and full enough to make me jealous. Check. He traced the outline of his tie next. Silk. Designer insignia. Tied double Windsor without a dimple. Check. He patted the front of his Italian suit. Check. He pivoted just enough to see that his pants weren't riding up on his socks. Check. Zipper. Check. He took a deep breath, filling his lungs with fragrance from the daffodils. With his chest thrust forward he was preened and ready to face his adoring public. Almost. Zipper again. Compulsive check number two.

"Call once you're in Denver. You can leave a message with Grace if I'm in the theatre."

I suppressed a desire to roll my eyes. He had called the operating rooms the theatre and even spelled it in the Queen's English ever since his days as a trauma fellow in London. It fit him. The problem was, he was near the pinnacle of surgical perfection and he knew it. I caught myself smiling again, because this morning I'd decided I was going to allow myself to think the curse words that would make my pastor father blush. "Of course."

Denver, hah. I was going to be sunning on white Caribbean sand. I was not going to visit my nursing-home-bound mother for a week. I was not raising money for the medical auxiliary to replace the monitors in the ICU. I was going to seduce the choir director from my father's church, drink frozen mango daiquiris, and make love for longer than three minutes.

I stood and interposed myself between my husband and his adoring reflection. "Kiss me goodbye."

He paused. I was interrupting his routine. He leaned his head to the side to check his part.

"You're perfect," I whispered. "Now kiss me goodbye."

His face danced to the right, trying to avoid my lipstick. I countered. I wasn't going to settle for duty. This was no time for a peck on the cheek. I wanted this last embrace to mean something. Down with superficiality and haste. Up with passion. I wanted to live each moment. Mechanical was out. I wanted spontaneity, maybe even a little aggression.

"Wendi," he whined. "Your lipstick."

"I'm leaving," I said. "I want to kiss you goodbye."

I felt his will eroding. He wouldn't fight. Henry didn't do mad. Maybe that was what drove me crazy about him. He couldn't ascend an emotional mountain peak. With Henry, it was all flat roads. The ice cream was all vanilla in his world.

I pushed up on my tiptoes and puckered for a final memorable Stratford kiss and suddenly remembered our very first time.

I was his patient. I'd heard of his reputation and sought him out after my gallbladder no longer agreed with my desire for cheese pizza. It wasn't until my last postoperative visit that, looking up at the ceiling of his examination room, I felt guilty for how attracted I was to my physician.

Dr. Stratford stood over me and nodded his approval. "How's your appetite?"

When he touched me, I felt the heat in my cheeks. I tried to speak, but my voice cracked through the desert in my mouth. "It-it's fine. Good, really."

He leaned closer, inspecting the small scars. "Without a gallbladder, the bile will drip slowly into the bowels all the time, not intermittently like before. Some patients experience a loosening of their stools for a few weeks after surgery, but that's normal and should go away."

I had no idea what he was talking about. All I knew was that every time this man touched me so tenderly, I found myself breathless, longing for something more than his clinical exam. He nodded, and I saw the edge of a smile sneak upon his lips. He stood proudly, admiring my abdomen, touching gently and staring with all the attention of a sculptor approving of the curve of his work.

It was to be my last visit. I'd recovered sufficiently to be outside his watchful eye. I gathered the gown across my body, covering the pretty lace unmentionables I'd worn just for him. They were a departure from my normal modest Hanes and a definite venture away from the narrow path of my church life, but I knew that he'd have me strip to the bare essentials. I'd even worn red lipstick, trying on three shades that morning before choosing.

I'd fallen for him hard by then, and he was my savior.

I dressed behind a flimsy curtain while he sat on an examining stool and listed the reasons I might need to contact him. Redness of the wound. Fever. Chills. Increasing pain.

"Dinner," I said, pulling back the curtain.

"Excuse me?"

I giggled. "Reasons to call you." I shrugged as if my heart wasn't beating in my throat. "Dinner sounds like a great reason."

He stood and retreated, but I wasn't turning back. If I walked out of that office without a date, Dr. Stratford would disappear from the room and my life would never see fulfillment. "I — dinner," he stammered.

I pushed forward until our breath mingled, and he looked like at any moment he might call for his nurse, who'd exited after my exam. "Is that a yes?"

He stood speechless.

"Kiss me," I ordered. Where that came from, I'll never know. *Somewhere between my childhood dreams of being an Air Force cadet and the fantasies I'd had about my surgeon for the last four weeks*, I thought.

To my surprise he obeyed, hesitating for a moment because of my lipstick, I'm sure. Our lips met and our future was sealed. After a second or two, he pulled away and gasped. Where my red-lace panties failed, my desperately forward behavior scored. He pulled me forward and kissed me again.

Now, seven years and countless Stratford kisses later, I rose on my tiptoes and puckered for a goodbye. As his face danced right to avoid my lips, I mirrored his movements, a perfect man-to-man defense. I wasn't going to let him get away. "Kiss me."

He complied, and my lips met his. Passion met obligation. Freedom and lipstick versus responsibility and duty. I won. He responded by pushing me against the mirror.

"Easy, tiger," I said, straightening his tie. "You need to give Grand Rounds."

He looked at himself and wiped his lips on a handkerchief. He turned towards the garage, having regained his professional demeanor. He cleared his throat and nodded at me. "Goodbye, Wendi."

"Goodbye, Henry."

I watched him disappear through the doorway into the garage, thinking I'd enjoyed our first embrace more than our last. I reached beneath the waistband of my jeans and snapped the edge of my fancy lace panties. *It's odd*, I thought. *I haven't worn that particular pair since my first kiss with Henry.* But this morning, I had gotten up with a new resolve to live from my heart, and I found them, like so many of my dreams, crumpled and nearly forgotten in the back of my undies drawer. *Imagine that*, I thought. *My entire relationship with this monotonous man has been framed by the same pair of unmentionables.*

I took a deep breath.

I'd said goodbye.

It was time to pack. Out with stuffy business suits. In with things two-piece and revealing.

CHAPTER 2

I lifted the curtain from the front window and watched as Henry drove away, his Mercedes pausing at the end of our one-hundred-foot driveway. His turn signal was on, another obsessive behavior that I couldn't understand. Who in heaven's name was behind him to see it, anyway?

He sped on towards Route 29, which he would take south into Charlottesville. I glanced at my father's church across the street and let the curtain fall. I analyzed my emotions. Knowing this was the last time I would watch Henry leave from this window, what should I feel?

Sad? Hardly.

Despair? Don't make me laugh.

Guilt? Maybe a little. All good church-goers feel guilty.

But as of this morning, my plans would take me far from the fold of good Christendom. My Christian life was a prop, an implant of sorts, something I'd worn for so long to look proper that I'd forgotten what naked felt like. But I was done with that. I'd put on for so long, I was cancer-sick of the act. What began as a one-act play at a wilderness church camp had settled over me as a life-role. Today, I planned to shed my skin and let the world see a bit of the snake within. Was I the proverbial wolf in sheep's clothing? Perhaps, but I'd grown so used to the wool sweaters of Christianity that I wasn't so sure I could recognize the real me.

Today, I was taking off the wool. Goodbye perfect house. Goodbye perfect husband. Should I feel remorse? I shook my head to answer my own question, aware that I was departing from a life-path that was predictable and comfortable, if a bit boring. I felt like a child ready to jump rock to rock to cross a rushing stream. I was ready to find my way, reaching my toes forward into the future, testing the stability of a stone and then committing to a launch that promised freedom of new life at the risk of a slippery fall.

Mostly, I was aware that I felt little of the loss that I thought I should feel. Henry was a surgeon, a provider comparable to few. He'd certainly lifted my social status. He had given me everything I wanted.

But nothing I needed.

Henry was gone.

I had dreamed of this moment for months. I was about to do what I imagined millions of nice Christian women dreamed of doing but dismissed as out-of-the-question outrageous.

Henry's gone.

I took a deep breath. I hadn't even left him yet, and already a familiar guilt tugged at my conscience. I pushed it away, determined to give it a shove so hard it wouldn't threaten me again. The moment called for music, something danceable—another sin. In my teen Sunday school class they always called dances "foot-functions," so as not to raise the eyebrows of crotchety Miss Fogberry. From today, I would dance.

I pulled a CD from my private stash and ejected one of Henry's symphonies. "Thirty-nine Minutes of Bliss (In an Otherwise Meaningless World)" by Caesars. I pressed the forward diamond on the front of the player and waited for the sounds of "Jerk It Out." I gave the volume knob a healthy twist and bobbed my blonde locks to the rhythm. I danced back into the foyer and performed for the mirror, shaking my hair and my Christian backside with such liberty that I laughed out loud.

Jesus would like this, I thought. He must not have been a pew-sitter akin to Miss Fogberry.

After the song, I lifted my hair and thought about keeping it. It was fun bouncing it from side to side. I shook my head. Nope. Today it's history. Along with this house and my marriage.

I contemplated my position and wondered how someone arrived at a place like mine, a life so whitewashed that no one saw the real me. On routine days, I thought I'd even fooled myself, accepting my appearance and my words at face value. I'd never intended for it to be this way. I never thought I could be bold enough to leave my husband, my family, or the church.

It wasn't that I didn't have good reasons. If anything, I should have run from the sheepfold at fourteen, the moment a trusted leader in my father's congregation robbed me of my innocence. But instead of running, I followed my mother down a path of deception, outwardly smiling as my soul-wound festered, red with pain. And month by month, I tried not to cry. And soon I mastered a smile so natural that even I had trouble recognizing the real thing.

But today wasn't a day to mull over my past. Today was a day for rebirth of the new me. I was a woman with a purpose. I marched

down the hall towards my bedroom, a physical attempt at corral-
ling my emotions into a fence of confidence.

I flopped my American Tourister onto our king-size bed. I'd
packed with Henry watching. That wasn't fun. This was going to
be. I opened the bottom drawer of the mahogany bureau. It was
easily a foot deep and four feet wide. In one motion, I dumped the
entire contents of the suitcase into the drawer and whumped it shut
with my foot.

Then, I entered estrogen central, my walk-in closet. It was big
enough to house my Mercedes and contained a wardrobe easily
double the value of my car. I'd hidden a few things in the back
behind my furs. It was silly, I knew, because Henry had looked
in there once in six years, and even then, he backed out pale and
breathless.

I replaced the business attire with four bathing suits and three
cocktail dresses, including one with a slit so high up the side that I
was sure Miss Fogberry would get angina if she was still alive. *God
bless her lemony soul,* I thought, adding a sexy black teddy. With
each item, I imagined my sister's approval. Unlike me, Rene had
lived her life in open rebellion against our parents' wishes. She was
a bold, in-your-face sinner, and I envied the happy way she gulped
life, like she'd just surfaced from the bottom of a pool thirsty for
air. Rene was evil. When she was thirteen, she paid for one movie
ticket and got lost in the theater to watch three different films. She
lived with her boyfriend in New Orleans, a city brimming with
temptations I blushed to discuss. But Rene was an honest sinner,
and I an R-rated actress in a G-rated life.

I threw in my Nikes, a pair of running shorts, and a sports bra
because I knew that "all-inclusive" meant I had a week of calorie
excess coming my way.

I looked at my stand-up jewelry chest, momentarily frozen.
Then I twisted off my one-carat diamond and pushed it into a felt
ring slot in the top drawer. I frowned, a sudden lump in my throat.

I would miss my ring more than Henry. I loved that ring. Perhaps I'd get it reset in a stylish divorce pendant. Would that be tacky or what?

My wedding ring came off with more effort. Henry had designed it for me. It had three intertwined golden cords, based on some verse in the book of Ecclesiastes. *A threefold cord is not easily broken.* I had no idea Henry even knew the Old Testament contained the book of Ecclesiastes. I cradled the small ring in my hand and gave it a goodbye squeeze. Our wedding had been perfect, a fifty thousand dollar extravagance that Henry paid himself because my father wasn't able. Everything had to be just so for my obsessive husband-to-be. Flowers. Gown. Reception. Cake. The right guests. The correct champagne. I sighed. *We had an awesome wedding ceremony, didn't we, Henry?* Sometimes I wondered whether, if we'd spent five thousand on the wedding and forty-five thousand on things that developed our relationship through common interests, things would have turned out differently.

After a deep breath, I set it gently in its resting place beside the diamond.

A moment later, I caught myself staring without seeing. It was time for change.

I'd said goodbye to Henry. Goodbye to my diamond.

I checked my watch. It was time to say goodbye to my hair.

I freshened my lipstick. I'd already kissed one man and planned to kiss another.

I backed my sedan out and avoided looking at my front yard, but diverting my eyes didn't quell a stab of guilt. It seemed I was doomed to live under the shadow of the Almighty. At this hour of the morning, the sun pulled up behind my father's church and dropped a shadow of the steeple cross right onto a bank of ivy next to the drive. A daily reminder of my failure to be a good Christian.

I paused at the end of the drive and shook my head at the pitiful row of golden willows I'd had Jack plant. Jack was my piano teacher and seven years my junior. He supplemented his income by doing landscaping. He directed the choir at the church across the street, and I planned on rolling in his arms before the sun dropped too far into the Caribbean that night.

The trees were supposed to reach fifteen feet in two years and were part of my plan to block out the condemning shadow that fell across my turf. It was bad enough living in the same town with my father, and worse yet that Henry insisted the lot across from the church was perfect for so many reasons, including its proximity to First Baptist.

I'd conceded to buying the property in a weak moment when Henry and I watched the sun set over the Blue Ridge Mountains while standing next to a for-sale sign. He'd brought two plastic glasses and a fifteen-dollar bottle of chilled champagne. My worst university dates had gotten me tipsy and tried to see behind my brassiere. But not Henry. He just wanted me high enough to approve of his plans for his perfect house. I, being his perfect wife and slightly intoxicated, said, "Why not?" But it was evening, and I didn't know about morning shadows then.

I growled under my breath at the scrawny trees and broken horticultural promises and made a left turn.

Ten minutes later, I entered Trendsetters and went straight to Ellie's chair as Ellie motioned me in. "Morning, Wendi. I didn't expect to see you for a couple weeks."

I smiled sheepishly. "Do you still know my original color?"

Ellie's jaw dropped. "You're such a beautiful blonde." Her hands went to her hips. "You love being blonde."

I shook my hair. "Henry loved me being blonde."

The hairdresser sighed.

I pulled out a magazine page that I had folded in my purse. "There," I said, pointing at the model with her hair just above her ears. "Make me look like that."

She shrugged. "That I can do. But you need to tell me your story."

Ellie. She cuts my hair. She massages my soul. "Got all day?"

"Give me the *Reader's Digest* version. You've got my ear until ten."

Three hours later, I paced my kitchen waiting for my piano teacher, Jack Renner. I looked at the kitchen clock, a black kitten with a tail and eyes that flicked back and forth with each second. Kitty told me that in three hours Jack and I would be on our way to Jamaica and a week of freedom from responsible behavior.

I double-checked our ticket itinerary that I'd printed and slid it in the front pocket of my carry-on next to a brochure promising white sand, blue water, and a variety of water sports. I wondered if Jack liked snorkeling. Maybe we could learn to windsurf together. The flyer mentioned live Reggae bands. We could stay up late and sleep in. Or go to bed early and skip the bands. I'd packed outfits for either possibility.

There was only one small detail that needed to fall into place.

Well, OK, it was a huge detail. One that I'd reserved for the last possible minute so I could chicken out and no one would be the wiser.

I hadn't asked Jack to go.

CHAPTER 3

I heard his car in the driveway and scurried to the foyer, checking my new do in the mirror. What if Jack didn't like it? I shook my head. *Ridiculous. I look great.*

I think.

The doorbell rang. I froze and counted to twenty. I didn't want to appear too anxious. I yelled, "The door's open," and ran to the piano bench where I appeared to be absorbed in an Alfred's piano instruction book. At thirty-two, I should have been a virtuoso, but I was only in level two. Most third-graders played better than I did.

I didn't look over when I heard his steps. Instead, I stumbled through my half of a duet entitled "Teasing Mr. Hanon."

"Wendi?"

I glanced his way and played on as if intent on my work.

I stopped when I felt his eyes fixed on my face. "Yes?"

"Your hair."

I shrugged as if I'd forgotten all about the change. "Oh that."

"Wow," he said, smiling.

I smiled back. This man couldn't hide an emotion.

And I loved him for it. If he liked something, he'd say it, politically correct or not.

"I love it. From the back I wondered if I had the right house."

I laughed and held up my hands, which flopped outward, palms up. "It's the real me." I paused. "Finally."

He squinted at me.

I explained. "I've been bottle-blonde too long, Jack." I let my eyes linger on his face a moment before turning back to my Steinway grand piano and continuing with my voice quiet. "I thought it was time for a little honesty on my part. No more masks." I hesitated and added, "What you see is what you get." I offered a sideways glance. Was he listening to me?

I rested my hands on the keyboard. A Steinway piano. Good grief. With my skill, I should be playing on some yard-sale cast-off. The piano was a gift from Henry. He insisted on it when I said I'd always wanted to learn. I'd mentioned it almost in passing, but he'd picked up on it, and the very next week, when I returned home tired from a consulting job, there it was, ready for me to unleash fingers that seemed more suited to adjusting a volume knob.

It's ironic, I thought. Henry bought the instrument that turned my heart to this younger man at my side. Jack the honest. Jack the open book. Henry described him as artsy, but I called him my renaissance boy.

I glanced at him a second time. *What you see is what you get, Jack.* I screamed it in my mind. He wasn't getting the vibes.

"Shall I play it with you?" he asked.

I looked back at the duet. "Sure," I whispered, my voice suddenly hard to find.

He set the metronome. "Let's try it a little slower. One, two, ready, go."

We played it together. Jack made even my baby steps sound decent. He embellished the edge of the song with added grace notes, something I was convinced he'd do to my life as well.

I remembered the first time I'd seen him play. He gave free performances in my mother's nursing home every Sunday afternoon. I was so smitten, I'd asked him that very day if he'd take me on and teach me.

Week after week, he patiently walked me through my lesson, demonstrating again and again proper hand position and counting. Every lesson, I let my wrist droop, knowing he would gently remind me with a touch to lift my hand into place.

We played two more elementary duets and laughed at my mistakes. "I practice every day. Honest I do," I said.

"You're doing fine." Jack the encourager. "It takes time to get really good."

I kept getting distracted by his left thigh against mine. My leg felt like it was on fire. I glanced at my watch. We should be getting to the airport soon, and I needed to give him time to pack.

I turned my head as he leaned forward to flip through my books, looking for a playable piece. When he straightened, I let my lips stroke his left ear. A light touch. It could have been an accident. I waited for his response. He didn't pull away. So far, so good, I thought. I touched him again, a little longer this time, my lips soft against his earlobe. Still, he didn't pull away. "Jack," I whispered in his ear.

I listened as he swallowed, and I sensed his head push ever so slightly against my lips.

I felt that someone had switched my heart for a galloping horse—no, a *jack*-hammer, I thought. I breathed his name again, my voice hot against his face.

He turned into me, allowing my lips to slide across his cheek. When my lips were at the edge of his mouth, I pulled away, my eyes intent on his, searching for desire. I saw it there, for an instant, just before he blinked and covered his mouth with his hand. "I—I'm sorry," he gasped.

Jack the open book. He wanted to kiss me.

But something held him back. Jack had moral scruples, and I was a married woman.

When he leaned forward, I placed my fingers on his lips and intercepted his kiss. "Not here," I said. "Not just yet."

He pulled up, confused. "I shouldn't."

"Stop," I said, tapping his wonderful mouth. "Listen," I whispered. "Go with me to Jamaica." I paused, capturing his eyes. "Leave with me today."

His jaw dropped. I coaxed it closed with my hand and leaned forward so that I could talk with my lips against his ear. I teased at his hair with my fingers.

"I've already purchased the tickets, Jack. Just say you'll go."

"I—" his voice halted.

"Just say yes, Jack," I whispered. "I want you to go with me."

"But you're married." He pulled away and stood up, nearly stumbling off the bench. "We're not married."

"Look at me and tell me you don't feel something special." I stood and stepped towards him. "I know you."

He stopped backing. He was cornered against the curve of the Steinway. "But we—"

"Papers, Jack. I'm married on paper. Not in my heart." I stared at him. *I'm going to have to play it firm.* I pressed him against the piano. "What does your heart say? What do you *feel*?"

I pushed my face into his neck. "I know what I feel, Jack."

"I am attracted to you," he stammered. "You're a beautiful woman. I—"

"I'm tired of doing everything for the right reasons. Everything for someone else. And nothing for me. I'm tired of living a lie."

"So you want to run away. Just like that?"

"I've been dreaming about this for months, Jack. Tell me you don't feel the same."

"You're married."

"For now. You didn't tell me how you feel."

He walked away from me and let the silence grow between us. When he finally spoke, I thought my heart would escape my chest. "Every night I fantasize what would happen if Dr. Stratford died." His cheeks reddened. He told the truth because lying to me wasn't in him. He shook his head slowly and stared at the carpet. "I find myself wishing for some kind of lethal illness. For a fatal accident." The last words surged forward until his throat abruptly closed in the beginning of a sob. This honesty was hard even for Jack.

I walked to him and took his hands in mine. I looked into his brown eyes. "It seems we've both been stuffing away our feelings."

He looked at me with innocent eyes, afraid to smile.

"So go with me. I'm packed. Our flight leaves in an hour and a half. We can be strolling on white sand together before the sun sets."

"Mrs. Crumley is expecting me."

His next piano student. I wondered silently if she'd fallen for him too. "Call her and cancel. You need a few minutes to pack."

"Just like that. We disappear together."

"Henry thinks I'm going to a meeting in Denver. He won't suspect a thing." I teased him by pushing out my lower lip in a pout. To my surprise, he kissed me. I wrapped my arms around him and let him taste my lips.

After a moment of delight, his indecision returned. He pushed me away and shook his head. "This is crazy!" He walked across the room towards a large stone fireplace. I trailed behind him like a puppy on a leash.

"Of course it's crazy. If I know you like I think I do, you've never done anything irresponsible in your life." I slapped his shoulder. "Wake up and live, Jack. Look at us. We were made for each other."

"I don't know. Reverend John—"

"Please don't bring my father into this. I've spent my life doing what that man wanted. And look where it's taken me."

"You're doing pretty well."

"I've divorced my heart."

He sighed.

"Starbucks?"

I shook my head. We'd fallen into a routine. After each lesson, we'd have coffee together at Starbucks, sitting at a corner table to go over my music theory book. "We have a plane to catch," I said. I tried desperately to capture his eyes. "Come with me."

He took a step towards the front door. I couldn't voice my fears. *Don't do this, Jack. Don't leave me alone. I'll be crushed. We love the same things! Music. Art. Travel. Double mocha lattes.*

He continued walking until he reached the foyer, when he turned to face me. "Don't get me wrong, Wendi. I want to go. It's just—" His voice trailed off.

I shook my head at him with tears welling up and threatening my mascara. "Just walk out that door and go to your next piano lesson. But I promise that for the rest of your life you'll live with the haunting question, 'What would have happened if I'd obeyed my heart?'"

He shook his head slowly.

My voice began to crack. I cried through the next sentence. "Here," I said, pulling a little box from my pocket and shoving it in his hands.

He opened it and saw a gold pocket watch on a chain. He snapped it open, saw the little picture of my face inserted opposite the watch face, snapped it closed again, and saw the engraved heart on the front.

"It's my heart. I want you to have it."

I suddenly felt so adolescent. I was twelve again, giving Jimmy Pearson a ring behind the bleachers.

He stood clutching the little locket in his hand. Speechless, I watched as he slipped it into his pocket. "It will be our secret," he said. "Wendi, I can't—"

I stopped him with a kiss on the cheek. "Don't say 'no' yet. Drive away. Follow your heart. I'll wait for you."

He looked as if he might protest, so I added, "Thirty minutes. Then I'm leaving for the airport. Go to your next lesson or go home and pack. The choice is yours."

I shoved him towards the door. "Just do something," I added, choking up, "before I lose it completely."

He opened his mouth, but I held up my hand. "Go!"

He let himself out. I closed the door and dropped my head against it with a thump. I lifted it again and let it drop. Maybe it would make the pain go away. I turned and slid to the floor with my back against the door.

What had I done? I was a member in good standing at the church across the street, and I'd just given flight to the bird of my inner feelings.

I took a deep breath and wondered if I'd lost my mind. I'd thrown myself shamelessly at my father's choir director. I'd shown him my soul, naked and unpretentious, and he'd walked away.

My heart ran ahead as I studied my trembling hands. No matter what, I'd done it. I couldn't believe it. I'd actually followed through with an insane plan to escape my perfect life. My perfectly boring life. I was free. Exhilaration pulsed in my soul, circulating through my veins until it reached my face to show itself in a smile so wide my cheeks hurt.

My next thought scared me to death and buried my smile in the anxiety. I'm going to be thrown out of the church, disgrace my husband, and burn in hell.

I closed my eyes, pinching back tears and contemplating a sacrilegious prayer:

God, I hope Jack comes back.

With my hands knotted behind my head, I paced the house. When I passed the bookshelves next to the fireplace, I saw my wedding photo album sticking out from the neat row of books beside it. I pushed it back into place and wondered how long it would take Henry to notice that I'd cut my face out in the shape of a valentine to put in the watch I'd given Jack. I didn't use any of the photos of me alone. I used one of me standing beside Henry, one I didn't mind desecrating.

I paused with my hand coming to rest on a pair of binoculars that I used for looking at the cardinals playing in the backyard birdbath. Then, I ran to the back deck and strained to see if Jack's car had reached Route 29. From my vantage point up the hill from the highway, I had a partial view of the intersection. I pressed the binoculars to my eyes to see Jack's blue Honda Accord pull up to wait at the light.

If he turned left towards Charlottesville, he was heading towards Mrs. Crumley and his next piano lesson. If he turned right, he was heading home to pack! I held my breath. I strained to see the back of his car, but his signal lights were hidden behind the dogwood leaves. I moved right a few feet, then left, aware of the drone of an eighteen-wheeler barreling down Route 29 from town.

Jack's light turned green. Binoculars in place, my eyes were fixed on a circle with Jack in the center. I needed to see his taillights. Was he turning right or left? His car edged forward and then disappeared. I saw the flash of a side of a silver truck and a glimpse of the blue Accord as it flipped out of view. Two seconds later, I heard the sharp report of metal against metal. I pulled the glasses away, squinting over the treetops towards the highway.

"Jack." I spoke his name in disbelief. I'd personally witnessed the destruction of dozens of smaller vehicles at the hands of eighteen-wheeler behemoths.

"No," I cried. "No, no, no!"

CHAPTER 4

J esse Anders wiped sweat from his forehead and explored the gap in his smile with his tongue. He downshifted his rig, turned down the music and picked up his cell phone. *Let Dr. Stratford try to cut me off again.*

He fumbled with the numbers, folded his cell, and cursed his trembling hands. He'd dreamed of this moment for months. How could his emotions betray him now? Inside the refuge of his smoky cab, his heart hammered out his resolve.

He checked his rearview mirrors and marveled at his luck. *No one is following. No one saw.* With phone open

again, he willed his fingers to cooperate. Slowly, he dialed the surgeon's number.

He listened as he was patched through to Dr. Stratford's voice
mail. *Typical high-brow behavior. Won't stop to talk to me.* Anders
nodded to himself. *He'll learn who's in charge.* "Hey, Doc!" he said.
"It's a new day. And we need a new start." He paused. "Maybe now
you'll understand just how painful it is when someone you love
gets hurt."

No." I lifted the binoculars up to my eyes and scanned the
roadside. Neither vehicle was in view. I could hardly believe
what I'd witnessed. One second Jack was in view, the next he was
gone, launched out of view by a speeding truck.

A second later, I was in motion, clawing at the screen door to
throw it open, then vaulting over a leather ottoman on my way to
my Mercedes.

I sped down the road towards the highway in a blur of anxiety. I had fully expected some negative fallout from my plummet
from grace, but not so soon. I drove down the hill as if swimming
through a tangle of emotions threatening to strangle me. Guilt.
There it was, sitting on the seat beside me. I thought I'd abandoned
that copilot in my desperate search for the new me. But predictably, in a swing of the pendulum, my old life came slamming back.
Shame enfolded me, the airbag deployed as a result of the wreck
I'd made of my life.

How could I have been so stupid as to think that Jack would
leap into my arms and save me from my desperation?

Was it so bad, wanting to stop the hypocrisy?

All the way to Route 29, I couldn't help feeling responsible
somehow. I behaved shamelessly and Jack paid the price.

That's ridiculous. God doesn't behave that way.

Or does he?

I approached the intersection and pulled onto the shoulder. Where was Jack's car? Where was the truck? Could it be that I misunderstood the whole thing? Cars were speeding by. It seemed like normal Wednesday traffic. With morning rush hour over, traffic was sparse. Jack?

I grabbed my cell phone and walked along the highway. Broken glass littered the road. My heart quickened with my pace. "Jack!" My voice disappeared into the wooded roadside. Twenty yards to the north, I saw a disturbance in the grass beside the road. A fresh rut cut an acute angle off the highway. I ran ahead, scanning the ditch. There, partially hidden by a bank of honeysuckle, was the blue Accord.

The car was upside down, and the smell of gasoline pungent. I approached from the passenger side and dropped to my knees. "Jack?" I touched the edge of the shattered passenger window. It moved, so I stood and kicked it with my shoe. I dropped to my belly in the soft dirt. "Jack?"

That's when I saw him, hanging from his seatbelt. "Jack!" I screamed.

No response.

I punched 9 – 1 – 1 on my cell phone.

"State police, 9 – 1 – 1. What is the nature of your emergency?"

"There's been an accident. Just north of the intersection of Azalea and Route 29. A car is off the road east of the highway. The driver isn't responding."

"I'm dispatching a paramedic crew, ma'am."

"I smell gas."

"I'll have a crew there soon."

"I'm afraid of fire."

"What's the condition of the driver?"

"I'm not sure. Hang on." I went to the driver's side. The window was gone. "Jack?" I touched his cheek, and recoiled. Blood dripped from his forehead.

"Is the person breathing?"

"The car is upside down." I looked at Jack again. "He's breathing!"

"Don't move him."

"I'm afraid of fire."

"Help is on the way."

I knew better than to try to move him. I stood and ran to the edge of the highway. After a three-minute conversation in which the male 9 – 1 – 1 voice told me four times that help was on the way and that I should stay calm, I saw the approaching lights of the rescue squad. I waved my hands in the air and ended my phone call with the stay-calm voice.

I pointed to the car. "He's over there. A truck hit him."

A trio of paramedics ran to the car carrying large orange tackle boxes.

I was used to crash scenes. But not ones with people still bleeding. I didn't remember my own accident that launched me into a plastic life of regret. From the looks of Jack, he wouldn't remember this either. Perhaps that was a necessary grace.

Feeling uneasy watching, and not wanting to lose it completely, I withdrew into the shell of my life's work: accident reconstruction. I retreated to my car and retrieved my evidence kit. A police cruiser pulled off the road behind the rescue squad just as I was measuring the distance from the point of impact in the middle of the intersection to the final position of Jack's car. I stepped it off behind my rolling measuring wheel, like a person might walk a dog on the end of a stiff leash. Then, I took digital pictures of the scene, carefully documenting the dispersion of glass and fender molding on the highway, the ruts on the roadside, and the car from every angle, including close-ups, which would allow me to measure the amount of deformation. From the distance and weight of the car, I would calculate the speed of the truck.

A Charlottesville police officer approached me. He was Schwarzenegger-built and took off his sunglasses before speaking. "Hello ma'am. Did you witness the accident?"

"I was watching from my back deck," I said. I pointed to the wooded hillside. "I live up there. I saw the light on Azalea turn green. The car pulled out and was broadsided by a truck."

"Did you see the type of truck?"

"Silver. I'm pretty sure it was an eighteen-wheeler."

He put back on his glasses. "Pretty sure," he muttered.

I looked beyond him to the paramedic crew. I looked twice to see if the patient was really Jack. They had him on a stretcher with a large yellow collar around his neck. In a moment, they loaded him into the back of the rescue squad. "Where will you take him?"

"University."

I nodded. Of course. To the trauma team. To Dr. Stratford, king of trauma.

"The truck couldn't be far. This only happened a few minutes ago."

The officer disappeared into his cruiser, leaving me, as the rescue squad siren warbled a get-out-of-my-way warning. I watched it go, fighting the urge to cry.

I stood helplessly beside the road with a question hanging paramount in my mind. *Was Jack turning right or left?*

I had to see if his turn signal was in an up or down position.

I walked back up the road, wishing the signal into an up position. I was just about equal with the police car when the Accord exploded into flames.

CHAPTER 5

I drove to the University of Virginia hospital praying to a God I was sure I'd offended, wrestling with my alligator of unbelief. I'd run boldly away from God, and now, with disaster all around, I wanted to cover my bases. It wasn't that I doubted his existence. I just doubted that he loved me.

I parked in the pay deck across the street and walked to the emergency room, where I found Henry quietly teaching a resident about airway management. She was stunning, blonde and tall with a full figure noticeable behind her white coat. Henry leaned close as he made one-two-three points on the tops of his fingers.

I clasped my left hand, suddenly conscious of my bare fingers. "Henry," I said.

He wore a pair of green scrubs and a white coat embroidered with his name over the left breast pocket. "Wendi?"

"I came to check on Jack Renner."

His eyes narrowed. "What'd you do to your hair?"

I hadn't even remembered. "I had it cut. And dyed." *I did it for Jack*, I thought. "How's Jack?"

"Aren't you supposed to be on a plane?"

"Henry, Jack just had a horrible accident." I hesitated. "I couldn't take a trip now." *Not without Jack.*

"He's in the scanner," Henry grunted, then studied me. I looked away. I didn't want him to read me. I couldn't tell him. Not yet.

"He'd just left our house after my piano lesson. I saw the whole thing from our back deck."

"The paramedics mentioned a witness. I had no idea it was you."

I steadied my voice. "Is he going to be OK?"

Henry stepped away from his resident and took my arm, ushering me towards a bank of X-ray view boxes and away from the path of a patient stretcher being pushed by a mob of white-coats. "I've got a good team this month. Ulrich is with him in the scanner." He looked over at the female resident. "Cindy, check on the boys in CT. Tell them I want an update on patient Renner." Then, back at me he said, "I'm so sorry, Wendi. I'll find you a new piano teacher."

Did he actually think that would calm my heart? My temper rocketed and in seconds, I launched from guilt and sorrow into an orbit of white-hot rage. "You insensitive pig!"

His jaw dropped. I felt the eyes of patients and nurses. The ER environment blurred through my tears.

I needed to disappear. I pivoted and stomped through the double doors leading out of the ER and into the hospital beyond.

Michael Ulrich, M.D., looked through the viewing window into the CT scanner, watching a blood pressure and cardiac monitor hooked to his newest trauma patient. As an intern, Ulrich represented the front line, the first to be called by the nurses and the first to be blamed if things went south. "Eat when you can," he whispered. He retrieved a blue Starburst candy from a bulging coat pocket. It looked like it was going to be a long day, and working for a perfectionist like Dr. Stratford was a royal pain.

The door to the CT command console opened, and Chief Resident Cindy Swanson entered. "The monitor says his pressure's sixty-two."

"I've opened his fluids."

"Have you started blood?"

"First unit is in."

"And his pressure is still down. When were you going to let me know about this?" Cindy touched the shoulder of the CT technician. "How much longer?"

"Thirty seconds on the head. Then I'll give a bolus of contrast for his belly." He shrugged. "Should be out of here in five minutes tops."

"Make it three."

The tech glanced over his shoulder. "When did you dye your hair?"

"When I started trauma."

The intern smirked. "We all find our ways to cope."

She paced the small room, muttering, "Load the boat, Ulrich, load the boat." She quoted from a surgery training principle. When the patient is going down like a sinking ship, you need to keep your higher-ups informed, so that if the boat goes down, your bosses will be with you.

Ulrich nodded, unwrapped another piece of candy, and threw one to his chief resident. "Load the boat," he echoed. "Should we tell Stratford?"

"Call blood bank and get another unit of packed cells. I'll call him as soon as the scans are out. When they break to give contrast, I want you in that room squeezing an IV bag."

"I'm on it."

"That's what I'm afraid of." She paused. "I think we need to keep Stratford happy. I don't think his home is a cheery place just now."

"What gives?"

"His wife just blew up at him in the ER. Right in front of everyone." Cindy shook her head. "Maybe I'll have to comfort him."

"I'll pretend I didn't hear that."

Cindy leaned towards the window and looked at patient Renner. "Pressure's down to sixty. We need more blood. Stop the scanner. I need to get to my patient."

"Fifteen seconds," responded the technician.

"I'm going in there."

The tech shrugged. "It's your ovaries. I'll be done in ten."

She walked to the door and held the handle until the tech counted down to zero, then rushed to Renner's bedside.

Ulrich called the blood bank and watched the CT images come up on the screen. "Call neurosurg," he yelled. "This guy's got an intracranial bleed."

Cindy joined him. "It's an epidural."

The CT tech nodded. "Starting the abdominal scan."

"This guy needs a craniotomy," Ulrich said.

"Something else is brewing. I'll bet he has a belly full of blood." In a moment, Cindy started smiling, pointing at the screen. "Look at that! You can see an arterial blush. That's an actively bleeding spleen." She picked up the phone.

In a moment, she spoke again. "Dr. Stratford. Looks like it's going to be crowded in the operating room. Our patient is hypotensive with a ruptured spleen and a large epidural hematoma." She nodded and replied, "Yes, sir." She hung up the phone and pointed a finger in Ulrich's face. "Take a lesson. As an intern you only need to know six phrases." She lifted a finger to begin. "Yes sir, no sir, my fault sir, yes ma'am, no ma'am, and my fault ma'am."

Ulrich nodded. "Yes ma'am," he said, smiling.

Cindy didn't smile back. She barked instead. "Now, let's roll!"

I paced the hospital halls trying to quiet the internal rumblings I'd spewed out on Henry in the emergency room. I'd thought plenty of curse words in my life, but other than at a college party when my tongue had been sufficiently lubricated, I'd kept them inside. We daughters of pastors don't curse, and we certainly don't call our husbands insensitive pigs.

He had it coming, I thought. *I shouldn't feel guilty for giving him what he deserved.*

But I did feel guilty. I sighed. Guilt. My modus operandi since I'd put my mother in a wheelchair.

And I despised the way everyone in the emergency room stared at me. Like I was a freak on a circus stage. I'd come into the king's lair and dared insult him.

I stomped down a long hallway following a sign directing me to radiology. I'd spent my whole life on stage. First as the minister's daughter, and then as the surgeon's wife. And I was a compliant actress, good at playing the roles assigned to me. I shook my head. I was done with stage life. I wanted to join the audience and gawk at someone else for a change. I'd been trying to break free from passivity since I was a teen. Today was my latest and most desperate attempt. But today, like every other time, I'd fallen back into captivity. I was a slave to the stage, and I sensed the director wasn't happy.

Wearing a mask turned me into a volcano. I'd been dormant for years, with lava somewhere beneath the calm. But not today. The plates had shifted, and rage found a vent through my smiles.

I looked up to see the doors to the CT scanner open. A patient on a stretcher was the center of attention, pushed through the doorway by two resident physicians. The patient's face was a bloated plum topped with hair gelled with matted blood and attached to a body by a cervical collar from chin to chest. A white tube exited puffy lips. *Jack?*

I recognized the tall blonde.

"Is that Jack Renner?" I asked.

The female stood between the stretcher and me and addressed me formally. "Mrs. Stratford, that is confidential information, isn't it?" She spoke as if I was a child.

I sent darts back in her direction. What was in her craw? "He's a friend of ours. He's a member of Dr. Stratford's church," I said, invoking my husband's name.

Her face twisted with sarcasm. "You mean the insensitive pig?" She pulled the stretcher forward, brushing against me. "Your husband is one of the most compassionate men I've ever met."

I felt heat in my cheeks. *Don't mess with me today!* I clenched my teeth. I should have known that the residents would defend their lord. I pivoted and watched her hair bouncing off with my dying boyfriend. I knew her color. I'd worn it just that morning.

"Where are you taking him?"

The resident snipped, "We've got work to do here. Why don't you visit your mother? Dr. Stratford says you go to the nursing home whenever you feel guilty."

The gall of this woman! How could she mouth off to the wife of the head of trauma? I strained to see her name tag. Cindy Something. I opened my mouth to respond, but couldn't think of anything with a PG rating.

I followed helplessly. "You'll regret this!" I called.

She ignored me. A twenty-something man with a wide girth pushed with one hand and held up a bag of IV fluid with the other.

He looked back at me. "We're off to the OR. It will be a few hours until we know anything."

I slowed and let the stretcher pull ahead. There was nothing I could do here, and so far, all I'd managed to do was make a huge scene. Twice.

I headed back out of town, north on 29, letting tears flow. I thought again about visiting my mother, but decided Cindy Short-timer was right. I would only be doing penance for the mess I'd made of things today. Besides, my mother wasn't expecting me for a week. A week I was supposed to be spending in Jamaica with Jack.

I slowed at Azalea Drive to turn right and saw that the Accord was about to be loaded onto the back of a wrecker truck. It was charcoal black, unrecognizable. I pulled over and got out of the car. I had to know.

I walked up to the car and reached through the glassless window on the driver's side. The turn signal knob was deformed, a melted glob. I touched it, then pulled it down. It clicked. I pushed it back up.

I sniffed. *Jack was going home to pack.*

I wanted to cry again. For joy over his decision or for sorrow that he was fighting for his life. I had no idea what was wrong with him, but the image of his bloody, swollen body was etched in my memory.

I brushed back a tear and smiled at a man from Ray's Wrecker Service.

At least Jack's in good hands. Henry Stratford is the best.

I walked back to my silver Mercedes and drove home to pray.

ChaPteR 6

Contemplating what might prove to be the world's shortest affair, I watered the golden willows. *What had it been, ten minutes tops?* I let the water run slowly for a full five minutes on each of the six trees at the front edge of the lawn. Short of fidgeting in the waiting room, it was all I could think of doing to kill time while Jack was in the operating room. It was my tribute to him, linking me to something he had started. Letting the water flow was the closest thing to prayer I could do without feeling guilty for trying to seduce him.

I pressed my thumb over the end of the hose and let the wind carry the spray towards a bed of azaleas, another project of Jack's. I used to love them, but now every branch swayed in the wind, each bud a fist shaking in the face of God.

After thirty minutes, I'd watered the lawn, but not my soul. I still had at least an hour before Jack was out of surgery if the intern's predictions were true. I changed and headed for Dogwood Acres Nursing Home.

At the nursing home, I quietly entered the large front visiting room to see my mother's wheelchair parked in front of the TV. Her back was to me. Instead of approaching, I straightened my spine and walked directly into the administrator's office.

I paused at the desk of his receptionist, a girl barely out of high school, chubby and destined for mediocrity. "May I help you?" she asked, smiling.

I looked at the bag of fast food on her desk and thought about introducing her to fresh vegetables, but stopped short when I saw her dimples. This girl seemed genuinely happy. I ate salads for lunch and hated my life. Maybe I should be eating fried cholesterol and smiling. "I'm here to see Mr. Williams."

"Do you have an appointment?"

I looked past her through the partially open door. Mr. Williams had both elbows on his desk with his lips fondling a disgusting mound of cow on a bun. He too was smiling. I decided I hated them both. "No," I said, walking past. "I'll only be a minute."

I pushed open the door. Here in this facility, I'd always found it easier to escape passivity. In fact, my guilt over putting my mother here made the leap into aggression seem the normal thing, even for me. Here, it seemed, my aggression was justified. I was making up for past sins by standing up for my mother's rights.

His chair jerked upright. "Mrs. Stratford, what a nice—"

Skip the social pleasantries, I thought. *You respect me because I donated a new piano for the front room*. But only because I loved to listen to Jack. Momentarily distracted by the mayonnaise on his cheek, I cleared my throat. "I want Mother moved to the east wing."

"But east is full," he began. "I can't—"

"Give her the O'Cleary room. I read her obituary just this morning."

"But Mrs. Thompson is already scheduled to move into that room."

"Mrs. Thompson hasn't known where she is for ten years. My mother needs a room with a view of the lake." I stared down at the administrator, who carefully set aside his burger on an unfolded foil wrapper. It was a precise and gentle movement, something I'd reserve for a Faberge egg.

"Harry Thompson is already moving his mother's things."

"Tell him there's been a change of plans. My mother has been here six years. She deserves that room." I kept my eyes on Mr. Williams' face, which reddened above his tie.

My mother wouldn't speak for herself. I had to be her advocate.

I could see his turmoil. But after a moment, he relaxed, the crisis passed, and the wrinkles on his forehead melted. He must have remembered our last few battles and decided fighting with me wasn't worth the misery. At my tally it was Wendi Stratford, seven; Dogwood Acres administration, zero. "OK," he said, "I'll make it happen." He looked back at his burger. I could see he wanted to take a bite but was reluctant in front of me. Perhaps that's why he'd conceded so quickly. I'd have to remember that. Interrupt his lunch and he'd give me anything.

"Thank you," I said.

As I reached the door, he cleared his throat and I turned back.

"Did you get contact lenses or something?"

Men! I tried to be pleasant. I'd gone from long, blonde, and straight to off-the-ears wavy brunette, and he couldn't tell. I smiled. "Nice of you to notice," I said, winking. *What an idiot.*

I walked back to the front room and surprised my mother from behind. I hugged her boney shoulders and graced her cheek with a kiss. "Hi, Mom," I said. "My plans changed. I'm not going out of town after all." I knelt in front of her and took her hands in mine. She closed her hand around a Kleenex. Crumpled facial tissues, a Ruth trademark, so necessary when she drooled. "Would you like to go back to your room and continue where we left off?"

She smiled, her face breaking into an uneven soil. The right, wrinkled, plowed with life's grief. The left, flaccid from paralysis, smooth, twenty years of worry erased in one traumatic moment. Her eyes communicated her joy. She nodded. "Oh Wendi," she exclaimed. "Wonderful."

I wheeled her to her room, a retreat with a hospital bed, a nightstand, and a worn leather recliner that she refused to have recovered. It sat next to the window and absorbed the afternoon sun. The one stand-out feature was the wooden shelving along the wall opposite her bed. Burdened with books, the shelves proudly displayed a long road we'd traveled together. Twain, Dickens, and Tolstoy crowded shoulder to shoulder with Jane Austen and James Fenimore Cooper. We'd been far away in time with Homer's *The Iliad*, solved crimes with Sir Arthur Conan Doyle, and felt the closeness of African humidity in Conrad's *Heart of Darkness*. Ruth and I had blushed through *The Canterbury Tales* and plodded through *War and Peace*. I picked up F. Scott Fitzgerald's *The Beautiful and Damned* and opened to chapter four.

I thought about the book and the deceptive nature of desire. Fitzgerald was looking into my soul. I smiled, quelling my turmoil, and glanced at my watch. "Now, where were we?"

Dr. Henry Stratford stood opposite his chief resident, a shared body open between them. They worked as an efficient team, exposing, tying, dissecting, and packing away warm intestines to visualize and care for the flood of bleeding from Jack Renner's liver and spleen. They shared air, but not germs, the masks filtering out even the smallest of microorganisms that are normally spewed into the atmosphere with every breath.

"There, yes, uh-huh, yes, OK, uh-huh." Henry guided and encouraged his resident's every movement with running commentary. "Careful, OK, now off. Hemostat," he said, opening his palm to allow the scrub technician to hand him an instrument. "Metzenbaums, tie." He lifted the shattered spleen, squeezing the irregular edges together. He looked up at the blood-pressure recording. Eighty-two. His voice was like that of someone talking about the need for rain or a dislike of black olives. Without a hint of tension, he spoke of the critical decision in front of them. "OK, Dr. Swanson. What next? Splenorrhaphy? Splenectomy?"

"We've already packed the liver. He's unstable. I say take it out."

The attending surgeon smiled behind his mask. "Of course. Right angle," he said, holding out his hand. He pointed to the splenic artery as it snaked beyond the tail of the pancreas. "Take the artery here."

"Tie," said Cindy.

"Good," he said, watching her slide the knot down over the vessel. "When did you change your hair?"

"I didn't think you noticed."

"I notice everything."

The anesthesiologist's voice came from behind a sterile drape at the head of the table. "Make it snappy, Stratford. I'm giving this guy zero anesthesia at this point and his pressure is in the pits."

Henry didn't raise his voice above his normal cool. "Just give more blood, Newton. Just give more blood."

When I arrived in the surgery waiting room, my father, John Aldridge, greeted me warmly. *Of course*, I thought, *my father the pastor would be here, wouldn't he?* Somehow I hadn't thought that I'd have to deal with him today of all days.

My feelings for my father were complicated, and being with him only made me more aware of my own inability to believe. He was the world's kindest man, and I loved him for it. If only being kind would win him my respect. My father was a perfect man of the cloth. He was sacrificial in service, followed the will of God as best he knew it, and preached of things too wonderful for me to believe. And for that, I thought him the King of Naïve.

"Hi, Dad." I gave him a hug. "Any word about Jack?"

He shook his head. "Not yet." He still had his arm around me and turned me to face a man and woman sitting in the middle of a row of vinyl chairs. "This is Steve and Miriam Renner, Jack's parents." He lifted his hand towards a younger woman sitting beside Miriam. "And this is Yolanda Pate, Jack's fiancée."

My mouth went dry. *Fiancée? I had no idea.* Somehow making myself move in the midst of my shock, I reached out my hand to Jack's parents. "I'm Wendi Stratford. I—" I shrugged. "I'm one of Jack's piano students."

Daddy put his arm around me again, giving me a squeeze. "My daughter. Her husband's Dr. Stratford, the one who is operating on Jack."

I smiled pleasantly. Of course. The pastor's daughter, the surgeon's wife. I almost forgot my identity.

I sat down on a chair in a row opposite the trio and tried to look outwardly controlled. Inwardly, I scolded myself again. I'd been envisioning a future with Jack, playing a mental fantasy without really knowing his life. *He never mentioned being engaged!* I offered a weak smile. "Jack had just finished giving me a piano lesson. I walked out onto the back deck after he left and heard the accident at the bottom of the hill."

Steve Renner looked like Jack plus thirty pounds with white hair. His wife was still brunette, with black-rimmed glasses sitting halfway down the slope of her skinny nose. Her hands were knotted in her lap, lying on an open magazine. "Did you see anything?" she asked.

"The flash of a side of a silver truck." I paused before adding, "Nothing else."

Yolanda, Jack's fiancée, had long blonde hair and streaked mascara. *She wears her hair just like I did. Until this morning.* Her eyes met mine as I judged her Miss Virginia features. "I'm finishing my degree at Mary Baldwin. Jack and I were planning a tour of France for our honeymoon. He never liked the thought of just going to the Poconos like everyone else. They have heart-shaped tubs and everything. But Jack wanted to experience history and art," she added, waving her hand in the air.

TMI, sweetheart. Too much information. I smiled. "Sounds like Jack."

"I have one more year until I'm done with an elementary education degree. Jack wanted me to go into something we could count on. Music doesn't always pay the bills, you know."

I shrugged, thinking about the golden willows Jack had planted for me. "There's always landscaping."

"Jack and I met at a sorority function. One of my girlfriends hired him as the entertainment. When he plays, I think I've just died and gone to heaven. He wrote a song for me once. I cried for a week. He taped it for me. I think my roommates wanted to strangle me. I must have played it a thousand times."

I think I want to strangle you. Jack is in love with me! At least, he said he prayed my husband would die. I looked at my father. He'd sat next to me opposite Steve.

"It's obvious we all care very much about Jack. I believe God cares for him as well. Would it be alright if I led us in prayer for Jack?"

Dad the pastor. Why can't you just be a regular guy and let these people believe what they want?

I studied their faces for a moment. Tears brimmed the edges of Miriam's eyes. "That would be nice," she said.

Not the hands, Dad. Not the hands!

My father held open his hands, extending one to me and one to Mr. Renner. To my surprise, Steve Renner gripped my father's hand with a slap. Yolanda sniffed, extended her hand to me, then returned a tissue to her lap and extended her hand again. I looked at it, fresh from dropping her tissue. Wondering if I had my hand-sanitizer, I hesitated, then opened my palm.

Dad prayed with his usual heartfelt fervency. For healing. For peace. For God's will.

I felt too guilty to pray. What was I going to pray? Heal Jack so I can run away with him and destroy flaky Yolanda's life?

After the amen, I glanced around. Dad, the Renners, and Yolanda dabbed their eyes. Was it only me who was too cold to be touched by my father's sincerity?

Yolanda sniffed. "Jack prays like that. You can tell he means what he said. It's the oddest thing, really. The thing that makes me feel closest to Jack isn't when we kiss. You might think that I'd feel closest to him then, and I do feel close, but it's when we pray. That really brings us close."

I wanted to call her unchristian names and tell her to shut up, that Jack had his right turn signal on when he was blindsided, and that *when he wakes up you have another surprise coming: Jack is in love with me!* I looked away towards the doors leading from the operating rooms and tried not to think of Jack kissing this girl. *She's not your type, Jack. She may be cute, but she'll talk you into a coma within a week.*

Before Jack's cutie could go on about honeymoons, kissing, prayer, or Jack's piano-playing, Henry J. Stratford, Jr., M.D., Ph.D., F.A.C.S., F.R.C.S., pushed through the double doors. My father tilted his head towards the approaching surgeon. "That's Dr. Stratford now."

We stood and gathered around Henry.

Henry smiled, the air around him calm. I'd grown to merely tolerate his proud demeanor, but at that moment, I found myself reassured by his cool confidence. "We've finished the operation," he said. He gestured towards the chairs we'd just left. "Let's sit and chat a bit."

Henry sat next to me and John, opposite Steve, Miriam, and Yolanda.

My father made introductions.

Henry nodded. "I'm sure glad to meet you." He leaned forward and began to speak in even tones, talking of the surgery and the possible tough road ahead.

I hung on every word.

"The neurosurgery team worked on him first. He had a fracture here," he said, pointing to his left temple. "An artery was cut by the bone, bleeding into his brain."

Miriam and Yolanda gasped.

Henry paused. "The surgeons were able to stop the bleeding and remove the blood that was pressing on the brain."

Steve Renner verbalized the question we all wanted answered. "Will he be OK?"

"We'll know more in a few days. We'll keep him in a medication-induced coma until then." He paused, meeting each of their faces with his gaze. He even looked at me, and without his saying so, I knew he'd forgiven me for my outrageous behavior in the ER. He was pure compassion and confidence. "We'll take him back to the operating room tomorrow and remove the packing over his liver. There is a good chance for a full recovery."

I looked down and realized he'd slipped his left hand into my lap and I'd been gripping it with the tenacity of a drowning sailor holding a life rope. I lessened my purchase on his thumb and hoped it would pink up again soon. "Sorry," I whispered.

He gave me an I-love-you triple squeeze before letting me go. It was something we did at the end of every date during our engagement, but that had been lost in the weariness of subsequent years.

I looked away. *Not now, Henry. I'm leaving your perfect world. The renaissance boy is the one I want.*

Yolanda leaned forward. "Can we see him?"

"In a few hours. Check in the ICU waiting room. The nurses will let you know when you can visit." Henry stood. "But don't expect too much. He'll be on medications to keep him asleep and to keep him from fighting with the ventilator. Until we take the ventilator tube away from him, he won't be able to speak."

Steve Renner nodded and extended his hand. "Thank you so much."

"Sure." Henry glanced at me. "I'll be home late."

Of course. Stay as long as Jack needs you. I recognized the irony in my thoughts. I'd resented his late hours until he was staying for someone I loved.

Two hours later, we were allowed to see Jack, or at least a body they claimed was Jack. ICU rules mandated no more than two visitors at a time, so his parents were ushered in first. Two minutes later, Steve practically carried out his wife, whose face seemed pale under the fluorescent lights. The visit aged her. She slumped in a vinyl chair with her shoulders thrown forward and hid her nose behind a facial tissue.

Chatty Yolanda and I were next, as my father had gone on to visit other church members. Jack's nurse met us at the double doors leading to the unit. Her name was Brenda Lee, and she'd helped take care of me during my stay in that very unit.

She greeted me with a hug. "Wendi!"

I gripped her tightly. "Oh, I'm so glad it's you."

She took me by the hand. ICU grads often become fast friends with their nurses. We paused at a sliding glass door leading into

Jack's cubicle. There she turned. "Jack isn't going to look much like himself, OK?" She looked at Yolanda. "Are you his wife?"

"Fiancée," she said timidly.

"Jack's head has been shaved for surgery. He's on a breathing machine, so he has a tube going through his mouth into his windpipe," she said, pointing to the front of her neck. "There are other tubes, one in his nose draining his stomach fluid, one in his bladder draining his urine, and one in his chest draining some blood and air." She paused, talking slowly, making sure we were listening. "It's often quite traumatic seeing loved ones this way. His face is quite swollen, and I doubt he looks anything like himself at all."

Yolanda nodded, already paling.

"Ready?"

"Sure," I whispered.

Yolanda gripped my arm. Brenda slid open the door and a curtain to allow us into his room.

I was prepared for him to look different, but this man was not Jack. This man's eyelids bulged with fluid, swollen purple slits pushing out of white cheeks. Instead of hair, he had a curving row of staples and what appeared to be another drain exiting from the center of his head. Brenda hadn't mentioned that. His chest rose and fell in a mechanical cycle, unnatural and accompanied by the whispery bellowing of the ventilator.

Yolanda sniffed. "Jack?" She moved to his side and started to reach for him and pulled back, holding her hand to her chest.

"You can touch him," Brenda coached. "But he cannot respond to you or speak. He's on medicine to keep him in deep coma."

I resented Yolanda's tears and her presence. I wanted time alone to mourn the man I loved. *Jack?* I searched his face. He had a small mole on his left cheek, shaped like a miniature map of Africa. I used to look at it when he sat next to me on my piano bench. The mole was untouched, an island of normality in a sea of bruised flesh. *This is Jack.*

I moved to the other side of the bed and took his hand. I cared little if it mattered to Yolanda. Jack was turning right. Tonight Jack and I were supposed to walk on white sand and drink mango daiquiris while the sun melted into the Caribbean. I let tears flow. *Don't leave me, Jack.*

My next thought was classic Wendi. *This is all my fault.*

Yolanda gripped his right hand and I his left. Jack hung comatose between us, a warm shell of a body we hoped he would inhabit again. Yolanda cried loudly and stumbled out of the room.

I traded glances with Brenda, who moved to my side. I felt her searching my face. "Who is he?" she whispered to me.

I sniffed. "My piano teacher."

She shook her head. She knew students didn't usually cry when their piano teachers were comatose. I felt her arm around my shoulders.

"He'd just left my house when the accident occurred."

"Look at me," she said.

I obeyed.

My friend stared past my tears. "Does Henry know?"

I covered my mouth with my hand and shook my head. *What am I doing? I'm being honest. I've stopped covering up.* I immediately cleared my throat. "We've never—"

"Shhh," Brenda said.

"Henry's a wonderful surgeon," I said.

She nodded her head. "Of course."

I steadied my voice. "This was my room, wasn't it?"

She nodded. "Spend a minute here. I need to record his vital signs in a moment." She squeezed my shoulder and disappeared into the ICU beyond the curtain.

I watched the dancing of the cardiac monitor on the screen above Jack's head and remembered waking up in an ICU just like this. I was fourteen years old, pregnant, and scared. I lifted my eyes to the light above the bed and the thousands of dimples in the ceiling tiles. I used to stare at the ceiling and let my eyes blur, transforming the dots into faces. I remembered.

Pain. There is something in my throat. Where am I? I opened my eyes. My stomach ached. I listened to a rhythmic electronic beeping noise. My heart.

A face appeared in front of me. A floating face, a smiling man. Handsome with short wiry hair. "Well, hello to you," he said.

My mouth was sand. I closed my lips around a tube.

"You're in the hospital, Wendi," the man said.

I liked his voice. Strong, reassuring.

"You were in an accident. You've had surgery and you're just waking up. Don't try to speak." He touched my forehead gently as his eyes fixed on my face. "Can you lift your head?"

I strained. My stomach hurt. Did my head move?

"Good, good," he said. "Let's get rid of that tube."

An accident? What about my baby?

What happened? We were on our way to the clinic.

Is my mother OK?

Brenda touched my shoulder. "I need to get back to caring for Jack. Would you like to visit again tonight?"

I shook my head. "I'd better get home for Henry," I whispered.

I laid Jack's hand back onto his bed, but not before I'd given it a triple squeeze, willing his subconscious to feel the message I was sending.

When I looked up, Henry was there. He ignored me. Here in his kingdom, patients were priority number one. His eyes scanned the monitors, taking in everything in seconds. "How's his urine output?"

"One hundred last hour," Brenda responded.

Henry slid back the sheet to inspect his abdominal dressing. He outlined a sanguine stain on the bandage with his pen. "Let me know if this gets bigger." He laid his stethoscope on Jack's chest and closed his eyes to listen.

Then he touched Jack's shoulder and brushed the back of his fingers against his patient's chin. "Fight, Jack, fight," he said.

Here, Henry was pure compassion. He lifted his eyes from Jack, looking towards me, but I couldn't meet his gaze. Instead, I slipped out, comforted that Jack was in Henry's care.

CHAPTER 7

At home, I tried to lose myself in preparing dinner. I had no appetite, but I wanted Henry to eat. I simmered a clove of garlic, salt, and a sprinkling of oregano in olive oil, and poured it in a roaster over a half chicken. I set the oven to 400 degrees and retreated to my laptop.

I downloaded my pictures of the accident and stared at the screen. I looked up the weight of the Accord, checked data from side-impact crash tests, and measured the amount of side-door deformation. The distance the car traveled after impact was dependent on multiple variables, including whether it had slid on its roof or its wheels, as well as the speed and mass of the truck. From my examination of the highway, the Accord hadn't flipped until it hit the grassy shoulder. There was no paint on the highway to suggest the roof impacted the road.

The energy transferred from the truck to the Accord was dependent on only two factors: speed and mass of the truck. I decided to give the trucking company the benefit of the doubt and assumed the truck was at or under legal weight. But even if I assumed a maximum legal weight, the amount of deformation of the Accord and the distance traveled after impact made the speed of the truck come out in excess of eighty miles per hour. If the truck wasn't maximally loaded, the speed was even faster.

I looked at my calculator and tried to comprehend the number. I hadn't even added in a fudge factor that accounted for the complete reversal of the Accord's forward progress before it was flipped up and off the road.

I closed my fist and decided I would help the law nail the driver. This trucker needed to pay. If he got off with reckless homicide after I was through with a jury, he was lucky.

I picked up the phone and called the desk of Charlottesville detective Chris Black. He picked up after the fifth ring and sounded tired. Come to think of it, he always sounded tired.

"Detective Black."

"Chris," I said, "Wendi Stratford."

I listened as his chair squeaked. "Wendi, my favorite blonde consultant." His voice dripped with sarcasm.

"Not any longer."

"You'll always be my favorite."

"I'm not blonde anymore."

"What?"

"Long story," I said. "I need help."

Chris sighed. I'd bent his arm for favors so many times. "Wendi, Wendi."

"Hit-and-run on Route 29 this morning. A truck and a Honda Accord. Has the truck been located?"

"It'll cost you. Two double mocha lattes at Starbucks."

"One."

"What's your interest? Have the insurance attorneys enlisted you already? I know we haven't."

"The Honda's driver was a friend of mine."

"Was? Is he dead?"

"Not yet." I felt my heart quicken.

"You're asking for personal reasons. What makes you think I'd give you department information when you're not consulting?" He paused. "Especially after the way you embarrassed my men—"

He couldn't forget our last court battle, when we ended up on opposite sides. My accident analysis had proven a pizza delivery boy was traveling in excess of sixty miles an hour on a country road. I'd saved an insurance company a three-million-dollar payout. "I was just doing my job."

"So convince me to help you."

I took a deep breath. I was going way out on a limb. "I'll bet it was a drunk driver. Or an overworked driver fudging his logbook asleep at the wheel. Or maybe something more sinister."

I heard cowboy boots thud onto the floor and another squeak of Black's chair. He snorted. "What do you know?"

"The truck was traveling in excess of eighty miles an hour. No tire skids."

"That hardly seems like something sinister." He laughed. "You're paranoid."

I pulled my fingers through my hair, still amazed at the feel of my ears without a load of hair. I played with the bristles at the nape of my neck. "It's my job to be paranoid."

"I don't know anything. They haven't found the truck."

I wanted to curse.

He continued. "Remember what happened the last time you dreamed of foul play?"

"It seems I managed to save an insurance company a huge payout."

"And incur the wrath of a multi-kazillion-dollar pizza delivery chain."

"So I'll eat DiGiorno."

"I'm serious, girl. You've forgotten the death threats?"

"Unsubstantiated crap. We still don't know who was responsible for that."

"Exactly. We don't know." He sighed. "I just want you to be careful. I don't want any more middle of the night rescue-me-I'm-being-threatened calls."

"We're not talking about me, remember? We're talking about a Honda Accord being demolished by a hit-and-run trucker. No one is threatening me."

"Just let me play detective. That's what I'm paid to do."

"My faithful protector." I tapped my perfect nails against the Corian kitchen counter and groaned. Today wasn't going according to plan. "I know you love me," I teased. "Just do me a favor and let me know if you hear anything."

"You're not blonde anymore? Really?"

"Chris, you're not listening."

"I'm listening. I'll call you if I hear anything. But listen, if you think dying your hair can stop me from telling blonde jokes about you, then you've—"

"You don't get it," I interrupted. "My roots were never blonde."

"You act blonde."

"Shut up."

He laughed. I could imagine him sitting in his chair with his thumb in his belt as his belly did a little chuckle dance above his pants. "I'll call you, sweetheart."

I hung up. Chris was so helpful. And so annoying.

I plodded to my bedroom and stared at the suitcase sitting by the door. I didn't have the heart to unpack my dreams, but was too scared to leave it out for Henry to snoop through. So back into the closet went my revealing swimwear, the cocktail dresses, and my black teddy negligee, but not before I shed another tear for Jack.

Predictably, Henry wasn't home when normal people ate supper, but I didn't want to face him anyway. I fixed him a plate and withdrew to hide under the covers of our king-size bed.

There, I hugged my pillow and marveled at how horribly my day had departed from my plan. My heart longed for beauty and intimacy, yet here I was stuck with a Buick-size closet of designer clothes and a husband who approached our relationship like another item on his checklist of successes. Job. Check. Blonde, busty wife. Check. I wanted to be the beauty at the center of a romance. I wanted to be pursued, to be desired. So how had I ended up feeling like an actress in my own life?

I brushed a tear from my cheek. Instead of experiencing new love, I was back in my own bed worried that Jack might not survive the night.

Why, God? Every time I decide to take steps to reclaim my life, disaster strikes. Why are you punishing me?

I shouldn't have asked the question. I knew the answer my mind would conjure up. Even if it didn't come from the throne of God, the answer was immediately with me. *Because you're unfaithful, child.*

Images of Jack's swollen body prodded memories of my own ICU experience into focus. First memories of a plan gone awry joined hands with guilt in an attempt to rob my sleep.

I looked at the nurse standing by my bed. "What happened?"

"You were in a car accident, Wendi. You're going to be OK."

My hand touched my stomach. "What did they do to me?"

"You had surgery. Your uterus was ruptured." Her eyes searched my face.

"M-my baby?"

She shook her head.

Her message was understood, but the news didn't hurt me. I was on my way to end the evidence of my affair with a married man.

The nurse gripped my hand. "There was a lot of bleeding, Wendi. You almost died." She seemed to hesitate. "The surgeon needed to remove your uterus to save your life."

My uterus? I felt my throat tighten. I won't be able to have children! The irony hit hard. I wanted children, just not that child!

I'd lived my life in the shadow of my father's church. I strayed from the path and this was what I got?

"My mother, how's my mother?"

"She's still in surgery. The neurosurgery team is working on her now."

"Neurosurgery?"

"She had a skull fracture. I don't know any more."

Great, I thought. This is what Mom gets for scheming this up to protect Daddy's all-important ministry.

At eleven-thirty, I heard Henry arrive. I listened as the microwave beeped. He'd found the chicken. Ten minutes later, bathroom noises followed and Henry slipped in on his side. In a moment, I felt his breath on my neck. I pressed my eyes with my pillow, drying my tears. I tried to make my voice sound as if I'd been asleep. I moaned, "How's Jack?"

"He's ten units down." His hand slipped around my waist. "If he can be stabilized, I'll have him back in the OR tomorrow."

I shuddered as Henry moved his hand beneath my pajama top. I kept my body stiffened against his touch, and my face away from his. "Just hold me." I bit my lip.

Henry's hand froze in midcaress, and I listened to him sigh. "Just hold me" isn't a concept understood by husbands hungry for more.

He held me a few moments while I steeled myself against the emotions threatening to erupt. His were not the arms I desired. His were not the kisses I craved.

"I'm sorry," he whispered. "I was insensitive this morning."

My breath escaped in a sob. The dam had burst. I cried while Henry the husband did what most men do when their wives cry. He misunderstood my needs and tried to solve the problem. I needed a shoulder, not a solution.

"Why don't we take off next weekend? We can go to Smith Mountain Lake."

I didn't want a weekend retreat with Henry. I didn't want him to apologize. I wanted a divorce. If only it weren't spelled with a capital D in my mind, maybe I'd be strong enough to tell him. I sniffed. Maybe he thought I was crying because I'd been so brash. "I shouldn't have called you an insensitive pig."

"But I am an insensitive pig."

At that, I turned and looked at him, unable to conceal my surprise. Admitting his pride was as close to humility as Henry ever got. I nodded. I shouldn't have apologized. "Sweet of you to admit it."

He seemed pleased with himself. In fact, apparently happy that I'd accepted his apology, he seemed to think the coach was waving him on towards third base. He placed his hand against my skin. He was like most husbands in that respect, I thought; he equated a successful apology with sex.

I turned away from him. I was still dreaming of Jack. There was no way I could let Henry run the bases tonight. Not even if it was three minutes like our usual. I couldn't.

I wanted to scream. My plans were on hold, if not destroyed. And somehow phoning Henry to clue him in from Jamaica seemed easier than telling him at the bedside of my wounded boyfriend. Besides, if I mustered the courage to tell Henry it was over, it would just bias him against giving Jack the care he needed. I'd better wait until Jack was clearly out of the woods. If only the woods weren't so big and my boyfriend so lost inside them.

As much as I trusted in Henry's ability to provide quality medical care free from emotional attachment, this would be too much. Besides, emotions had gotten in the way of Henry's patient care before. I knew too well how quickly a clinical exam could turn into something more alluring. He'd fallen for me, hadn't he? Henry rolled the opposite way, ending our cozy chat and leaving me to wrestle with conflicting emotions.

I shut my eyes and tried not to remember Henry's exam room and how much I once longed for a surgeon's gentle touch. He had been my knight in shining armor once. He'd rescued me from an uncooperative gall bladder, and, briefly, I'd been the pursued beauty in the fairy tale. But Henry stopped pursuing my heart, and I'd resumed my life of plastic smiles.

There, in the darkness, as my husband's breathing transitioned into the deep nasal whistles of sleep, I wondered if God had yanked my leash today. For the second time I'd wandered off the straight and narrow, and something disastrous had goaded me back into the fold. The last time I'd returned to the sheepfold but felt like a wolf. The mask-of-happiness life I led sitting on the back pew of the church had left me empty and launched me into my plan for a prison break. I sighed. My plans had been foiled, and I remained trapped in my husband's perfect life.

I buried my face in my pillow and whispered my commitment to a man I hoped would be my Moses and lead me from the drudgery of Egypt. "Jack Renner, I love you." The words slipped out so easily, and tasted dangerous and delightful all at once, like stolen candy. I'd imagined whispering it to Jack a thousand times. We were to be together tonight. "I love you, Jack," I whispered again, my heart pulsing like a love-sick teen's. It seemed even more delicious and precarious to say it in bed with Hubby Henry.

I'd whispered it tonight. Maybe tomorrow I would be brave enough to raise my voice. I was done with safe. I was sick to death of my hypocritical guilty life. But now freedom was locked in an ICU bed, and my husband held the keys.

That's when I remembered my fancy panties. I slipped my hand into my pajamas and smiled, letting the lace catch on my matching nail polish.

Tomorrow morning I would start with Henry's Cocoa Krispies. Maybe I'd even skip my vitamin. Life on the edge. No more fiber.

CHAPTER 8

I woke up on day two of my wonderful Caribbean vacation in bed with Henry's nose whistling. It used to be endearing.

I dressed in estrogen central, so my husband wouldn't see my red-lace undies. Then, I dripped Ethiopian coffee, added French vanilla creamer, and left the house before Henry. I wanted to park my Mercedes up the hill on 29 and watch the Azalea intersection.

I parked in the front of an Exxon facing the highway and lifted my travel mug beneath my nose. I watched the light at the bottom of the hill through the steam rising from my coffee. For six cycles I timed the yellow caution. It lasted a full five seconds, plenty of warning for routine traffic. Unless it had been changed since yesterday, the light seemed to be operating fine. From this position, everything seemed in order. There were no visual obstructions. No overhanging tree branches obscured the traffic signal, and because the road ran north and south, the sun shouldn't have been a factor either.

I looked at the steam from my mug fogging the side window and remembered my commitment to eat Cocoa Krispies. I returned home in time to find Henry performing an English muffin dissection. He talked without looking up. "You're up early."

"I wanted to time the light at the bottom of the hill."

"So?"

"So I think the light is working fine. At least now it is." I poured more coffee into my silver mug and leaned across the table. "Henry, did you really tell your chief resident that I visit my mother when I feel guilty?"

I watched an almost imperceptible twitch of his lip before he spoke. "You do do that, you know."

"I visit my mother every week."

"You feel guilty every week."

This may have been true, but I was in no mood to hear of it from Henry. "Your resident was rude to me. I don't think the university should train surgeons like that."

"She was defending me."

"So you know what she said?"

He looked over the top of the *Wall Street Journal.* "There is very little that goes on in my department that I don't know, Wendi."

"I want you to fire her."

"She's already been reprimanded." He lifted his paper to hide his face. "She's a good resident."

"She's mouthy."

"She's got spunk."

"She disrespected me."

"And you disrespected me, remember? She was only defending the boss. That's what good residents do."

I stuck my tongue out at the front page of his paper. It was immature, but I was done with holding back. If I didn't feel like smiling, I wasn't going to smile, Christian or not.

I watched as Henry walked to the foyer to do a preflight inspection. It was Friday, and he always rode his motorcycle on Fridays. It was the one irony that I loved about him. How a trauma surgeon could get on a bike after all the damage he'd seen, I'd never understand, but if anything could bring a smile to his serious face, it was the rumble of a cruiser. His was a Triumph Rocket III, cherry red and 2300 cc strong. I only knew it because he'd told me twenty times, and of course Henry J. Stratford, Jr., M.D., would only drive a motorcycle with two names and a suffix.

On Fridays, he discarded his suit for a leather jacket. He looked in the mirror and checked his hair, tie, jacket, pants, and zipper. And zipper.

I walked up behind him. "Are you operating on Jack again today?"

"If he's stable."

I kissed his cheek. "Do a good job."

He looked at me as if I'd told Santa Claus to give out gifts for Christmas. He walked towards the garage with his Friday motorcycle swagger. "Always."

I listened to the rumble of the Triumph and watched from the front window as safety-first Henry signaled and then revved the beast onto Azalea Drive. I let the curtain fall and plodded back to my kitchen. I'd just topped off my coffee mug when the doorbell rang.

Odd, I thought. *No one calls on me this early.* With the angst that the unexpected usually prompted in my gut, I walked to the front room where I could discreetly view the front porch. I peered around the edge of the drapery and felt my heart quicken. It was my hero, my open-sinner baby sister, Rene.

I flung open the door. One glance told a troubled story. Her hair unwashed, raccoon-circles of weariness beneath her usually sparkling eyes, and her shoulders thrown forward with a burdened duffle hanging from her hands, which were clasped in protection in front of her. This was hardly Rene, the sister who burned through life leaving little behind but smoke and the memory of her irritating laugh that made me so jealous.

But above her downward chin I saw the first hint of the strength I wanted as my own. She grinned at me through the unwashed kelp of her hair. "Aren't you going to invite me in?"

I stumbled over the duffle and pulled her into an awkward embrace and found myself on the verge of tears. She had no idea how much I needed her on that day of all days. I held her for a moment, unable to find my voice. She smelled of stale cigarettes and coffee. When I pulled away she looked down, and kicked at the army duffle at our feet.

"What are you doing here?"

"I'm selling dictionaries door to door."

"You look like hell," I said, surprised at my vernacular.

Rene's eyes widened at my comment. "Sales have been off."

I shook my head and looked at the Saturn in the driveway. "Been driving all night?"

"Almost. I napped for an hour in the parking lot of the Almighty across the street waiting for you to get up." She shrugged. "When I saw Henry leave, I figured it was safe."

"Safe?"

She nodded and avoided my eyes. The smile was lost, and her expression hinted at a story.

I pushed her towards the door and picked up her bag. I groaned at the weight. "What's in here?"

She pushed a strand of rebellious brunette hair behind her ear. "Everything."

"Coffee?"

"I need a bed."

"You need a shower."

"That I'll take."

"You can stay in the guest quarters downstairs. Sleep for a few hours." I stared at her for a few seconds before adding, "Then we'll talk."

She didn't argue. I followed her down the steps.

"You can't smoke in here."

She sighed her frustration but didn't fight back. Something was seriously wrong.

I pointed to the bathroom. "There are fresh towels on the rack. I'm going to run a few errands. I'll be back by noon."

She filled a glass with water from the bathroom faucet and lifted it to her lips. Her voice cracked. "Cheers."

After watering the willows and making a run to Kroger to stock the pantry with comfort food for my reunion with Rene, I saw her emerge from the basement. My head was in the refrigerator when I heard her voice. "Got anything to eat around this joint?"

I lifted two raspberry wine coolers. I opened one, but she waved me off. I felt my jaw slacken, but I kept the surprise to myself. I'd bought them just for her. "Coffee then?"

She sat on a barstool at the edge of the counter. "I shouldn't."

I shook my head. An alien had taken over my sister. I looked back in the fridge. "Orange juice?" I squinted at her, testing one more time. "I've got vodka."

"Juice is fine," she said, never lifting her eyes from the counter.

I set a glass in front of her and filled it. "OK," I said. "What is it? Randy?"

My first guess hit the mark. I saw it in the lines at the corner of her mouth that appeared when she was tense.

She played with the juice, slowly shaking her head. Randy was a jazz musician, a sax player, and Rene's newest in a short string of bad relationships. She pressed her upper lip with the glass. When she finally met my eyes, I could see the tears threatening her fresh mascara. "I'm pregnant."

"Rene!" I gasped. "That's wonderful."

She glared at me. "No. It's not." She gulped the juice and wiped her mouth with the back of her hand. "For you, it would be wonderful. But not for me."

For me, it would be a miracle. Henry and I had married, knowing that biological children without a surrogate would be impossible. I've got ovaries and plenty of estrogen, but no uterus to house a baby. But Henry had allowed me to dream. We'd even talked of asking Rene to carry the child for us and he'd allowed me to design a nursery. It was part of Henry's five-year plan. Tenure. Check. Blonde wife. Check. A male child came somewhere after the home in the suburbs and the Mercedes, and somewhere before an elite preschool where Henry J. Stratford, III, could get a head start in Latin. "Rene," I replied softly, "I didn't mean—"

"I'm on my own, Wendi. Randy's out of the picture."

I sipped at my wine cooler and sat at the kitchen table, hoping she'd spill the story without my prodding. She did.

"This was his idea. He had this romantic idea of being a little family." She looked into her empty glass. "We were going to get married," she sniffed. "I missed my period last month, but I didn't let on. I wanted to be sure so I could surprise him."

She paused, and I was getting impatient. "So?"

"So by the time I was late again this month, I went to the clinic for a test. That's when they told me I was right. I was pregnant." She looked away again and wiped her eyes with the sleeve of a white blouse.

"I'm not getting this, Rene. You wanted this, right?"

"I did want this." She pushed the glass across the Corian countertop. "Once. But not now."

I waited for more.

"He thinks I cheated on him."

"Is he crazy?"

"I had to have a blood test at the clinic. They said it was all routine," she mumbled. "Part of the pregnancy workup." Again, she halted. Her story was in neutral, and I was flying ahead.

I stared at her, wishing I could push her forward. *Talk to me, Rene.*

Her eyes met mine and in a moment I could see the terror she held there. It was only a flash, but I knew, perhaps as only a sister could, that her fear was nearing a life maximum. I leaned forward. "What, Rene? You can tell me."

"I'm HIV-positive."

CHAPTER 9

Rene let the words hang for me to digest.

My baby sister, daughter of a Christian minister, pregnant out of wedlock. And HIV-positive.

I couldn't speak. I gathered my sister in my arms and cried. HIV haunted the halls of gays and drug abusers. Not heterosexuals. And certainly not respectable families like ours.

After I collected myself, my words tumbled forward in a rush. "But it's treatable. There are good drugs now. Antiretrovirals or some such pills," I said, waving my hand in the air. "I've heard Henry talk of it. It doesn't mean you're gonna die or anything. At least not for a long time."

She didn't respond. I don't think I was encouraging her.

My next thought was to kill the saxophone player. "Randy did this, that no good—"

"Wendi!"

"What?" I said, folding my arms across my chest. "I just started cussing yesterday." I nodded, assured this was an appropriate time. I shrugged. "Maybe I'm just tired of holding it in."

Rene shook her head. "He tested negative, Wendi. He didn't give it to me."

My hand went to my mouth. "But who—"

"Don't look at me that way!"

I didn't know how else to look. I turned away. "Who then?"

"It's a short list. All before Randy." She looked up. "I didn't cheat on him."

I didn't like Randy. "You should have."

She laughed, obviously surprised at my new brazenness. "You warned me about dating a musician."

I thought about my love for Jack and how many stupid things I must have said while living a plastic life. I pulled hard on the wine cooler in my hand and set the empty bottle on the counter. "So why come here? Why now?"

"Don't make me say it." She shrugged. "Where do I always go when I'm in trouble?"

"Why?"

"You have an ego problem, don't you? You just want me to say it, don't you?"

I was completely lost. "I'm family. That's why you're here."

"Dad and Mom are family. And I'm not there." She huffed. "You're together, Wendi." She gestured her hand around the house. "You've arrived. You've got a great husband, a great job. You're the daughter Dad always wanted." She walked to the refrigerator and emptied the carton of OJ into her glass. "Unlike me."

"You don't know me."

She let my comment fall.

I thought about spilling the story about the outward Christian frosting over the cake of my scrumptious evil heart. And I almost did. But just as I was taking a breath to begin, I saw a glint of hope in her eyes, a hope built on the me she thought I was and not the me I was about to reveal. I cleared my throat instead and offered an implant smile.

"What did you tell me when Simon left me?"

I opened my mouth, but my head was blank. I chewed air searching for advice long forgotten.

"What did you tell me when Grandma Aldridge had a stroke? What did you tell me after your accident?"

She'd come to a well looking for water, but I was dry. I had no idea what wisdom she expected.

She stared at me, but I just sat there empty and unresponsive. At least at that moment, I didn't offer a platitude I didn't believe in.

She put down her glass and touched my shoulder. "You told me God cares about us. That he's watching out for us even when it's dark."

I said those things. But no one ever asked me if I really believed it.

Guilt. My conscience attacked. I'd been nothing but an imposter, and now my sister wanted comfort that I couldn't manufacture.

Rene had always seemed the strong one to me. Confident. The one with the on-the-edge life. But now, with tears in her eyes, she was broken, and I couldn't come up with the everything's-gonna-be-alright message she craved. I studied her a moment, looking at the soft curl of her mousy brown hair and her lovely eyes. Sitting there in a petite frame was a warrior, and I knew she had the will to fight or she wouldn't have come. I just needed her to find the spark again.

My voice was paralyzed. I couldn't tell her the words I wished I believed. Instead, I crossed the kitchen and gathered her into my arms. She fell into me, crying into my blouse. I probed her hair, unable to speak.

"I'm afraid I'm going to die."

What was I to say? I opened my mouth in search of a phrase with a ring of truth, anything that might sound remotely close to a cozy blessing, even an "It's gonna be OK," but I couldn't say it. To say anything only propped me up as a poser, an actress in a play I'd promised to leave. Somehow to speak meant turning my back on a man lying on an ICU bed fighting for his life. A man who had to live if my dream of being free had any hope at all.

And so, with my soul barren, I simply held her and let my frustration vent in tears.

We must have cried for minutes on end. All I knew is that when she lifted her head, my blouse was soaked and her hair completely tangled. Somewhere in the middle, I'd found enough of my voice to whisper, "Oh Rene," and that had uncapped a second well and our tears flowed with new force until her sobs quieted once again.

When we separated, I turned back to the sink and leaned against the counter. "Why don't you talk to Daddy?"

I heard her huff. "I can't."

I understood. She'd not spoken to him since he'd told the congregation of her refusal to set aside her immoral ways. It was an ugly affair, a churchy event that seemed to me an inability to stand up to the church elders rather than the following of some biblical principle as he claimed. It was a year before I'd landed the perfect husband, the perfect future, and the perfect life.

I shook my head. I couldn't say the things that she wanted to hear.

I listened as Rene found the Kleenex box on the counter. She was never timid about blowing her nose. I looked at her, standing in a pair of capri jeans and a white blouse, which she left unbuttoned from the collar, one, two, three. Always one more open button than I dared.

I swallowed and reached for my own collar. I fumbled with a button and tugged the neckline open. This was the new me. More cleavage. Less whole-wheat.

I opened the refrigerator again. "You need to eat. How about a toad in the hole?"

She smiled. Daddy always called his special breakfast that, an egg fried in the middle of a piece of toast with a circular cutout. "Sure."

I worked, relieved to have something, anything to do but talk. Every minute or so, I glanced at her. She sat picking at her fingernails and saying nothing.

Finally, when I set the plate in front of her, she spoke again. "Randy changed the locks on his house. My bag was sitting on the porch yesterday evening when I got home."

I called Randy a bad word. The words tingled from my tongue bittersweet. I enjoyed it, but felt anxious, like a child testing a murky stream with a big toe.

Rene giggled.

"What?"

"You cussing." She shrugged. "It's funny."

I put my hands on my hips, incensed. I took a deep breath and scowled. I paused for a moment, searching for just the right way to emphasize the word before launching boldly ahead. I found another word that would have sent Miss Fogberry after the dishwater soap to cleanse my tongue. I launched it into the air, smiling. There! Uncharted waters.

This was too funny for Rene or just beyond reason, something akin to snow skis in hell or Mother Teresa with an AK–47. She began laughing hysterically, holding her stomach and swaying until I thought she might slip from the barstool.

This, of course, was funny to me and I responded in a proper giggle of my own.

When Rene finally regained her composure and began to eat, she ate like a wolf. I turned to the skillet and started a second toad in the hole.

She imitated Daddy's voice, the deep, croaky imitation of a frog he used every time he served us this breakfast when we were little. "Ribit. Riiiibit."

I joined the little chorus. "Ribit. Riiiibit."

We laughed again, and I marveled at how her mood had responded. A hug had worked so much better than the words I'd failed to offer.

"You can stay here," I said.

"I'd rather Daddy didn't know." She looked down. "At least for now."

I shrugged. "OK." I looked at my mischievous kitten clock with her eyes darting back and forth and thought about Jack. "I need to go to the hospital. I have a friend who was in an accident."

She shifted in her seat.

"Don't worry," I said. "I'll be home long before Henry."

Cindy Swanson peered across her surgical mask and studied the eyes of her attending surgeon, Henry Stratford. The eyes could communicate so much, something she had learned well in her years standing across the table from surgeons during her residency. With the mouth covered by a mask, she'd relied on her ability to read approval, displeasure, or anger from the small rectangle of the forehead and eyes.

She hoped the signals she sent were getting through. She'd taken extra time that morning with her mascara and eye shadow. Nothing extravagant or showy, just a subtle application to improve on nature's gift. She'd flirted with him before, but only in the brash banter that the surgeons so often used in a group. But now, seeing that the situation with his wife was fertile for her advances, she longed for an opportunity to express her feelings in private.

Dr. Stratford was the most compassionate man she'd worked with. So capable and confident, but so warm in his communication with his patients, a rarity among her other surgical teachers, who left the handholding to the nursing staff.

The game she planned was a dangerous one. With only six months left of her training, an affair with a supervising attending could be an assurance of an excellent recommendation or a blight on a career yet to begin. She knew in her head to stay away, but her heart prompted her forward. Surely she could be a more natural match for Henry than the bimbo that dared to insult him in public. She dreamed of fanning the sparks of physical attraction she felt whenever Henry leaned close to her to assist her through an operative case. And their love of surgery could lead to years of shared intellectual joys as well. *Certainly more than that uptight brunette he married. I can't imagine she could provide the intellectual challenge to keep Henry interested year after year.*

She removed the series of towel clips holding the skin together, allowing it to part to reveal the underlying fascia. "Scissors," she said, holding out her hand.

The technician placed the instrument in her open palm.

"Get the suction ready," Henry said.

She snipped the suture holding the abdominal fascia together. With all of the packing against the liver, the suture popped as she cut, and the sides of the abdominal wall opened like a book.

"Slowly now," Henry coached. "Remove the packs from above the liver first."

She obeyed, lifting out one blood-soaked pad after another. When they were all out, she held her breath. *Was it going to bleed?*

They peered into Jack Renner's open abdomen.

"Should I stitch the liver?"

Henry shook his head. "Better leave well enough alone. It's not bleeding. Let's get out of here."

"Should we drain it?"

"You know the answer to that."

Just like an attending. Always testing. Always teaching. "We'll need a Jackson-Pratt drain."

Henry's eyes smiled. "Good."

"Closing music," Cindy said. "Let Dr. Stratford choose."

Henry looked at the circulating nurse. "I'm in the mood for the Stones."

In a moment, "Beast of Burden" began prodding them home.

Cindy smiled behind her mask. Henry was full of surprises. "I've got the preliminary data for the trauma outcome predictor chart review. Can I bring them by your office?"

"Sure. After this case?"

She glanced at his eyes. He was all business. "Oh, I've promised the med students I'd meet them for a teaching session. Can I bring them by tonight? Will you be in your office at seven?"

"I can be."

Excellent. The department should be empty by then. "I'll come by." She let her gloved hand rest against his as she asked for a suture. It was a casual touch, something that could have been unintentional. She let it stay there until the technician complied with her request.

She felt her heart quicken. Dr. Stratford and her alone after hours. *Perfect.*

I left the house fighting guilt, so I visited Mom and read a chapter of *The Beautiful and Damned* before heading to the ICU waiting room. There, as I entered, I saw Steve and Miriam Renner sitting beside Yolanda, and all three behind a collection of luggage. Miriam stood and hugged me. "Your offer is such a lifesaver!"

I pulled away gently to see my father standing behind her. "These dear folks were staying at the Ramada, but he's retired and I knew you had the guest suite. I told them it would be no problem."

No problem for you! I tried not to cringe. For as long as we'd lived across the street from the church, my father had offered my guest quarters to missionaries, visiting preachers, and other company. The parsonage is much too small, he would say, calling at the last minute on Saturday eve. It didn't seem to bother Henry, but he was never home anyway.

I tried to send my father a stern look behind Mr. Renner's back, but he waved me off, knowing I would comply. I was about to object and tell him the guest quarters were taken, but I didn't want to betray Rene's confidence.

"Tell her, Steve. Tell her," Yolanda gushed.

Mr. Renner cleared his throat. "Jack is waking up."

"I thought they were keeping him on the ventilator," I said.

"Your husband operated on him this morning and removed the packs. He said the bleeding had stopped, and as long as it was OK with the neurosurgeons, they were going to try him off the ventilator ahead of schedule," Miriam said.

"Does he know you?" I asked.

Yolanda hugged me and squealed, "We haven't seen him yet. The nurse is supposed to come get us as soon as he can speak."

Great, I thought, *I'll probably have to visit with Yolanda. I need to talk to Jack alone.*

A few minutes later, Brenda, Jack's nurse, came out with news. Jack was off the ventilator, still a bit groggy, but able to speak a bit, and she would let us visit two at a time.

She led the Renners away, and I was left with Yolanda and my father in the waiting room. I pulled my father aside and whispered, "How could you invite them to stay without asking? How do you think Henry will feel about keeping the family of one of his patients?"

"It's church family, honey. We always look out for those in the fold, you know that."

I refrained from rolling my eyes. "I don't like it."

"It's probably only a few days. Then Jack will be out of the woods and they will be going home again."

I watched as Yolanda paced, twirling the blonde hair over her right ear with her finger. Her nervous energy made me want to scream.

A few minutes later, Steve escorted Miriam onto a waiting room chair.

I touched Steve's shoulder. "How is he?"

"His memory is a bit blurry."

Miriam sniffed.

Yolanda wanted details. "Did he ask for me?"

Steve shook his head and took Yolanda by the hand. "I'm not sure he knew us, Yolanda. This may take some time."

"Surely he'll remember me. Did you ask him what he remembers?"

Miriam nodded. "I could see it in his eyes. He recognized me. I told him I was his mother. I told him his fiancée would be coming in. I told him you were very beautiful and that he'd made a wise choice."

I wanted to barf. *Jack loves me!*

Brenda opened the door to the ICU and looked at me. "Next?"

Yolanda grabbed my hand. "Go with me, won't you? I'm not sure I can see him alone."

I tried to smile, but managed only a nod. "Let's go."

Brenda led us to Jack's side. His head was still swollen and shaved, but the pressure monitor entering his scalp had been removed and I recognized the first hint of a smile.

Yolanda was the first to speak. "Hi, Jack." Her hands were folded across her chest as if she was afraid to touch him.

"Do I know you?"

I watched Yolanda's jaw slacken as Jack held up his hand and continued. "Wait, don't tell me," he said, his voice strained and just above a whisper.

We leaned in to hear.

"The man and woman who were just here, they told me my fiancée was coming in." He shook his head. "I'm afraid things are a bit fuzzy."

He stared at us with bloodshot eyes and nodded. "But the woman said I had good taste and that my girl was very beautiful." He looked away from Yolanda and took my hand, cradling it in his. "You must be my fiancée."

Yolanda pulled my hand from his. "Jack!"

His expression was blank. "What?"

"I'm your fiancée!" she screamed. "Don't you remember?"

He studied her for a moment and shook his head, and then turned to me. "You look familiar," he said.

Yolanda shook her head. "He's brain damaged!" She fled the room sobbing as Jack gathered my hand back in his.

"You," he said, "are very beautiful. You must be my girl."

CHAPTER 10

J ack still held my hand as Henry appeared at the edge of the ICU bed. I felt immediate heat in my cheeks and stuttered as I pulled my hand away. "Jack, you've lost your memory. I'm Wendi Stratford. The woman who just left was your fiancée." I smiled sheepishly at Henry. "He thought I was Yolanda."

Jack coughed. "Yolanda?"

"Yolanda is the name of your fiancée." I tilted my head towards the exit. "The woman who just left."

"I don't know a Yolanda," Jack said. He looked at me. "I was engaged?"

Henry walked to my side. I nodded. "You were engaged." Henry touched my arm. "This is my husband, Jack. He's your surgeon, Henry Stratford."

Henry took Jack's hand, feeling his pulse at the wrist. "What year is it, Jack?"

"Two thousand eight."

I looked at Henry. "How can he know this and not remember his fiancée?"

Henry shrugged. "Perhaps the injury has robbed his recent memory."

"I remember you," he said, looking at me.

I feared what he might say. "You were my piano teacher."

Jack smiled. "I remember playing the piano."

"Do you remember teaching me? You were at my house just before your accident."

He looked from me to Henry and back to me before shaking his head. "'Fraid not."

It took me a few seconds to remember to breathe. *You don't remember?!* I paused, wondering how this new development affected my plans for our future. I'd shamelessly confessed my attraction to him, brazenly throwing myself in his path. But now, he didn't remember. My mind raced around the possibilities, each thought a new stream breaking away from the banks of my old dilemma.

It dawned on me ... my sins had been forgotten. I wasn't sure what to feel. In part, I was relieved. No one knew of my bold departure from my former life. I squinted at Jack. This was an unexpected development, perhaps something I could use to my advantage. I'd just been handed the chance to drop the golf ball of my life back onto the fairway after hopelessly losing it in the trees. It was a life do-over, a heavenly mulligan from heaven's golf pro.

I was suspicious. "You don't remember being at my house before your accident?"

Jack seemed to be chewing over my question. He looked over me for a moment before replying. "I was at your house?"

I watched as Henry laid his stethoscope on Jack's chest. "Take a deep breath," Henry coached. He moved his instrument to a new location. "Again."

Here, Henry was at home, fluid in his environment. He smiled reassuringly at Jack. "I'll need you to do something today. Something that's going to hurt, but something's that's very important. I need you to cough." He paused. "You need to do this to prevent any complications like pneumonia. Do you think you can do that for me?"

Jack nodded. "I'll try."

Henry demonstrated how to brace a pillow across his abdominal incision to make coughing less painful.

Here, Henry was compassionate.

Watching my surgeon husband took me back to the time he took care of me, a time when his tenderness swept me into love. For a moment, I felt the heat of an old flame.

Was this bout of amnesia an unexpected gift to me, a burying of my adulterous behavior? Was God giving me a second chance at walking the straight and narrow?

Or was I cursed to return to my plastic life?

Henry gently touched Jack's shoulder and smiled. "Can't blame a guy for thinking a woman like that would be a great fiancée. She's beautiful," he said softly, winking at me. "And she's mine."

My heart ached. Henry never showed this type of flirtatious behavior in front of others. *Don't do this now, Henry. I was done with loving you and the masks I've been wearing!*

Part of me wanted to grab Jack's hand in mine and tell him that the reason he remembered me was that we were destined to be soul mates, that undoubtedly his subconscious was sending him subtle memories of our plans.

The Baptist part of me, the reliable, stable, smile-at-everyone-in-church part of me, held back.

I looked at Jack. Innocent Jack. Even with his amnesia, he seemed incapable of dishonesty. He thought I was beautiful, so he said it. What-you-see-is-what-you-get Jack.

I looked back at Henry. Capable, compassionate, and today, a rare gem: flirtatious.

"Get strong, Jack. You have a good man pulling for you," I said.

I slipped out of the cubicle and waited for Henry. A few minutes later, he stepped away from the bed.

"We've got problems," I said. "My father offered our guest quarters to Jack's parents and his fiancée."

"Nice of him to ask."

"You know Daddy." I shrugged. "But that's not all. Rene showed up this morning. She's separated from Randy and needs a place to stay."

"Sounds like a good evening to work late," he said, looking past me to the nursing station. "I've got some research data I need to work on. Don't count on me for supper. Besides," he added, "I'd like to be around for a few extra hours since Jack has just come off the ventilator, to make sure he flies."

Since when do I count on you for supper? I sighed. "OK."

"Just put Rene in the nursery. You can blow up the air mattress in there and let Jack's family have the guest suite downstairs."

I nodded.

He seemed to be scanning the nursing station. He didn't look at me when he talked. "I'll be home late."

With that, he walked away, leaving me alone.

I traded glances with Brenda, my nurse-girlfriend. I didn't feel like baring my soul. Jack had forgotten me. I walked from the ICU feeling alone and guilty.

I gave the Renners and Yolanda directions to my place. "Come for dinner at seven," I urged. It was the Christian thing to do.

Then, I rushed home to prepare dinner and figure out what to do with Rene.

When I arrived home, Rene was hanging up the phone. I looked at the sheet of paper in her hand. She'd scribbled a phone number for a family planning clinic in Northern Virginia. I immediately recognized the clinic's name and felt a stab of guilt. Years before, my mother had made a similar appointment for me.

She jerked the paper back and held it against her chest.

"I know what you're doing, Rene."

"And I know you'll try to talk me out of it," she said. "But you don't have any idea what it's like to be in my shoes."

I know exactly what it's like to be in your shoes. Except for the HIV. I nodded. "Is that what you want me to do?"

"Of course not."

"Then why did you come home? You could have stayed in New Orleans and gotten what you wanted without the family hassle."

Rene looked away. I'd struck a nerve. Maybe she didn't realize it, but I knew any family member of mine couldn't go forward with a decision to have an abortion without at least a little internal conflict. Except for our mother.

What she didn't know, and I wasn't ready to tell her, was that I'd headed down that same road myself with my mother's guidance, all in the name of protecting my father's precious ministry. *"What John doesn't know can't hurt him."*

Rene's eyes started tearing. "I can't take care of a baby, Wendi. HIV-positive mothers can't even breast-feed without putting their babies at risk."

"So the answer is killing it?" Immediately, I felt guilty for my comment. I had no business judging her.

"You don't understand."

"I understand guilt."

"That's your problem." She said, stomping towards the basement stairs.

"Rene," I said, calling after her. "Look, I'm sorry. You don't know everything about me. You can't begin to assume you know why I react like I do."

She whirled around to face me. "You think I've got what I deserved."

"What are you talking about?"

"You think God is judging me."

"Rene, I'd never say you deserved this!"

"You don't have to say it."

"You're projecting your own feelings on me. Do you think God is punishing you?"

Our eyes locked for a moment before she turned away and spoke in a volume just above a whisper. "Maybe."

I shook my head. "God doesn't work that way." As soon as I said it, I mentally berated myself for saying the words I didn't believe. I'd given that up. Besides, I still thought my car accident was because I slept with a married man.

We looked at each other silently for a moment, me not admitting my hypocrisy and Rene a guilty mess. "Will you drive me to the clinic? They said I need someone to drive me home."

"Why don't you think about this for a while? There's no rush."

"I don't want a baby."

"And maybe I do." The words were out before I could stop them, before I'd even had time to consider the truth of my own desires.

She started down the stairs. "You're insane."

I called down after her. "Dinner's at seven."

"Hooray. I get to argue with Henry."

"Good news. Henry's not coming home for dinner."

"Why don't we go out? Is The Hardware Store still open?"

"It's not just us. Daddy invited a few guests."

"Daddy?"

I sighed. "I couldn't say 'no.' Our choir director was in an accident. He's the friend I visited in the hospital. His family is in town. Dad is always offering my guest suite to church folks."

"So I go to Motel 6?"

I shrugged. "You stay in the baby's room."

At seven, I welcomed Steve and Miriam Renner, Yolanda, and Rene to the table. We sat in the alcove off the kitchen, a bay-windowed area with a view of the setting sun. It was nestled at the back of the house and looked away from my father's Baptist church across the road. It was my favorite place in the house, with windows opening into the wooded area leading down the hill towards Route 29.

I set the last of the dishes on the table and smiled. I exchanged glances with my guests. Obviously, they were waiting for some sort of blessing before the food was passed. I cleared my throat. I could do this. I'd heard my father do it a thousand times. *Hypocrite or not, here I go.* "Let's say grace. Thy abundant blessing we receive from thy hand. To thy service give us strength." I paused, promising myself never to talk in an ancient language to God again. Down with artificial sweeteners, up with things natural like sugar and talking to God in my own heart language, even if it wasn't PC. "Amen."

We chatted nervously about the weather and the food, a spicy sausage lasagna, garlic French bread, and mixed green salad. It was as if we tiptoed around a minefield, trying not to mention Jack or his amnesia, so as not to injure fragile Yolanda.

When Jack's parents started talking about his condition, Yolanda shook her head, obviously tortured by the discussion. "Did I tell you that Jack is going to write a song for our wedding?"

Miriam nodded. "I think you mentioned it. Has he sung it for you?"

"He said I'll hear it when everyone else does," she said, wiping the corner of her eye. "He's such a hopeless romantic."

At that moment, I decided the appropriate honest response would be to slap her. But I seemed plastered into a mold I couldn't escape, so I just nodded and tried to smile. I glanced at Rene, hoping she wouldn't open her mouth and act like she was gagging herself with her finger.

I wondered when life would settle down and let me remove my happy-mask. Maybe when Jack was out of the woods, I would find the chutzpah to confront Henry and Yolanda with the truth: Jack loved me. For now, I was afraid of telling the truth to him because I wanted him to care for Jack. Since my plan A to escape my plastic life had failed, perhaps and I'd have to shift to plan B.

If only I had a plan B. I considered my options: *Smother Yolanda while she sleeps in my guest room, then run off with Jack once he recovers.* My mind raced ahead. *Perhaps I could just work a trade with her. I'll give Henry to blonde Yolanda and she'll give brain-damaged Jack to me.*

I smiled, thankful for the respite of my secret monologue.

Yolanda frowned, her brain obviously launching forward to the next emotion. She looked at me. "Do you think his memory will recover?"

I was used to this. Just because I'd married a doctor, people asked me for medical opinions all the time. I was immediately conflicted. I kind of liked the present situation. Jack seemed to have forgotten Yolanda and was enamored with me. My sin was buried, and no one was the wiser for my craziness. On the other hand, here I was, trapped playing gracious host to the competition, and supportive Christian sister to Rene. If Jack recovered and remembered my proposition, he'd likely force me out of the closet, scandal would ensue, my father's ministry would be tarnished, Yolanda would lose, and Henry would be humiliated.

And Jack and I would live happily ever after. At least in my fantasy.

Yolanda leaned forward. "Wendi?"

"Oh, of course," I said halfheartedly. "Don't most people get their memory back?"

Rene scrapped the edges of her dessert goblet. "I heard of one man who woke up after an accident and thought he was a woman."

I scowled at my sister. "Thanks for sharing."

She stood up. "I think I'll turn in early." She turned around when she was in the kitchen and said, "Wendi, can you give me a lift to my doctor's appointment tomorrow? I'm due in Arlington at 11:30."

I stared at her. It was just like her to ask me in front of a crowd to assure I'd maintain my hospitality façade. I sighed, just enough to let her know I was annoyed, but casually enough to suggest that I might be merely fatigued. "Sure." I sent her a telepathic sister message with my eyes. *This discussion isn't over, Sis. We'll talk later.*

I reached for another helping of mousse. Maybe I wasn't being honest about everything, but at least I wasn't going to hide in the kitchen and have another dessert after my guests had gone like I usually did.

Ahhh, I thought, rolling the creamy fluff around my mouth. *Life is short. Next time I'll start with dessert.*

CHAPTER 11

A soft knocking interrupted Henry's thoughts. He looked up from his desk to see his door opening. Cindy Swanson entered and closed the door behind her. "Hi, Dr. Stratford." She wore a white lab coat, which she quickly shed, hanging it on the inside of the door next to his. She was in green scrub attire, having chosen a men's top a size too big and gapping at the neckline as she leaned forward over the desk and laid a folder in front of him.

Trying not to be distracted, he fumbled with the report, opening it to the first page. "It looks like you've put a lot of work into this."

She walked around and sat on the edge of his desk. Her perfume was intoxicating. She lifted her hair and laid it behind an ear graced by three small golden hoops. "I need you to read through the statistical analysis."

He lowered his head to read and felt her hand on his shoulder. She slipped behind him, with her fingers massaging his neck. "You've been stressed," she said, kneading the tension from his shoulders. "Is everything all right?"

Her touch was magic. How long had it been since Wendi had spontaneously touched him like this? He felt warmed and alarmed all at once. Cindy was young. Young, pretty, and smart. He relaxed as she continued to work, but tensed as soon as he felt the front of her scrubtop brush the back of his head. Caution lights flashed a warning. He lifted his hand and laid it on hers, interrupting her touch. "Thanks."

Instead of taking a hint, she slipped back around and leaned against his desk again. Even in scrubs, she was beautiful. Her lipstick was perfect and her eyes were embellished with just the right amount of mascara. "Is everything alright at home?"

"Oh, you know, the regular stressors." He looked up and met her eyes. "Surgery is a difficult mistress to compete with."

"There's an understatement." She looked away. Was she blushing? "I guess that's where having a spouse in medicine would come in handy. I could totally empathize with your schedule demands."

He pulled his eyes back to the report and turned the page, but she put her hand on his and whispered. "We're alone, Henry."

No resident ever called him Henry.

His throat was immediately parched. "I, I, we—" *We what?*

She lowered her face to his. When he didn't move away, she smiled. In a moment, she had slipped into his lap and the warmth and taste of her mouth was the only thing on his mind. Without thinking, his hand went to her hair, his lips responding. But as he fell further and further into the forbidden, the caution light in his brain flared to an urgent red. He found his voice and pushed her away.

"No."

Her face was inches from him, her breathing fast and warm against his face. She stood up and sat again on his desk. "I'm sorry, I—"

"Cindy, we can't do this." He paused, thinking. "Not now."

She looked away. "Not now?"

He took a deep breath. "Not now."

He watched as a smile crept upon her face. She kept her eyes locked on the floor.

He picked up the report in front of him. "Why don't you give me some time to look at your data," he said. "Then we can get together again."

She nodded. "OK," she said, lifting her eyes to meet his again. She pulled a tissue from the pocket of her scrubs and moistened it with her tongue. Then, she rubbed the lipstick from the edge of his mouth. "There," she said. "Now you're perfect."

R ene tried to lose herself in a novel, but couldn't concentrate. Every few minutes, she lifted her eyes from the pages to look at the colorful way Wendi had decorated the nursery. She'd used a Noah's ark theme with a rainbow wallpaper border and a little mobile of animals hanging above a white wooden crib.

Rene rose from the rocking chair and snapped a little smiling elephant that hung in the mobile. She watched the elephant spin. This room revealed a Wendi she'd not known before. Wendi the confident, she knew. Wendi the righteous, strong in the face of her own disability, she knew. Wendi the competent expert witness, she knew. But this ... a motherly Wendi?

Rene twisted a ceramic little ark sitting on a round base. A familiar lullaby began to play.

She sat down in the chair and began to rock.

And then she began to cry.

I n spite of the late hour, Henry took the long way home, relishing a moment of alone time straddling his Triumph. He needed space to think, and as he rolled on the throttle, he enjoyed the immediate response that pulled him back and away from the handlebars.

He accelerated through the gears and spoke her name from within the sanctity of his full coverage helmet. "Cindy."

The memory of their contact excited him, warmed him, and terrified him. Since Wendi had blown into his life, no other woman had held such an allure. One moment he relived the experience of Cindy's embrace, the next, he berated himself for letting down his guard. He was a tenured professor and a prominent member of the Baptist church. He had to avoid the appearance of impropriety. Was there any way to enjoy the hidden delicacy that Cindy offered without tarnishing his image?

He felt the tension of conflicting emotions. He was angry that he'd let himself down, risking so much for a little pleasure, but with every bit of rage, there arose within him a memory of her perfume, the feeling of her breath on his lips and the desire for more.

He turned up Azalea Drive, climbing the hill towards home and the wife he once thought would satisfy him forever.

He thought of Wendi and his patient, her piano teacher. He remembered the blush of her cheeks as he walked in and found her holding Jack's hand. Jealousy was a thorn that pricked his soul and drove him towards despair. He could not endure the humiliation that losing his young bride would cause.

As he parked in the garage, he thought again of Cindy, and his hand went to his mouth, rubbing the edge of his lips as he remembered the softness of her touch. He shook his head and fought off the emotion he'd often chided his wife for battling: guilt. Kissing Cindy, as wonderful as it had seemed ... was wrong.

Was that why it excited him so?

He let himself in the house quietly, expected everyone to be asleep. He removed his shoes and walked into the foyer, glancing into the living room to see that Wendi was up, her long, blonde hair cascading over the back of the couch. He watched her for a moment with her unaware, and again felt a pang of conscience. He approached from behind, thinking perhaps that she slept. *What better way to absolve my guilt than to show her my affection?*

He leaned over and planted his lips on her cheek.

Immediately, she pulled away and screamed.

The sound was enough to scare him. He jerked away to see that it wasn't Wendi at all. It was Jack's fiancée! "Yolanda," he said. "I-I thought you were my wife."

Her hand rested on her cheek, covering the violation. "Your wife?!"

"Y-yes," he stuttered, "the blonde hair."

She shook her head. "Your wife looks nothing like me!" She stood and backed away with the couch between them. "You dare to assume that I—"

"Until yesterday, I wore my hair exactly like you."

Henry looked up to see Wendi.

Yolanda pointed at Henry. "He kissed me!"

"Wendi, I'd forgotten about your haircut. When I saw her there, I thought it was you."

Wendi picked up a small picture frame from the mantle of the fireplace. It was a recent photograph of her and Henry taken at the lodge at Wintergreen Ski Resort. She held it up for Yolanda to see her long blonde hair. She laughed. "Henry is a lot of things, but a womanizer isn't one of them."

Henry stepped back and laid his fist over his heart, watching Wendi as remorse closed around him. *Could I ever really walk away from you?*

That night, I lay in the dim light of our bedroom and stared at the ceiling. "I'm worried about Rene," I whispered.

Henry sighed. "She's a big girl."

I faced him. "She's pregnant."

Henry lay there, considering my words. Then, "Not exactly a convenient time for Randy to toss her out."

"It's complicated, Henry. She's HIV-positive."

He touched my cheek with his fingers and rolled my hair behind my ear. "Wendi, I'm so sorry."

"Randy accused her of being unfaithful."

"He's been tested?"

"He's negative. That's why he thinks she cheated on him."

"You believe her?"

I sighed. "Of course." I curled away from Henry pulling his arm around me. "She wants an abortion. I'm supposed to take her to a clinic tomorrow."

"Abortion? She needs time to think this through."

He stayed quiet for a moment, and I felt his breath on the back of my neck. "What are you going to do?"

"I don't know."

He stroked my hair and whispered. "We've got a nursery, Wendi."

I gasped. "What are you saying?"

Henry didn't answer. He just snuggled towards me and kissed my neck.

I was floored. In a thousand years I would never have suspected that from him — that he would speak my heart. Something in me twisted, a flare of regret for what I was giving up. This was the Henry I'd longed for. Without thinking, I reached for him. "Sometimes you surprise me, Dr. Stratford," I whispered, pulling his hand to my mouth. I kissed his hand and then cradled it in my own.

We stayed that way for a few minutes as I reminded my heart of why I'd fallen for this man. Yes, he worked late and made me fight for second place, but he was compassionate and thorough with his patients, something that gave me comfort since he was the one in charge of Jack. The pendulum of my heart stood still, threatening to arc in the opposite direction from the one I'd been on: an arc towards loneliness, emotional isolation, and divorce.

He kept nuzzling my neck, and if I understood anything about the male psyche, I suspected he was enamored by the idea of making love to a short brunette, rather than the long blonde I'd been for him for so long.

"You would adopt Rene's baby?" I asked softly.

"A boy would be nice," he said.

A boy. Of course. It was part of Henry's obsession with a perfect life. First the perfect wife. Then the perfect family: oldest son, younger daughter, separated by two years.

This was not on my agenda. This was the end of day two of the new me. I was supposed to be in Jamaica with a new love. I was not supposed to be dreaming of beginning a family with my image-sensitive husband.

But just then, I wondered if Jack's amnesia might not be a second chance with Henry. I closed my eyes and pushed my body against my husband's. There was something comfortable about being with Henry that night, and amazingly, he seemed content to just hold me without demanding more.

As I neared sleep, Henry's voice filled the silence. "I'm so sorry," he said.

I didn't understand what he meant. Perhaps it was his embarrassment over kissing Yolanda. Maybe he was sorry about Rene or about being home late. I wasn't sure, and he didn't volunteer more. "Shh," I said, comfortable in his arms. Just then, I didn't want to know any more. If this was guilt, it was a new emotion for Henry.

I felt his body shudder against mine before he whispered again, "I'm so sorry."

CHAPTER 12

The next morning, I drove without speaking, the rhythmic squeak of my windshield wipers and the pelting rain the only noise between us. Rene kept her face towards her window, leaving me alone in my thoughts.

Invariably, my mind was drawn to my own trip to this same clinic. It was a day that changed my life.

Mother drove. I stared out the side window and thought about a man who said he loved me. At least until I carried his baby. "Did you threaten him?"

My mother focused on the traffic. "I only helped him see what was best for his family, Wendi."

"You threatened him."

"I don't expect you to understand."

I sulked. She was the one who didn't understand. The only thing she understood was her husband's standing in the community and protecting his ministry. My baby, his grandchild, was someone he'd never know about. Mom had seen to that. I watched as we passed a vineyard on a Virginia hillside.

When I turned back, I saw her brush a tear from her eye.

"What? What makes you cry now?"

"It's not like I wanted it this way," she said. "I've dreamed of being a grandmother, you know." Her voice cracked, and for a moment, she pressed her hand against her face.

When she refocused on the highway, it was too late to swerve. A pickup truck was in our lane, across the center line and closing fast. My scream was the last thing I remember.

I gasped at the freshness of the old horror. Rene looked at me. "Everything alright over there?"

I felt heat in my cheeks. "An old memory, that's all."

"Why are you doing this?"

"Doing what?"

"Taking me to an abortion clinic. It's about the last thing I'd expect from you."

"You're my sister."

"All the more reason to impose your beliefs on me."

I clenched my teeth. I needed to come clean. Out with the truth. Down with the good-Christian mask. "I'm sick of being a hypocrite."

"You feel like a hypocrite for taking me to the clinic?"

I shook my head. "No."

"Then you think what I'm doing is OK?"

"No." I sighed. "It's complicated, Rene. I think abortion is wrong, but I'd feel like a hypocrite if I didn't take you."

"But you—"

"I'm not who you think I am, Rene. I'm not the good little pastor's daughter that you seem to think." I glanced at her. I had her attention.

"Just because you were bold enough to cuss in front of me doesn't mean—"

"I'd be a hypocrite for not taking you to the clinic, because I was in your shoes once, and I wanted someone to take me."

She tilted her head and squinted her eyes in a question. "What?"

I took a deep breath and blew it out through pursed lips, wondering if I could spill it after all these years. My and my mother's darkest secret. "Remember my accident?"

I kept my eyes on the road, but could appreciate her nod out of the corner of my eye.

"I was on my way to this same clinic that day."

"What?" Her voice was tense. "You were pregnant?"

I glanced at my sister. Her mouth hung open as if this was incomprehensible. "But Mom was in the car. She was driving, right?"

I nodded slowly. "You're getting the picture. She was taking me to the clinic."

"Not Mom. She didn't know about the baby, did she?"

I felt an anxious cramp in my gut. "Who do you think arranged the abortion?" I shot a look at Rene before refocusing on the highway. "Even if I'd wanted the baby, she wouldn't hear of it."

"Mom?" She shook her head.

I watched as Rene wrestled silently with the news. After a minute, shock changed to emotion of a different sort. "That two-faced—"

My stomach tightened. "Just like me, Rene. Vanilla on the outside. But inside, pure chocolate."

"I don't understand."

"It's not *that* complicated. Mom was protecting Daddy. She was afraid of the scandal if the word got out that I was pregnant. We must keep up proper appearances," I mocked.

"But who ..." her voice trailed off.

I finished the question for her. "Who was the father? Bob Seaton."

"The youth pastor?"

"Now you're starting to understand the scandal."

"I'm not believin' this." She fell into a sullen silence. I felt her eyes examining me and then saw the shake of her head from the corner of my eye. When I finally glanced at Rene again, her head was leaning against the side window, her eyes staring out at the passing roadside.

"Maybe you understand why Mother loved Henry so much."

She didn't reply.

"They are both consumed with appearances. Henry's the perfect surgeon, the perfect husband with the perfect wife, the perfect back-row Christian. Mother was the perfect pastor's wife." I paused. "At least until I ruined her perfect life."

"You? What about me? I've never been the perfect pastor's daughter."

"But you were gone. Out of sight, out of mind. I was here for everyone to see."

"Why did you do this to me?"

"Do what?"

"Isolate me. Make me feel like the bad guy." She pointed an index finger at my cheek, holding it within inches of my face. "And all along," she said, mocking in a dainty voice, "you and Mother were covering up, pretending to be above my rebellion."

The accusation stung. And stuck. Everything she said was true, and I hated every word of it. "I know, Rene. And I'm sorry."

The rain increased, pounding the windshield. I felt my chest tighten as I turned up the windshield wipers. A moment later, I slowed and pulled onto the gravel shoulder. I looked at my blurred sister through my own tears. "I hate myself for it. And I want out. I don't want to fake my way through life anymore. I hate what it's done to me, and I hate what it made me do to you."

Rene shook her head and leaned over to turn on the car's flashers. She raised her voice to overcome the thunderous pounding on the roof. She squinted towards the road behind us. "You're going to get us killed, you know."

"Look at me," I coaxed. "I envy you."

Her mouth fell open. "You're insane."

I shook my head. "I'm serious." I looked away, unable to hide from her searching eyes. "You and I aren't as different as you think. But you never cared what others thought. You didn't care about Mom and Dad. You didn't care about the church—"

She grabbed my arm. "Don't say it."

I pulled away. "It's true!"

"No!" She seemed to hesitate. "I acted like I didn't care. But I always wished I could be the daughter that Daddy loved. I wanted to be you."

I shook my head. "Daddy loves the daughter he thinks I am." I looked back at her. She was crying too. "You're wrong. Daddy loves you. But he knew all about your life."

She huffed a protest. "So he shuns me. That's love?"

"Yes! That's the only way he knew to show it. He thought it would bring you back."

"He doesn't know everything. He doesn't know I'm pregnant. He doesn't know I've got HIV." She sniffed. "I always wanted to be you."

"Aren't we quite the pair," I said, my voice thickening. "I wanted to be you. You wanted to be me." I flipped the electronic door lock. I yelled to overcome the downpour. "Switch with me."

She yelled back. "What?"

"You drive the Mercedes for a while. Let's switch." I stared at her. "Come on, you drive."

"You're mad."

"I just want to be honest. Finally."

She shrugged as I flung open my door and jumped out into the rain. She made a mirror image dash around the front of the car. We collided in front of the Mercedes hood ornament.

It was the moment that the craziness of it all seemed to hit me face-on. I grabbed Rene to keep from slipping. She shook her head and lifted her face against the downpour, resigned to the drenching. Then she lowered her face to mine. I couldn't tell the difference between her tears and the rain. Both had mixed to throw her bangs into a tangle on her forehead.

"I'm so sorry," I cried.

She laughed. Laughed at me in my brokenness.

And amazingly, I found a chuckle escaping from my lips too. Honesty felt good. Soul-cleansing good, just like the rain. We embraced before she pushed me away. "Get in," she yelled. "Before we melt!"

It was a joke from our childhood. I used to tease her whenever we did anything bad. It started when she was in the eighth grade and she told me how she'd kissed Derrick Knicely in the little anteroom behind the pulpit in the church. She'd backed him up against the baptismal and dared to touch tongues, a wickedness I was sure God recorded. She wagged her head at me as she bragged. "So I'm the Wicked Witch of the West." I pointed my finger at her. "You'll melt if you get wet." She only laughed and imitated the evil laugh from the witch in *The Wizard of Oz*. "I'm melting!"

We ran around the car and assumed our new positions, me in the passenger's seat and Rene preparing to drive.

We waited in silence for a few minutes until the rain slackened. Then she turned to me and said, "Do you believe all the stuff Dad taught us?"

I wrinkled my forehead at her.

"You know, all the Christianity junk."

I didn't know how to answer. I knew one thing. If it was real, I hadn't experienced it. But I was a professional at looking like I believed it. "I believe in God," I said, looking down.

"Do you believe he loves us?"

I shook my head. "I don't know. I feel guilty most Sundays."

Rene tapped the steering wheel. "You know what's weird? I believe that part of what Dad taught. That God loves me."

"He taught you that?" I was tempted to scoff. "All I seem to remember is that I'm a sinner. I'll never be good enough."

"You know what's weird? I came home thinking you would help rescue me." She shrugged. "You know, the lost prodigal."

I touched her arm. "Maybe you'll rescue me."

She looked both ways and pulled out onto the highway, making a U-turn.

"What are you doing?"

"Going home." She glanced over at me. "You were supposed to talk me out of this clinic trip, Wendi. That's why I came back to my Christian sister when I was in trouble."

"What a joke."

She sighed. "So tell me about Bob Seaton."

CHAPTER 13

Henry looked at the log of missed messages on his phone and winced. *Jesse Anders.* The name brought with it a snow blanket of bad feelings. And now, with Anders in a corner, he was reacting, threatening to disrupt the snow into an avalanche of trouble.

Maybe I've misjudged him. Could Jesse really be a danger?

Henry shook his head. It seemed unlikely. And Jesse had waited too long to bring a legitimate lawsuit.

So why did he let the name tighten his gut and disrupt his control?

Henry told himself not to worry. That Jesse was a pest. A low-life druggie and no more, a disgruntled family member of a patient Henry would rather forget.

If only I'd had the guts to cut him off months ago.

I glanced at Rene. She wanted the scoop on Bob Seaton. I took a deep breath and wondered where to begin.

It was the season for our big Christmas pageant at the Baptist church. It was my father's baby, a huge community outreach deal, the one time of year that brought me as close to embracing the gospel story as anything ever did. It was as if the manger scene, the carols, the gifts, and the swell of the choir tempted my heart to believe that a God had been born of a woman. Almost. At least at Christmas, I wanted to believe, and for those days of pageantry, singing of a plan born long ago in the heart of God, my emotions convinced me I did, and I felt less of an imposter when I sang at Christmas than any other time.

Of course, that was before Christmas reminded me of Bob Seaton. He was the youth pastor in our church, the sort of guy the kids all loved. He was an athlete-turned-seminarian and had the body to prove it. I was fourteen. Naïve. My body was mature, but my head was adolescent, and to me and a half dozen other estrogen-crazed teens, Bob Seaton was the epitome of hot.

I'd returned to church to pick up the music I'd left on my stand during a practice. The building was rich with the smell of cedar garland and quiet except for my own footsteps. I sat on the front pew and tried to take it all in. Poinsettias, several large Christmas trees, and of course, a humble stable and the centerpiece manger prompted a longing within me. Was it all just a made-up story?

"Need company?" The voice was Bob's.

I lifted my hand to my cheek and hoped he didn't notice the dampness in the dim light. "I didn't hear you come in."

"Just locking up," he said, sitting beside me.

We sat that way for a minute. He must have known my need for silence. He leaned forward, and I sensed he was going to stand to leave.

That's when I touched his hand. "Do you believe it?"

His eyes searched my face.

"You know, the whole story is so wonderful. Jesus coming to earth." I hung my head. "I struggle to believe."

"You're not alone, Wendi. Everyone fights doubts at some time or another."

I didn't want to confess that my whole life was a big question.

He talked about how much he loved my solo, how the whole message of Christmas in my voice gave him chills. I found myself wishing I'd get chills over the message.

"Thanks," I said.

"Pray with me," he said, reaching out and taking my hand in his.

The prayer I don't remember. All I remember is the powerful sense that this man cared about me. I was aware only of the gentleness of his touch as he cradled my hand in his. When he finished praying I found myself facing him, our heads bowed together, our foreheads just touching and our breath mixing as I echoed his "amen" in a gasp of my own.

How exactly we began to kiss, I can't say. But I only remember feeling like no one would ever make me feel that good again and pushing away a little prompting that told me I was desecrating something holy there on the front pew of the Baptist church.

Rene pulled into my driveway, and looked at me, our first eye contact since my confession.

"Now what?" I asked.

"I think I'll go see an obstetrician."

I let my mouth fall open, then smiled. She was counting on me trying to stop her all along. Perhaps the Aldridge conscience in her was stronger than I thought.

She smiled. "Maybe."

I took a deep breath. "I'll go with you."

Saturday evenings meant Henry's favorite Caesar salad, grilled lamb chops, and rice pilaf. To say that we were in a nutritional rut would be to misunderstand my husband's compulsive quest for the perfect life. On Monday and Wednesday we ate fish. The fish, of course, was broiled. Henry's total cholesterol was a paltry 157. Tuesday was salad day, Thursday, pork or chicken. Fridays we dined at the Boarshead Inn and Henry had beef. Sunday after the service at First Baptist we took in the brunch buffet at the Omni.

But that night, Henry didn't show for dinner, leaving me to entertain the masses by myself.

Chatty Yolanda bemoaned the loss of her darling Jack. His overall condition had improved with the exception that his head injury left him without a memory or an apparent care for her. "What with the wedding coming up in a few months, he doesn't have time to fall in love with me before the ceremony!"

"Now, now," said Steve. "It's only been a few days. He's likely to remember something soon."

"Maybe you should take him some pictures," Miriam said. "Something to jog his memory."

The idea fascinated her. Immediately she left the table and brought back a small photo album she kept in her purse. It was the size of a four-by-six print, and it bulged with memories.

Rene caught my eye from across the table. "Maybe you should bring him a tape of you playing the piano."

I forced a laugh. "And torture the poor man?"

"I was thinking more of motivating him," Rene replied. "He'd realize how much you need a piano teacher." She lifted her eyelids. Touche. One point for my sister.

"Certainly Jack would remember this," Yolanda said, shoving a picture under my nose. It was a photograph of Jack and Yolanda in ski outfits in front of a black-diamond sign. "Of course I never went down that slope," she added.

"At least I play the piano. I seem to remember you hiding in the park when Mom thought you were taking piano lessons at Mrs. Thalheimer's." I smiled sweetly at Rene. One point for me.

"I know," Yolanda beamed. "I'll bet Jack has a picture of me on his nightstand."

Steve chuckled. "I'll go over to his place tomorrow and see."

Yolanda sniffed. "I have Jack's picture next to my bed. His face is the last thing I see each night before I close my eyes."

I wanted to gag. Better yet, someone gag Yolanda. Instead, I stood and started collecting dinner plates. Working would keep me from doing something drastic and reminding her that Jack thought I was his fiancée now. "Dessert anyone? I have vanilla ice cream and raspberry topping."

Yolanda patted her slender abdomen. "I'd better not. If I spend a week here, I'll never fit into my wedding dress."

I looked at her and tried not to wish her fat-fears upon her. I thought about my marriage vows and how Jack's amnesia, the very illness that upset Yolanda so, was the very thing that gave me another chance at doing the right thing. I offered a weak smile and sat in conflicted silence. It was right for me to hope good things for Jack, a recovery of his memory of his engagement to his precious Yolanda. But at the same time, if Jack recovered his memory, then my sin would no longer be my secret.

We sat around the table making the polite talk of strangers until way past dark. Yolanda suggested showing Jack another dozen or so pictures, and Miriam and Steve reminisced about Jack's childhood. I mostly sipped coffee and wondered what it would have been like if Jack and I had met before I'd fallen for my surgeon. By nine-thirty, when the phone rang, I welcomed a chance to escape.

I picked up the phone in the kitchen. "Hello."

It was Henry, his voice weary. "Sorry I didn't make it for dinner."

"It's OK," I said. "Are you coming home?"

"I'm on my way to the theatre," he said. "Someone with a crushed liver and a belly full of blood."

I wrinkled my nose and couldn't keep the sarcasm from my voice, "Sounds pleasant." I hesitated before continuing. "What's the likelihood of Jack recovering his memory?" I cleared my voice and hoped I sounded naturally curious. "Poor Yolanda is quite upset about him not remembering their relationship."

"But he remembers you."

I felt my cheeks flush. "Yes."

"Seems a bit strange. His memory is spotty." Henry sighed. "But I guess the brain is weird like that. Who knows? Most acute brain injury patients get slowly better. Let's just hope Jack is one of the lucky ones."

"Sure."

"Don't wait up. I'll be late."

I heard a click and looked at the phone. Henry was gone, off to save another life.

CHAPTER 14

Sunday morning was to be day four of my Caribbean vacation with Jack Renner. White sands, mango daiquiris, and clear water. Instead, I'd gotten the week from hell. A pregnant sister with HIV, my almost-lover with amnesia in the ICU, and now his adoring family and his brooding fiancée living in my house.

I got up early, leaving Henry making sonorous noises. I needed an escape, so I locked myself into estrogen central, slipped into a revealing two-piece bathing suit I'd selected for Jack, and lay down in my private tanning bed. I set the timer for ten minutes and tried to forget my misery.

I closed my eyes and fantasized about Jack and moonlit walks with surf tickling our feet. But Henry kept intruding. My thoughts drifted to Jack in the ICU and then on to Henry and the gentle way he showed his care and confidence. In another moment, I thought of walking hand in hand with Henry on the same beach.

My thoughts turned from Henry in the ICU to a continuous replaying of Henry's good-night phrase. *"But he remembers you."* Was Henry jealous? Was I more transparent than I thought?

The tanning bed didn't whisk me away to Jamaican sand. After ten minutes I was still hiding in the back of my walk-in closet with an economy load of stress. By today, I was to have been free of my hypocritical life for a full three days. Instead, I was still waking up the perfect wife next to the perfect surgeon in the perfect house in the perfect neighborhood. I sighed and pushed open the lid to my tanning bed. I'd just have to make due with small changes. I slipped off the little black bikini and looked at my selection of Sunday morning dresses. Then, instead of my normal designer fare, I put on a pair of nice jeans and a white cotton blouse. I'd always felt like such a poser in church, dressing to impress. Well today, I was going to dress for God alone. I figured there might be a lot of people in my father's church who cared what I wore when I worshiped, but God wasn't one of them. I buttoned the waist of my jeans and nodded my head. Henry and the rest of the uppity-up dressers could choke on their own piousness for all I cared.

I tiptoed through the bedroom, made Ethiopian coffee, and poured a big bowl of Cocoa Krispies and covered them with a light dusting of sugar.

After a few delightful minutes of silence, Rene plodded in and stole the first cup of coffee, then poured a second one for me. I added French vanilla creamer.

She sat across from me and sipped her coffee quietly.

"There's church today."

She looked up. "You know I can't go. The whole congregation must think I'm kin to the devil by now." She held her coffee mug with two hands like an offering. "Looks like I've proved them all right."

"And I guess I've proved them all wrong."

"How's that?"

"I'm not the woman they think I am either."

She nodded and stayed quiet. A few minutes later, I spoke again, this time in a whisper. "Henry was out until three. I hate it that he spends more time with his gorgeous blonde resident than with me."

"You're jealous."

"It's that obvious, huh?" I leaned toward my sister. "Sometimes I get so annoyed at his arrogance and his quest for polish. But I don't want anyone else taking him from me," I said, closing my fist.

Rene shook her head. "Henry's too smart to throw away his reputation on a fling with a gorgeous blonde."

I sighed. "You're right about that." For Henry, reputation and appearance was everything.

Henry came out a few minutes later in a gray suit, a white button-down shirt, and a designer silk tie. He looked at me. "Wendi, it's Sunday."

"I haven't forgotten," I said, feigning nonchalance. "Ready to go?"

"But you're—"

"I'm wearing this," I interrupted. "Do you think God will let me in if I'm not in a dress?"

He opened his mouth to respond, but must have thought twice after looking at Rene and me. He slowly shook his head, his expression the embarrassed look you'd give a man who walked into a crowded room with his zipper down. He held up his hands. His silence was judgment enough.

I set out breakfast cereals for my houseguests and walked across the street to church with Henry. Perhaps I shouldn't have gone at all, given my new quest for an honest life, but giving up church with Jack lying in the ICU didn't seem an acceptable way to win any points with God, so just in case he was watching, I decided to go.

I shouldn't have. Twenty people asked me the same questions about Jack. "What happened? How is he?"

I smiled and held it all in. *He was distracted by my suggestion that we run away together, so he pulled into the path of a speeding semitruck.*

Henry, the consummate poser, just kept smiling, complimenting old ladies' hats and politely refusing to give out professional information about Jack's progress. Of course, he seemed above taking any glory for saving Jack's life, but I could tell he was pleased that the gossip chain was alive and crediting him for a miracle.

In the parking lot after church, I watched as Deb Seaton ushered two fatherless teenage sons into a minivan. She caught my gaze, and I looked away. To her, I would forever be the other woman. I'd seen her at church sporadically over the last six months. Her boldness in coming back to the fellowship here since her husband's death was a credit to her resilience. She knew I'd never share the affair with the church. And since my mother was out of the picture, Deb didn't need to worry that my mom would pressure her not to speak. Her eyes were sad, not vengeful, and set within a face that looked weary of the hand she'd been dealt.

Every time I saw her, I felt guilty, and remembered our last encounter. It was two weeks after my release from the hospital. I wanted her to know how sorry I was. I needed to apologize for me, and for the way my mother had pressured her husband out of the church.

I stood on her front porch and rang the doorbell. I was never very good at being indirect.

She opened the door, and the words I'd practiced stuck in my throat, suddenly a desert. "What do you want?"

I felt tears sting my eyes. I sniffed. "Look, I'm so sorry."

She shook her head at me. I was an untrained puppy just caught next to my mistake on the carpet. "Stay away from my husband." The door slammed in my face, leaving me humiliated, still bearing the guilt I wanted to unload.

Deb closed the door to the van and stepped my way. I felt my heart quicken. I suddenly wanted Henry right beside me, but he'd been detained by another fan of his surgical skill. I glanced over to see him at the edge of the parking lot with a silver-haired woman bending his ear.

I looked at Deb, not knowing what to say. *So, long time, no see?* I folded my arms across my chest and prepared to defend myself.

"Wendi, can we speak?"

I couldn't imagine what I'd want to say to her. I tilted my head to the side and shot a second glance towards my husband. "Sure."

Deb kept her voice low. "Bob didn't commit suicide."

I took a step towards her and unfolded my arms. Her husband had died in a car accident six months before. Single car versus bridge abutment. The car lost.

"I've heard what you can do," she said. "I read in the paper about how you figured out that pizza delivery crash."

"Yes," I responded. It was my local claim to fame.

"I'm tired of everyone assuming Bob committed suicide," she whispered. "Is there any way to prove it was an accident?"

I puzzled over her statement. This was the last thing I expected out of her. I shook my head slowly. "Is this an insurance issue? Is his life insurance company not paying off because of this?"

It was an odd question, but I'd been consulted to figure out these sorts of issues before.

"It has nothing to do with that," she said. "I just want to know for me."

I paused, studying her worried expression. "You obviously don't believe your husband committed suicide."

"He wouldn't." She hesitated. "He couldn't."

"It's been a long, long time. Any physical evidence will have been erased." I paused. "Would we be able to make a conclusion from studying the old insurance and police photographs and reports? Not likely," I said, answering my own question. "You will just have to take your belief to heart. You knew him best. If you know he didn't kill himself, you'll just have to comfort yourself with that. Don't let anyone tell you otherwise." I reached out and squeezed her forearm. "I'm sorry."

I watched her eyes moisten. She nodded. "Thanks."

She scuffed a white sandal against the pavement and cleared her throat. "Bob was a good man, really," she said, looking away. "He never had another woman after you."

My heart pounded. *You mean he didn't seduce any more teenagers into his office for private Bible study?*

I put a clamp on my thoughts. She was trying to preserve her husband's memory with some decency. I didn't know what to say. "No one here knows about him," I said. "My mother saw to that."

She wrinkled her forehead and winced as her son blew the horn. With that, she scurried off to her vehicle.

Henry arrived at my elbow. "What was that all about?"

I looked in Deb's direction. "I'm not sure," I said. "Just a grieving widow wanting evidence that will help her sleep."

He let my statement stand. We walked silently across the street to the house.

Henry took me to the Omni for brunch. I wanted to take Rene, but she begged off, saying she had morning sickness. I'm not sure that was true, but I didn't press her.

We separated after a quiet meal, Henry retreating to his office and me to visit Jack in the ICU.

I passed the hospital cafeteria and was relieved to see Yolanda and the Renners having lunch. *Great*, I thought, *I need a few minutes alone with my piano teacher.*

A few minutes later, I pulled back the curtain to find Jack sitting up to a tray of liquids. Red Jell-O, cranberry juice, clear beef bouillon, and a cup of black coffee sat in various stages of consumption. "Mmm," I said. "Looks tasty."

He looked up. "Hi, Wendi."

"You remembered my name."

He sipped at his coffee. "Surprised?"

I shrugged. "Have you remembered anything from before the accident?"

He searched my face for a moment before answering. "Things are a bit fuzzy."

"Do you remember the day of the accident?"

"Some."

"Tell me what you remember."

"Did something happen that I need to know?"

I gave him my best stern look. "Don't play games with me, Jack Renner. Tell me what you remember."

I watched as a smile seemed to toy with the edge of his wonderful mouth. He needed a shave. He ran his fingers over his prickly scalp, gently feeling the staples. "I was going to your house to give a piano lesson."

I squinted at him. "You remember that?"

He nodded slowly. "That's about it," he said, folding his arms across his chest. "The next thing I knew, I was here."

"You remember the lesson?"

"Why?"

I tried to act barely interested. "You seem to have retrograde amnesia. I just wondered where your memory picked up."

He seemed to be concentrating on his Jell-O. He rubbed the back of his neck. "The accident must have wiped out everything just as I was heading for your house."

"Yet you don't remember your fiancée."

"The blonde? She looks vaguely familiar."

"I used to be blonde, Jack."

He looked down. "You were blonde? I wouldn't take you as the type. When I see you, I think what you see is what you get."

I put my hands on my hips. This was the very phrase I'd used the last time we were together before his accident.

Before I could comment, he spoke again. "What should I do about Yolanda?"

"Do about her?"

He looked at me. "She seems nice enough, and quite attractive, but she seems quite stuck on this wedding thing." He shook his head. "It's not like I can marry her. I don't know her."

I cleared my throat. "Perhaps you'll have to delay the wedding a bit."

"Until I can remember why I must have liked her?"

I held in a smile. "I guess. You can't marry someone you don't love, Jack."

He pushed away his tray. "Everyone tells me your husband saved my life. He seems like a wonderful guy."

"Sure," I said quietly. "The perfect man."

I looked away. I didn't exactly feel comfortable discussing my feelings about perfect Henry with Jack.

I listened to the electronic chirping of his cardiac monitor and watched a glowing green line dance across a monitor. Beep, beep, beep. Steady Jack.

"It must be difficult for you," he said.

I looked at him and frowned.

"I mean being the pastor's daughter in such a big church."

"Where did that come from?"

He smiled. "Just insightful, I guess."

"I guess." I shuffled my feet. "Maybe I should go. Let you get back to your dinner."

"Don't go. You didn't answer my question."

"You noticed." I took a step towards the foot of the bed and folded my arms across my chest, aware of my defensive posture. "I've lived most of my life trying to meet other people's expectations."

He nodded. "I'm the church choir director, Wendi. I know exactly what you're saying."

I allowed myself to smile. "Fair enough."

"But I think we're different," he said. He waited until our eyes met to explain. "I believe what your dad preaches."

I kept my arms folded. "And you think I don't?"

He shrugged without taking his eyes off me. I felt exposed, but not threatened. "Tell me, Wendi. I want to know if you struggle."

I forced a chuckle. "Do you have a few months?"

He smiled. His lips were chapped, but his teeth were gorgeous. Even in the fluorescent light with a two-day growth on his scalp, his features looked so fine.

I didn't feel like burdening him with my life story, but I couldn't seem to lie to his beautiful eyes. So I summarized my life in three words. "I'm a fake."

I let the words hang without explanation.

He didn't argue, didn't laugh, didn't speak at all. He just waited for me to go on.

"I don't want to be. It just happened. I've taken a thousand little steps, each one a small compromise, a separation of my heart belief and my mouth." I sighed. "Before I knew it, I'd become just like the hypocrite I accused my mother of being."

I heard the curtain move behind me. It was Brenda, Jack's nurse. "Guess what?" she said. "It's moving day." She began disconnecting wire leads from Jack's chest. "Dr. Stratford has given the order to send you to the floor."

"Where will you take him?"

"East 421."

She continued working, scurrying about the bed, readying Jack for the move. "You'll be able to have visitors more than two at a time."

Hooray. I can visit with Jack's parents and Yolanda at the same time.

I took Jack's hand. "I've got to go."

I pressed back the urge to kiss him. I wanted to tell him how thirsty my soul was for the attention he gave me, how it had been years since Henry wanted to know how I was on the inside, only caring about my bottle-blonde exterior. His eyes met mine, and he gave my hand a squeeze. Not fast, but firm. I was here to cheer him up. He was passing strength to me.

"Bye," I said, returning the squeeze. My eyes met Brenda's. She raised her eyebrows.

Outside, it seemed the air around me was thick with guilt. I was sharing my soul with another man. He may have forgotten my overt proposal, but I hadn't, and my heart felt sick. I'm a married woman. A Christian married woman. Christian women aren't supposed to have affairs. They're not even supposed to want to.

I walked down the hospital corridor promising myself that I wouldn't visit Jack again. I'd settled my question. He really didn't remember my outrageous behavior. All I was to him was a piano student and the wife of his wonderful surgeon.

I nodded my head to myself, telling my soul that it was the right thing to do. Henry was a good provider, after all.

I'm doing the right thing. I've been given a second chance. I sniffed. I'd laid aside my dream. Henry was my guy.

So why did it all seem so unreal?

ChaPteR 15

On day five of my wonderful Caribbean vacation I used Dr. Henry Stratford's name to get an urgent appointment for Rene with a University obstetrician. Alfred Bird specialized in high-risk obstetrics. I wasn't sure HIV constituted high risk, but I'd heard that Bird was the best, so I insisted on an office visit for my sister.

We sat in the waiting room reading outdated *Newsweek* and *National Geographic* magazines and spied on the other patients waiting to be seen. After forty-five minutes, my cell phone rang. It was Michael Chin, an insurance agent with State Farm.

"Hi, Michael," I said. "I'm on vacation. You're not supposed to be bothering me."

"Good morning to you too," he said, followed by a rapid chuckle. "You shouldn't answer the phone if you are on vacation." He plunged forward before I could protest further. "I'm in Ruckersville to file a claim for a client." Wind whistled in my ear, telling me Michael was outside, and probably walking. "A tractor-trailer cab coasted down a hill and slammed into some trees at the edge of a field. I'm no expert, but things don't quite line up here. The damage seems more severe than what I would have expected. I called the office and they suggested I see if you were available."

"I'm flattered. But I am on vacation. At least I'm supposed to be," I groaned.

"Come on, Wendi," he said, his voice low. "It looks to me like the truck has been scrubbed, but someone didn't get all the blue paint off the truck fender."

I looked at Rene. She was squinting at me and shaking her head. I couldn't leave her alone. "I'm sorry, Michael. Why don't you call Scott Jacobs? He—" I stopped and looked away from my sister's scorn. "Did you say blue?"

"Yeah. A small chip of blue paint is lodged in a crease in the bumper."

Jack's Honda Accord was blue.

"Can I come later?"

He sighed. "How long is later?"

"An hour," I said. Rene kept shaking her head, now faster. It would take me thirty minutes to travel up 29 to Ruckersville. "Two hours tops."

"For the best, I'll wait."

"Flattery will get you everywhere, Michael. Don't move a thing. I'll call you when I'm a few minutes from Ruckersville for directions."

"I owe you."

"Big time," I said. "I'm in Jamaica."

I flipped off my phone.

Ten minutes later, I was sitting with Rene across from Dr. Bird. He had a gray goatee and a generous waistline. He smiled when he talked and leaned forward when he listened. Perhaps his hearing was going the way of his balding head.

He nodded as he read the notes recorded by the nurse interview. "OK," he said, holding up one finger. "You've got HIV." Up went finger number two. "You're pregnant and," he said, lifting a third finger, "you're scared."

Rene nodded without speaking.

"I'm here to debunk the myths." He started raising fingers again, one by one. "First, HIV is treatable. It is not a death sentence. It is a chronic, controllable illness. Second, it is highly unlikely, if you follow my advice, that you will pass HIV to your child. Everything you've heard about AIDS orphans and babies dying with HIV in Africa is true. But this is Charlottesville, Virginia, and you have access to good medicine."

"Define 'highly unlikely,'" Rene said, forming quotation marks with her fingers.

"If we put you on three-drug therapy, your baby has less than one percent chance of contracting the virus."

"Do I have to have a C-section?"

Dr. Bird leaned back. "We'll check the viral load in your blood. If there are less than one thousand viral copies per ml, then there will be no benefit from a C-section birth."

Rene and I exchanged glances. This all sounded better than we had hoped.

"Of course, we will have to start you on antiretroviral medications right away."

"I don't feel sick."

"Doesn't matter," he said. "It's a precaution to keep the virus in check to diminish passage to your baby. During labor, we'll put you on IV AZT, and after delivery we'll have to treat your child with AZT and Bactrim. It's all part of a well-worked-out protocol."

Rene sat quietly for a few seconds. "I want to breast-feed." Her eyes met mine. "If I keep the baby."

The doctor shook his head. "I'm sorry. That would be risky to your child. You can pass the virus that way."

Rene looked at me again. We'd talked about this issue, and I'd given her different advice. I spoke up. "But I just saw a documentary about Africa. Uganda or some such place. The health workers are encouraging HIV-positive mothers to breast-feed."

"Again," he said. "That's Africa. This is America. You've got good water and formula. They don't. Stopping breast-feeding in Africa means the baby is likely to suffer malnutrition and die sooner than if it contracted HIV from its mother."

I nodded.

"Now," Dr. Bird said while picking up a folded patient gown. "Unless you've got other questions for me, I'm going to ask you to put this on." He stepped to the door. "I'll be back in a few minutes to examine you."

He left, and Rene and I fell into an embrace. "Stop crying," I chided, before tapping on her stomach. "Did ya' hear that, Junior? You're going to be alright!"

I arrived at the country home of Jesse and Linda Anders at one o'clock. There, I stopped at the edge of a long gravel lane behind Michael Chin's Dodge Dakota pickup. Michael joined me in the Mercedes and briefed me as we drove towards a single-story ranch perched on a small knoll. Two large dogs, a slobbering mutt and what appeared to be a Doberman, escorted us as we neared a home long overdue for a fresh coat of paint.

"Mr. Anders is a real case," Chin said. "I told him that I wanted an expert opinion about the accident and that I wanted you to examine the evidence. I mentioned your name and he got spooky on me."

"Spooky?"

Michael shrugged. "He made me repeat your name twice. A few minutes later he said he needed to make a run into town. He jumped in his pickup and he left me standing in his driveway.

"What'd he tell you about the accident?"

"He said he found it down there this morning." Michael pointed over a grassy field to a group of trees at the bottom of a gentle slope. "Anders claimed he parked it here at the edge of his driveway last night. Must have forgotten to set the brake."

The distance to the truck cab looked to be about one hundred meters. I decided to look at the truck first and get out my Nikon Total Station and record the measurements after the vehicle inspection. I opened the trunk and retrieved my digital camera and began walking across the field. The grass was long, and laid over in two discrete tire tracks leading to the truck.

I estimated the slope at under five degrees, something I could confirm later with my total station. With the tall grass, the truck's speed would have been hampered, making a high-speed impact improbable. The right front grille and the fender were dented, and the right headlight smashed. The truck rested against a large walnut tree. I photographed the scene, returned to my car, set up the total station, and did measurements. After an hour, I was ready to have the truck moved. I wanted a closer look at the front end. Chin was right; there was a dime-size speck of blue paint deep in a fender crease. Around it, the fender seemed to have been scrubbed with steel wool. Curiously, the bumper seemed to have been spared much of the impact. I knelt to the ground and looked beneath the front bumper. There, attached to the front frame, seemed to be some sort of mounting bracket. The damage to the fender was significant. But I couldn't understand why the bumper hadn't taken more of a hit.

Close inspection of areas of the dents on the wheel well revealed what looked like oxidation that had already started on the exposed metal. This had to be more than one night old for rusting to have started where the primer was scratched off.

It came to me as I walked back up the hill through the long grass.

"Does Anders have a garage?"

Michael pointed towards a large separate building behind the ranch house. "There, I guess."

"Let's take a look."

I followed him into a tall garage. It was dusty and smelled of motor oil. I found what I was looking for on the floor next to a workbench burdened with tools.

It appeared to be a metal grille, a substantial piece made of forged two-inch steel. Bolted to the front of a truck frame, it could have protected the truck from significant damage. It was scuffed with blue paint and flattened along one side.

"What is it?"

I smiled. "Just an old truck grille. Hmmm." I photographed it from six angles.

Michael just stood back and shook his head.

I walked back to the Mercedes to call Chris Black. "I think I've just been given a gift," I said to Michael.

"Whatever," He said. "Do your eyes always do that when you work?"

"Do what?"

He laughed and imitated me. His eyes darted back and forth over my Mercedes like he was reading a book.

I groaned. "Shut up."

In another minute, I was on the phone with Chris Black. "Detective Black."

"Chris, it's me."

"What is it this time, Wendi?"

"I've got news."

"Why don't you come down to the station so we can discuss it? I want to collect on my double mocha latte."

"I think I've found the truck involved in Jack Renner's hit-and-run."

I listened as he sighed. "Do you read the paper?"

"Sure."

"Well then you know I've got my hands full around here. A law student hung himself over the side of Beta Bridge down on Rugby Road." I listened to him tapping his keyboard. "What makes you think you've found the guilty party?"

"Some guy up in Ruckersville is trying to pull an insurance fraud."

"Ruckersville? What's the name?"

"Anders."

"Evidence?"

"A little. Mostly a hunch at this point."

"What do you have?"

"A truck with a blue paint chip the same color as Jack's car. It's a truck cab, could have been pulling a silver trailer like the one I saw hit Jack's car. This guy has a huge detachable metal grille covered with the same blue color. I found it in his garage."

I listened to the detective sigh. I knew he wasn't convinced.

"I haven't worked it up yet. I'll bring it by once I've finished my CAD drawings."

The detective coughed. "Do you have pictures?"

"I've always got pictures."

"Bring your camera by. We can download them here. I want to see what you've got."

"I need a chance to look at them first. I've got guests at home. I'll put them on my computer and bring them by your office in the morning."

"Bring the latte," he said.

"Fine. Nine o'clock?"

"I'll be there."

I arrived home to find a tearful Yolanda sitting on the couch between Steve and Miriam Renner.

She looked up as I arrived. "You're so blessed," she said. "You've got the perfect husband. He's got looks, a great job. He's so compassionate and," she added with her voice cracking, "he's crazy about you." She buried her face in her hands.

I traded glances with the Renners and mouthed, "What's going on?"

Miriam put her arm around Yolanda in a motherly gesture and looked up at me. "Jack has suggested they cancel the wedding. It's understandable. He was so sorry to hurt her, but he said he just couldn't follow through until his memory returned."

Steve nodded. "There, there," he said, patting Yolanda's knee. "Think about it from Jack's perspective. It would be like marrying a stranger. How weird would that be?"

"Steve!" his wife scolded. "Once Jack has a chance to get to know her again, I'm sure he'll feel the same."

Yolanda shook her head. "What if he's changed?" She stared at the Renners and me as if we could answer. We didn't have an answer, at least not one she wanted to hear. Jack could have changed. No one could have predicted his amnesia. Head injuries do weird things to patients.

I didn't know what to say. I knew that rejoicing that Jack remembered me wouldn't be appropriate. Instead, I just shrugged. "Anyone hungry?"

"I can't eat," Yolanda sobbed. "Unless it's cheesecake. I always eat that when I'm depressed."

I smiled. "The Hardware Store makes the best. I'll pick one up for supper." I left the mournful trio on the couch and headed for the kitchen, where I found Rene drinking a tall glass of OJ.

She made eye contact and kept her voice low. "Has the ex-fiancée stopped crying yet?"

"Not yet. I promised her a comfort cheesecake from The Hardware Store." I shrugged. "What else can I do?"

"Shoot her," she whispered. "Put her out of her misery." She seemed to hesitate. "Is that what I looked like?"

I narrowed my eyes at my sister and teased, "You've never looked that nice."

Rene held her head.

"What's wrong?"

"Just dizzy. A side effect of starting this medicine."

She nodded. "I've been thinking."

"Scary."

"I'm serious. I want to talk to Mom."

I shook my head. I knew what Rene wanted to do. She had confrontation written all over her. "Why don't you leave it?"

"I'm not in for a fight. I want to tell her about the baby."

I shook my head. I remembered telling Mother I was pregnant. "You'll be sorry."

That evening, the Renners retired early, Rene retreated to her room claiming her new medicine made her dizzy, and Henry didn't show for supper as usual. That left me dealing with the jilted Yolanda. By ten she was in a silent funk, teary and sober. That's when I made the mistake of opening my favorite wine, a 1997 Tulocay Cabernet, and pouring a glass for Yolanda.

The wine loosened her tongue. One glass led to three and the stories poured out uncapped. The day Jack proposed. The time she sprained her ankle at South River Falls and Jack carried her to the car. The first time she met Jack's parents.

I tried to get away. She followed me to my bedroom, telling more stories and sitting on the edge of my bed sipping the wine and sobbing about her lost future. By eleven, my prayers had been answered. Sort of. Yolanda had shut up. The only problem was, she had passed out on my bed.

I nudged her shoulder. She grunted once and kept snoring. It was no use. I pulled my quilted top cover over her shoulders and turned out the light, leaving her to sleep the night in my bed.

When Henry came in at midnight, I looked up at him from my fetal position where I'd curled up on our leather sofa.

"You didn't have to wait up," he said.

"I didn't. Yolanda's in our bed."

The question on his face prompted me to continue. "Jack wants to cancel their wedding. She was cryin' in her beer," I said. "Only this time it was my cabernet sauvignon."

"How'd she end up in our bed?"

"The poor girl followed me around the house like a lost puppy, telling me stories about Jack. She finally passed out while I was brushing my teeth. I didn't have the strength or heart to move her."

Henry sighed. He loved our bed. He spent six weeks researching the latest advances in sleep technology before selecting the Sleep System 6000, one of those memory foam mattresses that recorded the indentation from your body for a few moments after you got up. I liked the bed, but my enthusiasm fell short of Henry's love affair with the 6000, as he called it. I'd held a secret resentment towards it since the very day it arrived. I'd pushed my hand onto the top layer of foam and admired the imprint of my slender fingers before plopping down to check what kind of impression my body would make. I closed my eyes and let myself sink into comfortable bliss. That, however, was short-lived. I jumped up quickly to look, only to be aghast at the cavern left by my backside. I whirled around to look in the mirror. "Liar," I said, pointing to the 6000. It was comfortable. Expensive. And it made Henry happy. But I resented it nonetheless.

Henry plodded towards the bedroom.

"Are you going to move her?"

"I'm just going to get my toothbrush. We can use the guest room downstairs."

I was tempted to call Yolanda names that Christians weren't supposed to use. Instead, I caught myself smiling and snapped it off like a light. I was done with synthetic expressions of emotion. Instead of the name I was thinking, I compromised with, "I don't like her."

Henry stopped and turned to face me. "What's with you? The woman just lost her fiancé." He paused, as if wondering whether to continue. "Besides," he added. "You have to love that hair."

I held my tongue. That was below the belt. I glared at him for a second, reminding myself that I didn't need his permission to return to my natural brunette. I walked behind him down the hall towards the bedroom, stopping at the hall closet to pull out a pillow and a fleece embroidered with the University of Virginia Cavaliers mascot.

"What are you doing?"

I padded away with a heavy heart, sullen in my determination to punish my husband for his potshot. "I'm sleeping on the couch."

I'd wanted to start afresh with Henry. *Maybe I'll start tomorrow.*

CHAPTER 16

On day six of my Jamaican vacation, I awoke and ate Cocoa Krispies for breakfast. I almost didn't feel guilty, and I vowed to continue eating them until I could stop thinking about fiber and eat them without checking the side of the box to see that it had been fortified. Today, I needed to start with a bit of selfishness, as I knew sparks would fly when I took Rene in to see Mom.

Henry dissected an English muffin and ate in his usual silence, although I saw him lower the *Wall Street Journal* a time or two to look in my direction. Each time, he seemed fixated on my hair and unconsciously touched the edge of his sideburns as he studied my true colors.

I supposed Henry would never bring up last night's events again if I didn't, and this morning I didn't have the energy for a confrontation. My week had been nail-biting hellacious, and I needed a bit of an anchor in the storm. So I took comfort in the sameness of my quirky husband.

He stood and cleared himself for takeoff in front of the mirror. I pretended not to watch, but enjoyed it just the same. My pregnant sister might have HIV, my piano teacher might not remember that I tried to seduce him, his parents were staying in my house, and his fiancée was asleep in my bed, but I smiled, knowing some things just don't change even in the midst of extremes. I waited for Henry to do the double zipper check. I watched as he slipped a finger under the fly of his navy pants. Check. He leaned closer to the mirror for a final check of his nose. He sniffed twice and nodded happily. Again, he confirmed the zipper-closure and patted the front of his pants. He took a step away. I watched him hesitate and look back in the full-length mirror before doing a third zipper check.

I almost gasped. Henry never, ever did a triple check before. I wondered if I should point this out or question what catastrophic life event had brought this on, but decided against it. I knew his job stressed him at times. And so far, other than the zipper check aberrancy, I couldn't see that he was much worse for the wear.

I looked up to see the Renners carrying their suitcases into the foyer.

Miriam walked into the kitchen and helped herself to my Ethiopian java. "Morning, Wendi," she said. "We'll be out of your hair now. Steve is needed back in Philadelphia and I'm moving into Jack's apartment to stay until he's discharged and on his feet again."

Steve chuckled. "She won't last a week in that place. Too cramped," he said. "Miriam needs space."

I wasn't sad to see them go. I wished they would take blonde Yolanda with them. Rene and every other stressor in my life was enough to make me a bit crazy.

"I will miss the coffee," she said. "Where's Yolanda?"

I smiled. "Sleeping in." I avoided telling them about Yolanda's night. I'd let them discover it themselves when she got up with a hangover.

I watched as Rene plodded in wearing her pajamas. My sister didn't have a pretentious bone in her body. "Morning, everyone," she drawled using her best adopted New Orleans accent.

I watched in amazement as she poured a huge bowl of bran flakes. She mumbled something about needing to be careful about eating for two or some such nonsense. I wanted to tell her that the second person she was eating for was smaller than a peanut M&M, but held my tongue. Let her get fat. It would serve her right for saying my prom dress made me look chubby. I didn't care if it was fifteen years ago. I had a good memory for comments about my weight. Maybe that's why I resented the Sleep System 6000.

After breakfast, the Renners were launched, and I stood on the front stoop waving and feeling guilty because of the shadow of the cross on my ivy bank.

Before we went to see Mother, I spent five minutes watering each of my six willow trees. If they grew any slower, I'd be an old woman before they blocked out the condemning church- steeple-cross shadow.

Truthfully, I couldn't honestly say I was going with Rene to support her. I was just as interested in seeing my mom's reaction to knowing her second daughter was pregnant out of wedlock.

We drove to the Dogwood Acres Nursing Home so that we would arrive after breakfast. Rene was remarkably upbeat. I thought it was because she'd spent the previous afternoon on the 'net getting positive information about living with HIV, but I hadn't entirely ruled out illicit drug usage. No one had a right to be that cheerful in the morning, especially not someone with HIV, pregnant, and recently separated from a jerk-boyfriend.

I paused at Mom's door and took a deep breath before pushing it open. I gasped. A naked woman was on the floor, crawling towards the bed. It wasn't my mother. "Oh," I said, "Sorry! Wrong room."

"Don't leave me," she called. "Can't you see I need some help here?"

I exchanged glances with Rene, who seemed stunned at the sight of an old wrinkled bottom. "Call a nurse," the woman said. "I tripped getting out of the bathtub. I think I've broken my hip."

Rene ran into the hall calling for help.

I found a towel in the bathroom and placed it over the woman's back.

"Thanks." She shivered. "If you're looking for Mrs. Aldridge, she's over on east wing, number twenty. She got the room I wanted," she said. "One with a walk-in shower." She shook her head. "Stupid tub!"

Two nurses entered and I slipped out with Rene. I felt sick.

"What's wrong?" Rene elbowed my side as we walked. "Afraid your butt is going to get that wrinkly?"

"Shut up!" I said, lifting my hand to my mouth. "Oh, this was all my fault."

"What are you talking about?"

"I bullied Mr. Williams into moving Mom to the east wing to get her a nicer room. He gave Mom the nice room with a walk-in shower, and the naked lady gets Mom's old room and breaks her hip getting out of the tub."

"You didn't know. Stop it."

"Stop what?"

"Feeling guilty. It's not your fault."

I heard my sister, but my heart couldn't absorb it. We walked on in silence until we arrived at my mother's new room. I looked at Rene. "Ready?"

She nodded. I knocked softly and pushed the door open. Mom was sitting up with her head leaning forward over a plastic tub. My father was sponging her hair with a towel. I wasn't sure this was good. Would Rene open up in front of him?

Daddy looked up. After a moment of stunned silence, he erupted into motion and nearly stumbled in his haste to get to her. "Rene!" He enveloped her with a bear hug.

I heard her only whisper, "Hi, Daddy," before the strength of his hug silenced her. She dabbed at the corner of her eye, and I stood back to watch.

Mom cried. That wasn't unusual. She'd been hyperemotive ever since the accident. "Rene, Rene," she said.

My father looked as if he might cry as well. "You've come home." He always was a master of the obvious.

Rene moved to my mother and knelt beside her. "Hi, Mom," she said, taking her hand.

I expected more, I suppose, given the emotional exit Rene had made ten years ago, screaming at my parents about never seeing them again. I can't say that I blamed her. She'd been shunned by the church because she was living with her boyfriend. The elders insisted that Rene should receive the same treatment as any unrepentant member. In spite of my father's protest, the elders insisted that she leave.

She sat on Mother's bed opposite her wheelchair. Dad started brushing out Mom's hair and shaking his head in disbelief. After a few strokes, he sat in a chair, completely distracted by Rene's presence. I stood in a corner to watch. So far, my parents hadn't even greeted me. I took a step towards the window to see the view I'd argued to win for Mom. The lake was beautiful. A little chapel had been erected with a cross-steeple halfway down the walk to the lake. *Great*, I thought, *I asked for a view of the lake, and we have to look at that cross.*

"What's happened to you?" my father asked. He looked at Mom. "We thought we'd never see you again."

Mother held up her hand and placed it against her forehead, something she'd done frequently since the accident when she wanted to speak. It was as if words came slower to her now and supporting her forehead made it easier for her to speak. On the rare occasions that she did choose to speak, the left side of her mouth refused to cooperate, so the words were often slurred. This had always puzzled me, but the doctors say isolated bleeding in that part of the brain can do exactly what Mom's did. "Weef been praying for you," she said.

Rene nodded. "Daddy, I'm so sorry," she began. "I've really messed up this time."

My parents both shook their heads.

"I'm pregnant," she said, looking up at my father.

Again, there was a moment of silence. My father's face blanched. "Th-that's wonderful," he said. He touched Mother's shoulder as she nodded. "Hear that, dear? We're going to be grandparents at last."

I felt a spear in my back. If that wasn't a dig at my inability to conceive, I wasn't sure what it was. I wanted to point out that Rene was pregnant out of wedlock. Maybe they thought she'd gotten married. That must be it.

She took a deep breath and straightened, locking her elbows and putting her hands on her knees. "I'm single."

I watched as my parents exchanged glances. When my dad turned back, he took a deep breath, nodded, and smiled weakly. "We're here to help you. We'll support you."

"Randy's out of the picture." Rene paused, apparently as mystified by their acceptance as I. Perhaps she thought while she was on a roll without stirring waves, she might as well just unload the whole shrimp boat. "I'm HIV-positive," she said.

The tears that had moistened his eyes now spilled onto his cheeks. Dad's jaw dropped. "Oh honey, I'm sorry."

Sorry? What about God's judgment? What about "You got what you deserved for sleeping around"?

The right half of Mother's face wrinkled with worry. "Haff you ssseen a doctor?"

She nodded. "Wendi took me. My child will be OK. I just have to take medicine."

"Thank God."

Rene smiled. "Yes."

I was having trouble hearing. My sister just agreed with my father when he said, "Thank God." That was my role, going along with the Christian junk, even if it was only on the surface.

My father sniffed. "Why did you come home?"

Rene wiped her cheek with the back of her hand. "I was afraid you wouldn't take me back." Tears rolled down her cheeks as my father searched for Mom's ever-present Kleenex box.

"Rene," he said. "Of course we'd take you back."

I'd held my tongue until my gut burned. "So this is all you have to say?" I looked at Mom. Down on her from my corner stand. "You actually want her to keep this child?"

Rene stared at me, mouth agape.

Mom nodded emphatically "Of course!"

I hated myself for feeling so petty. When I was pregnant out of wedlock, my mother revealed her true colors and did what no one expected of a pastor's wife: she shoved everything under the carpet. And we suffered. I lost my chances to have another child, and she was left drooling in a wheelchair. I shook my head and avoided Rene's eyes. I couldn't speak.

Rene gasped. "Wendi!"

I backed away, turning my head from her view. When I got into the hall, I stumbled forward, not wanting to cry and not wanting anyone to see. I pressed my hand to my upper lip and sped up to a near jog to the exit. All I wanted was to get away from there and escape my self-pity.

Five minutes later, I sat alone in my Mercedes, nursing an old wound and the memory of another encounter with pain.

I'd been hiding in my room when another wave of nausea swirled around my head and sent me running to the bathroom. I emerged a few minutes later, having emptied my stomach and washed my face. I looked into my mother's stern gaze. "Wendi, what's wrong?"

I shrugged. "Just a stomach flu."

She shook her head. "When are you going to tell me?"

I walked into the living room, acting OK. "Tell you? What?"

"What are you going to do when you start showing?"

I glared at her. "You have no idea."

"Stop it, Wendi. You're pregnant."

She'd always been the perceptive one. My father was different. He would look at me, even inspect the subtle swelling of my lower abdomen, and think I was sneaking extra Oreos.

I held up my hands. "Yes."

Her eyes narrowed to slits. "I knew it! What'd you do? Seduce your camp counselor?"

I held my ground. "You don't know anything! Bob Seaton's wife doesn't understand him."

Mother's mouth fell open in a silent "O."

"That's right, Mother. Bob Seaton."

"Why that—!" Mom put her hand to her mouth. "You can't have a child! You're a child yourself."

"He loves me, Mother."

She huffed. "You don't know what love is."

"I don't need to listen to this!"

"How dare you do this to our family?" she shouted. "To your father's ministry?"

"That's what's important?" I touched my abdomen. "This is your grandchild."

She refused to acknowledge my comment. "I'll take you to a clinic," she said, as if talking about getting groceries. "We'll put this behind us, you and me."

"But Dad—"

"He'll not be told anything about this."

I heard a tapping on the window. It was Rene, pulling me from my past. I lowered the window two inches and kept staring straight ahead. "Do you mind telling me what that was all about?"

I shook my head.

She lowered her head to my window. "I thought you were excited about my baby too."

"I am."

My sister stomped around the car and got in. She just sat there staring at me.

I felt stupid and small. "Why didn't Mom say that when I told her I was pregnant?"

"That's what this is about?" Rene paused. "You want me to be treated as badly as you were? Thanks."

"Rene, no." I threw up my hands, my attempt at honesty. "Yes. I mean I don't know."

"Which is it?"

"It's complicated."

"I'm listening."

I looked at her searching eyes. "Down inside me, I don't want you to suffer." I hesitated. "When I look back on it, maybe I'm getting it all wrong. I'm sure she was distressed about it. Maybe she felt trapped, and decided that abortion was the lesser of evils. But when I remember it, I can only see it through the eyes of a fourteen-year-old."

"So what was that all about?"

"What would my life be like now if Mom had said that to me?"

"Why didn't you ask her?"

I was dumbfounded. "I'm not even sure she remembers. Besides, Daddy doesn't know. She kept it from him."

Rene nodded. "She was protecting his reputation." She added, "Daddy still thinks of you as his princess. He always called you that. You know what he called me?"

I knew. "Squirt."

"I wanted to be Princess."

"But don't you get it? It was all an act. I was a princess all right. He just doesn't know his princess had an affair with his youth pastor. He just doesn't know his princess dared to go against his teaching, lie, hide a pregnancy, seek an abortion, and put his wife in a wheelchair!" There, I'd laid it out. I glared at her, daring her to stack her sins against mine.

"You didn't do that to her."

"We were on the way to an abortion clinic, Rene. It was my fault."

"You were struck by a drunk driver. You didn't plan that."

"Maybe God did."

"If he did, then he put Mom in a wheelchair, not you."

I shook my head. "Look, I'm sorry. I'm mad at Mom, not you. I'm happy for you. I'm jealous for you, because bearing children will be an experience I'll never have." I took her hand. "Can you understand that?"

She gave my hand a squeeze. *I understand.*

My phone chirped. I looked on the readout. *Chris Black.*

I looked at my watch and answered, "It's not nine o'clock yet."

"I know, I know. I just wanted you to know that I investigated the Anders place myself. The truck's clean. If there was ever any blue paint on it, it's long gone now."

"What about the protective grille? Did he show it to you?"

"Didn't find it. If it was ever in that garage, it's long gone. He denied having it."

"That's crazy," I said, raising my voice. "The man is lying to you." I started the car. "Give me an hour. I'll drop by my house and load the pictures onto my computer. I haven't done the calculations from my mock-up yet, but I'm sure the truck couldn't have sustained that damage just by rolling down the hill." I shook my head. "What a jerk!"

"Ten minutes," he said. "I've got a meeting with the Captain."

"I can bring by my camera. At least show you the photos."

"Do that."

The connection closed. "Amazing," I said. "This Anders guy's not just a jerk. He's stupid to fool with me."

Rene looked at me. "I think I understand something. You love reconstructing accidents from subtle clues, right?"

"Sure."

"Maybe that's why you're so hung up on the why of your and Mom's accident." She smiled, as if she was sure she was on to something.

"You're wrong. The clues only tell me what happened, not the motive behind."

I pressed the pedal and let the powerful Mercedes engine push me gently back into the leather seat. If this guy hit Jack, I was going to hit him back.

Thirty minutes later, after promising Rene I'd not be long, I stood in Chris Black's office. I connected my digital camera to his desktop in preparation for importing and viewing the pictures I'd taken the day before.

I moved the cursor to the "import" button and frowned. An error message appeared on the screen: "The device contains no photographs."

"What?" I looked at the back of my camera. The digital read-out showed no stored images. I shook my head. "This can't be. I didn't have time to download the pictures last night because of my guests. But there aren't any photos here."

Chris squinted at me. "Who else has access to your camera?"

"No one. I keep it at my desk or in the trunk of my car."

"No one?" He sipped the double mocha latte I'd brought him. "Are you sure you used this camera?"

"It's the only one I use."

"You had guests?"

I nodded, thinking about each one. The Renners had retired early. Henry had come in late, and he knew better than to mess with my camera. That only left Rene and Yolanda. Rene wouldn't think of touching my professional stuff. That only left Yolanda. Could she have been messing with my camera?

Chris took the camera from my hand. "This is like mine. It only takes pressing this button twice to erase the whole thing."

I shook my head. "I did not erase my camera!"

"Come on, Wendi. Accidents happen." He chuckled. "You may have dyed your hair, but you're still blonde."

His attempt at humor fell flat. Not wanting to cuss, I bared my teeth like an angry dog.

He held up his hands.

I disconnected my camera and vowed to return to Anders' place to look around. Something strange was going on, and I was going to get to the bottom of it.

ChaPteR 17

I drove back home mumbling about the traffic and dis-tracted by my thoughts about Jesse Anders.

At a traffic light, I heard Rene saying my name. "Wendi!" She shook her head. "Sheesh! What planet are you on?"

"I was thinking."

"So was I," she said. "I want you to listen to me."

I made an exaggerated move to look at her. "I'm listening."

"I want you and Henry to adopt my baby."

My face must have paled.

"Wendi?"

"You're kidding, right?" I'd mentioned that very thing to her just a few days ago, but hearing her say it, sensing the real possibility...

"No," she urged, "Think about it. It's perfect. You guys are rich. You could provide the perfect home."

It looks perfect from the outside, I thought.

"Henry's got a great job."

"He's got a good job, yes, but—"

"You live in the perfect location." She paused. "I think Dad will be a better grandfather than father."

I pulled away from the light, trying to process the reality of having a baby. "You've seen how crazy it is at my house."

"It's only crazy this week because I dropped in on you and because of Jack's family."

"Maybe we're too perfect."

"What's that supposed to mean?"

I held up a finger from the top of the steering wheel. "We have the perfect house."

"You have the perfect nursery," Rene added.

"We go to the right church, the right country club, the right restaurants, sit in the right pew, eat the right food, drive the right cars, wear the right clothes, exercise in the right club." I forced myself to laugh. "It's driving me crazy."

"You'd be a great mom."

"You're not listening to me." Starting a family with Henry was not on my agenda this week. Just trying to keep from running away from Henry was on my agenda. I stared at my sister and wrestled with my conscience. I wanted to be honest, to tell her of my outrageous plans to run away with Jack and of the life I'd lived. Instead, I found myself smiling. "You really think I'd be a great mom?"

"The best."

I shook my head. "You're a moron."

"You're right. I can't be a mother to this child. I'm single. I smoke. What kind of example is that?"

"You're smart." I gestured with my free hand. "You can stop smoking."

"I'm HIV-positive."

"Irrelevant. Remember what the doctor said."

"The kid needs a dad. Henry would be perfect."

Would he? "Henry's never home."

"Ask him, Wendi."

She had a point about Henry. His resume looked great. And it wasn't because Henry didn't have the perfect plan for a perfect little family someday. "Henry looks good," I conceded. "But that's because he's obsessive about looking good."

"So maybe he can be obsessive about being a good dad."

"It doesn't work that way."

"Just think about it."

I sighed. This wasn't how I'd planned my week. I was supposed to be in the Caribbean with Jack. But, sans my midlife crisis, here I was in Charlottesville talking to my sister about adopting her baby into my perfect family. I thought about the children my husband took care of at the hospital. He could be so gentle.

I wanted to tell her how perfect Henry really was, how he carried three pens in his white coat, each one centimeter apart, how he tied his silk ties so that the longer tail hung two centimeters below the shorter, how he turned on the blinker at the end of the driveway. I opened my mouth to protest again, but halted as Rene interrupted. "Just think about it."

Instead of replying, I just smiled and turned up Azalea Drive. My plans to rescue my fake life had been foiled. I found myself swinging back towards believing that God might be working something out for my good. I wasn't there yet, but I at least wanted to be there.

I didn't have time to think about that anyway. "You didn't happen to look at my camera last night, did you?"

I watched her from the corner of my eye. Rene didn't flinch. "Of course not. Why would I?"

"The images on my camera have been erased. All those photos I took of a wreck up in Ruckersville."

"Don't look at me," Rene said.

"Yolanda," I muttered. "I'll bet that airhead was messing with this."

"Why would she?"

"I have no idea. But it was in my sight until I went to sleep. Maybe she got back up to mourn the loss of her sweet fiancé."

I pulled in my driveway. I must have looked frightening because my sister grabbed my shoulders. "What're you doin'?"

I checked my watch. "Time for the bottle-blonde to wake up," I said, uncaring that I was criticizing the color I'd worn for six years.

Rene followed behind, perhaps fearing that I was going to overreact, perhaps kill the floozy. I stomped into the house and down the hall to my bedroom.

I knocked on the door, softly at first, then a bit louder when the sleepyhead didn't respond. I looked at Rene. "Time to get up, hangover or not."

I tried the door. Locked. I knocked again. "Yolanda? Yolanda!"

I rattled the door. When she didn't respond, I reached above the door and retrieved a key resting on the molding framing the doorway.

A moment later, I pushed open the door. She was still in bed. "Get up, sleepyhead," I sang, throwing wide the curtains. "It's past time to—"

I stopped as the light fell on the pallor of her face. Her lips were parted, the color of lilacs in the spring. The covers were turned down to reveal her nakedness. Her chest was still. "Oh God," I said.

Rene shrieked.

Yolanda was dead.

CHAPTER 18

Call 9–1–1!" I screamed as I assumed a position with my ear next to Yolanda's lips and my fingers to the right of her windpipe. She wasn't breathing and had no pulse. I formed a seal with my mouth over hers and blew. Her chest rose, but only with force. She was stone-cold dead.

Rene shook her head and covered her mouth with her hand. "It's no use. You don't know how long she's been this way."

I felt helpless. I backed away, the eeriness of the situation beginning to dawn. There was an open pharmacy bottle on the table. I picked it up and read the label. "She's taken an overdose." I handed the bottle to Rene.

"Why would she do this?"

"Maybe she was upset over losing Jack." I stepped toward the door. "I'm calling Chris Black."

"Wait," Rene said, grabbing my arm. "Look at this." She pointed to the label on the little bottle. "Henry prescribed this. It's not even for her. It says Lanny Bedford."

I took the bottle from her hand. "Oxycontin," I read. "It's a powerful narcotic. But why would Yolanda have a prescription that belongs to someone else?"

"Weird."

I phoned Chris Black. A minute later I had him on the line. "Black," he said.

"Chris, this is Wendi. Something horrible has happened. I just got home with Rene. I wanted to confront Yolanda because I thought she'd erased the pictures from my camera, but when I went to check on her, she was dead. She's taken an overdose, I'm sure. She—" my voice halted with a sob.

"Wendi, slow down. What happened?"

I started crying. I felt stupid for not being able to answer Chris, but it seemed the last domino in my holding it together had just tumbled and now everything was going to fall. My almost-affair, Jack's wreck, my pregnant sister with HIV, a trucker who was trying to hide the truth, my erased camera, and now finding Yolanda's body nearing room temperature all erupted in a serious threat to my mascara. I bit my lip and closed my eyes. "Just come over. A woman committed suicide in my house."

I set the phone back in the charging cradle and looked at Rene. "We'd better not touch anything. The medical examiner will want to see everything like we found it."

I walked to the kitchen and called Henry's office. He was operating. *Lucky Henry. He has his refuge.* I plopped onto my leather couch in the den and waited while Rene paced and mumbled, "I can't believe this," over and over.

Ten minutes later Chris Black showed up with two young-buck officers, two boys looking like they were just a few years beyond puberty, Officers Bouchard and Mann. Chris made introductions and followed Rene into the master bedroom just as the phone rang.

I stopped in the kitchen to answer the phone. It was Henry. "Honey, my secretary said you called. She said you sounded upset."

"Yolanda committed suicide."

"W-what?"

"You heard me. She's dead, Henry. Rene and I just found her."

"Call the police."

"They're already here." I hesitated. "Henry, I need you here."

I listened to him sigh. He wasn't big on emotional support. "I've just started a big case. I just scrubbed out to call. Ulrich's in there by himself."

It was my turn to sigh. "Henry, there is a dead woman in our bed!"

"Maybe I can get Jackson to watch Ulrich. I can't leave him here unattended."

"I understand." As bad as it seemed, I knew he was trapped. He couldn't, under any circumstances, leave a patient already under anesthesia.

"I'll be there as soon as I can."

"Henry, there was an empty bottle of Oxycontin on the nightstand. It belonged to a guy named Lanny Bedford." I hesitated. "Henry, you wrote the prescription."

"I did?" I listened to him huff. "How did she get it?"

"Who is Lanny Bedford?"

Henry's voice was quiet. "A patient," he mumbled.

"What's it mean?"

He sighed again. "I don't know. I've got to run."

I walked towards my bedroom again, but Rene met me in the hall and motioned me away. "They're treating this like some crime," she whispered.

I followed her back to the kitchen.

"The detective has already called the medical examiner. They are calling a forensics team."

I shrugged. "It's probably all routine, something they'd do for any unexpected death."

Chris appeared at the edge of the foyer holding a notepad and pen. Immediately, his manner had me on edge. I didn't like his attitude and certainly didn't like his tone of voice. "When's the last time anyone saw her?"

"Last night. About eleven."

"Why was she in your bed?"

"She was pretty upset last night. Her fiancé just cancelled their engagement. She drank some wine. We were up talking in my bedroom and she passed out. I didn't have the heart to move her."

"Why was she staying here?"

"Remember Jack Renner?"

"Of course."

"Yolanda Pate was his fiancée."

"Why was she staying with you?"

"Good question," I moaned. "My father offered our house for Jack's parents and his girlfriend."

He raised his eyebrows and kept writing. "How did she get the narcotics?"

"I have no idea."

I watched as Rene and Chris exchanged glances. "I'll need to talk to Henry."

"He's in the operating room. I just talked to him."

"Let's see," Chris began. "Your piano teacher is critically injured in a hit-and-run accident. Now, his fiancée dies in your house." He looked at me. "Is all this more than coincidence or are you just having one hell of a week?"

I didn't have an answer. I remembered my camera. "Remember the photos I took of the truck? I think Yolanda erased my camera."

"Why would she do that?"

"No idea." I tapped my fingers on the kitchen counter. I had an idea. "Maybe," I said.

"Maybe, what?"

"Maybe someone really was trying to kill Jack, and Yolanda was concerned that I was starting to solve the mystery."

Rene pointed at me. "And maybe she hired someone to run Jack down and committed suicide when she thought she was going to be found out."

"Motive?" I asked.

Rene tapped her chin. "Check and see if she was the beneficiary of any insurance policy."

Chris frowned. "I thought Wendi's imagination was wild. Now I see it's a family trait."

"There is a connection somewhere."

The detective shook his head. "Maybe," he said slowly. "But unlikely." He looked at his two younger associates and then back to me. "Do me a favor, Wendi. Let me do the investigation here. It wouldn't look good for you to stick your nose into a death investigation when it happened in your own home."

Three hours later, the young police duo were still pacing, Chris Black had returned to his office, and Dr. Sig Eichmann, a state medical examiner, was completing his on-site examination of Yolanda's body and the death scene. Even though I knew Sig well and he had taught me so much in the past, every time I was tempted to go and see what he was doing, I thought about how he might misinterpret my interest and stayed away.

By six, the forensics team carried out the body, and Sig nodded at me as he walked through the foyer towards the front door. He stopped and reiterated the main points of my account. "Last seen around eleven p.m., deep sonorous breathing, fully clothed. The next thing you know was around ten this morning when you found her dead and without clothing."

I nodded. It was the third time he'd rechecked the details.

It was Tuesday, salad night at the Stratfords'. Henry insisted on it. I shook my head. I was going to order pizza, and Henry was just going to have to deal with a deviation from the nutrition schedule. Besides, he'd done a zipper check times three this morning, so he was already off scale for the normal perfect Tuesday plan. I called to Rene. "I'm ordering pizza from Angelico's. What do you like?"

She smiled and patted her stomach. "Junior wants Canadian bacon and mushrooms."

"Junior is the size of a lima bean," I said.

Rene gave me the finger.

I picked up the phone and ordered a supreme.

Henry Stratford slipped past his receptionist and into his office and closed the door. Then, he knelt on the floor and opened the bottom drawer of his oak filing cabinet. He found what he was looking for at the back of the drawer, lying flat beneath the hanging files. He stared at the document, his heart racing. He ran his finger down the list of names. There, halfway down the page, his finger came to a stop. "Lanny Bedford," he whispered.

Henry mumbled a curse and carefully placed the list back into the filing cabinet. A moment later he heard his name and whirled around to see Cindy Swanson sitting on his desk. "Cindy!"

"What's wrong, Henry?" She stared at him with squinting eyes above a mischievous smile. "What can possibly be so captivating in that filing cabinet that you didn't hear me come in?"

He stood and tried to regain his composure. "I-it's nothing. I was just recalling an old patient."

She reached for his forehead. "You're sweating."

He raised his eyebrows. "See what you do to me?" He looked beyond her to see that the door was shut and cleared his throat. "Look, Cindy," he began. "About last night. I sh—"

She shook her head and placed her palm against his lips. "Don't apologize to me. I'm a big girl, Henry, and I'm not sorry a bit."

He clasped her hand in his and pressed a kiss against her palm before releasing it. Instead of pulling her hand away, she tickled her way along his hairline and coaxed him forward.

After a kiss, he reluctantly stepped back. "We need to be careful."

She nodded. "I understand. Can you come over tonight?"

"I need to be at home."

"Wendi will understand. She expects you to be out late."

He felt himself weakening.

She made a face. A child pouting for her own way.

He planted a quick kiss on her forehead. "Maybe," he said. "Don't wait up."

At eight, Henry called and said he was managing a multi-casualty city-bus wreck. I was jealous. He had the operating rooms to retreat to and the obligation to set aside all of the confusion looming in our personal world. I had no such obligation. I wanted to look at my problems and say, "Sorry, I've got a life to save," turn away, and flee. Of course, I did have my consultant business, but I was officially on vacation this week, and thinking of that only made my misery more poisonous to me.

Rene went to bed early, having quickly reclaimed the downstairs suite that the Renners vacated. I wandered the house listlessly, carrying a glass of a Virginia wine. I drank more than I wanted, but less than would be required to quiet the worries that swirled about my head. In the midst of the trauma that this week had become, my sister had launched my thoughts in a new direction: motherhood. A week ago, my heart was steeled with a plan of escape. Henry was history. Jack was my future. Out with plastic. In with organic. But everything changed with Jack's accident and the fact that he'd forgotten that I'd seduced him.

As I watched Henry care for Jack, I felt a little warmth from the spark of what once attracted me to Henry in the first place. And I couldn't argue that Henry always tried hard to keep me happy.

Maybe God did give a care and was giving me a second chance to do things the right way. I surprised myself by allowing this thought.

Was Rene's baby to become the cement that Henry and I needed? I walked to the nursery to strip the sheets from the air mattress and found myself dreaming of a little one lying in the crib. I sat in the rocking chair and imagined midnight feedings, reading Dr. Seuss books, and cute little baby clothes. I picked up a quilted pillow and hugged it to my breasts. Could it be that my hopes for motherhood could come as early as December? I thought about Christmas and an extra stocking over the mantle.

Christmas with Henry alone had become a bore. I dropped hints and he bought everything I wanted. What fun was there in that? I wanted the unexpected. A surprise. Henry seemed obsessed with being sure I'd be happy with his purchases. Last year I offered to buy and wrap a leather jacket I'd seen, something I promised I'd wear while screaming in the wind on Henry's Triumph Rocket III. He revolted. He insisted on wrapping it himself after having me select the wrapping paper. I smiled at the memory. That was Henry. Sweet. Boring. But dead set on my happiness. But if I stayed with Henry, could I ever escape my plastic life?

I was standing with my hands on the edge of the railing when Henry came in behind me. "What's with the police tape across our doorway?"

I shrugged. "They told me it is routine. They're treating it as a crime scene until after the autopsy. Chris Black assured me it was routine."

His forehead was creased with worry.

"What's with the anxiety? Where's my ever-confident surgeon?"

He offered me a weak smile, one that faded when he started to speak. "When's the last time you had the alarm system serviced?"

"Monthly, Henry." I frowned. "The first Monday of every month."

"Who knows the entry sequence?"

"You and me." I paused. "Why?"

He acted nonchalant, but I could sense a fear beneath the calm. "The police are treating this like a crime. If someone else got in here, how'd they get in?"

"Henry, you're creeping me out."

He turned away. "We should change the entry code just the same."

"Fine, Henry. Shall we use our anniversary? Six One Eight Zero Two."

He nodded and stayed quiet for a moment. "So our bedroom is a crime scene. Where do we sleep?"

"We can use the guest bed downstairs. I'm not sure I want to stay in our bed after Yolanda—" I put my hand to my mouth.

He slipped his hand around my waist and kissed my cheek. "Hell of a day, huh?"

I inhaled his cologne and stared at the little animal mobile. "What's going on, Henry?"

"The world's gone mad," he whispered.

"Be serious," I whined. A moment later, I was caught off guard by my fresh desire to retreat into his arms. I pulled his arms around me and held him against my back.

He shook his head, nosing forward into my hair. "I don't know."

I couldn't face him just yet. I kept looking at the baby crib and wondering if we had a future together.

I took a deep breath and turned around. "Ever wish you could erase time? I'd like to do this last week over."

He shook his head. "What's done is done."

"Want to hear something else?" I said, searching his eyes in the dim light.

He nodded and put his hands on my shoulders, looking down at me. "Sure."

I took a sip of wine. My tongue felt thick and clumsy. "Rene wants us to adopt her baby." Before he could say anything, I put my index finger on his lips. "Don't, honey," I said. "Don't say anything. Just think about it."

He sighed. Adopting a child was in the future, but one this soon was a deviation from the Stratford master plan. "Is this something you want?"

I looked around the room. I'd worked for hours stenciling little animals around the top of the walls. I laid my head against his chest. A week ago, this was the last thing on my mind. "Maybe," I whispered.

"Will it make you happy?"

"Do you think I'd make a good mother?"

"What kind of question is that?"

I lifted my head and looked at him. "A serious one, Henry Stratford. I'm afraid I'll end up like my mother."

"She was a good mom."

I wanted to spit. My mother was the queen of implants. Her smile. Her role. It was all about appearance. I studied Henry for a moment and tried to focus. Maybe that was why my husband liked my mother. They were both all about image. "She appeared to be a good mother. That didn't make her one."

Henry let it pass. He was smart. "Anyway," he said. "You'd be a great mother."

I locked my fingers behind his head and pulled him into an embrace. At that moment, all my guilty emotions tumbled to the surface. I felt bad for having wanted someone else when Henry had been so good to me—even in the midst of his boring predictability. I'd been unfaithful to him, even if it hadn't gone outside my mind for more than ten minutes. I knew what Jesus said about lust. I'd already committed adultery in my heart.

I didn't realize I was crying until I felt the wetness on Henry's face. He lifted his face from mine and touched my cheek tenderly. "What's wrong, Wendi?"

At that moment, thinking about a baby in our little nursery, I felt I could really love him again. "Nothing," I sniffed. "I'm OK."

We stared at each other in the darkness for a moment before I tried my old line, the one that sealed our romance right in the beginning. "Kiss me!"

He obeyed. We moved together as he backed me up a step so that my foot nudged the edge of the air mattress I'd blown up for Rene. I tugged at his necktie. He gently lowered me towards the floor.

"Henry," I giggled a playful protest.

He must not have heard.

CHAPTER 19

The next morning, Henry stood, folded the newspaper into perfect quarters and proceeded into the hall for his routine. I sipped my coffee, keeping the mug close to my chin and watching him through the steam. He went through the whole routine, hair, teeth, tie, jacket, pants, and lastly, the double fly-check. Perhaps yesterday's triple check was a fluke. Either that, or something bad had infected his mind. I shook my head. Henry was way too predictable for flukes.

I watched him drive his Mercedes to the end of the driveway, signal, and pull out. At the last second, I saw him lift his hand in a feeble wave, so I followed his line of sight to a post just opposite the driveway to my father's church. There stood my father, waiting to cross the road.

Immediately I tensed, then chastised myself. *Why do I always do that?* I knew the answer. *Guilt.*

I hid behind the curtains so he wouldn't see me. I waited for his knock before answering. I pulled open the door. "Daddy, what a nice surprise." I tried to mean it.

"Hi, Wendi." He took a step forward. "Is Rene up?"

Of course. He's come to love on his prodigal. I felt my own disappointment surge. "Not yet. Shall I wake her?"

"No, no," he said, keeping his voice quiet. "I really wanted to talk to you." He walked in and selected an easy chair next to the piano in the front room.

I sat opposite him, immediately on the defense.

"Can I ask you to explain your behavior yesterday? The way you blew up over at the home?"

I looked at him. He was older than I remembered. He seemed to have aged overnight. Deep wrinkles creased the sides of his neck and forehead and gathered in little crow's feet beside his eyes. I shook my head. I couldn't betray my mother. I'd hurt her enough. "I can't explain it, Daddy."

His eyes were soft. Eyes that had absorbed so much of other people's pain. They were the same eyes I saw in the waiting room when he comforted the Renners. "You might try finding out who your mother is."

"What?"

"You don't seem to know her anymore."

I didn't understand. I knew my mother well enough. If only my father knew what I knew about his precious bride. How deceitful, how self-serving—

"She's changed," he said, interrupting my bitter reflections. He paused and leaned forward. He touched my hand, just a grace note, not sustained. "You obviously expected us to react differently to the news of our grandchild. Tell me why."

I bit my bottom lip and gave a rapid shake of my head. As I sat in quietness, it occurred to me that my mother not only had never told him, she probably couldn't tell him the truth. Perhaps she too had amnesia from the accident. I held up my hands. "It was a stupid comment. Who knows what I was thinking?"

He wasn't persuaded by my pass-it-off replies. "You can talk to me, Wendi." He stood up and walked away from me, and plunked a few high notes on the piano keys. "I should have made you practice when you were a child. Then you wouldn't be having to take lessons now."

"I like taking lessons. Jack's a great—" I paused. "Teacher."

He nodded. "I've made a lot of mistakes."

I watched as his old eyes brimmed with tears. My words came unbidden. "You were a good father, Daddy."

"You know what scares me the most?"

I shook my head.

"So many children get an idea of what their heavenly Father is like from their earthly dads." He looked down. "He's nothing like me."

"Daddy, don't say that. You were a good father." I stood up and held out my hands. "What, have I turned out so bad that you think you've failed?"

He smiled at me. "Of course not. You've always been the perfect daughter."

I watched him for a moment. His eyes carried a sadness that belied the words he spoke. "What is it, Daddy? Perfect not good enough for you?"

"Maybe that's it, honey." He gave me a hug and patted my back.

When he got to the door, he turned and said, "I'd love you even if you weren't perfect."

I opened my mouth to question him, but he'd made a dramatic exit before I could reply.

I walked to the kitchen, where I found Rene drinking coffee, sitting at the table. "How long have you been up?"

"Long enough to eavesdrop. Why didn't you tell him the truth?"

"I can't."

"You're protecting Mom."

"Shouldn't I?" I poured myself more coffee. "Haven't I caused her enough pain? She's stuck in that chair because of me." I glared at Rene. "And you want me to shred the last of her dignity by telling Daddy what a fake she is?"

"Is that what you think?"

"Do I have to spell it out for you? In church, she was all smiles, the successful minister's wife with the perfect family."

Rene huffed. "I ruined that."

I shook my head. "After you left, she seemed consumed with keeping what remained of her honor. Maybe she'd failed with you, but when I showed up pregnant, she couldn't stand to let anyone know."

"And maybe she just didn't want to lose you too."

"What?"

"She understood that if Daddy knew, you'd end up in front of the church elders, just like me. And then she'd be out two daughters, not just one."

"I don't believe it. You know what she said to me?" I gestured the quotation marks with my fingers. " 'How dare you do this to your father's ministry?' "

Rene raised her eyebrows and stayed quiet, sipping from the tall mug in her hand.

I sat across from her. "And why are you suddenly so cozy with them again? Have you forgotten that the church asked you to leave?"

She sighed. "I've not forgotten. But that was the church. Daddy never asked me to leave home. That was my decision." She looked in my eyes, as if pleading with me to understand. "This pregnancy, this HIV has a way of making me think. I'm at the bottom."

"Stop it," I said. "You're my hero. You had the guts to stand up to them. I only pretended to comply, but inside, I envied you."

"So talk to Mom. I think Daddy's right. I think she is glad about a grandchild. I think she's changed."

"What good will it do to confront her with the past? I'm not even sure she would remember." I paused. "We've never spoken about it since the accident. She spent days in a coma. She may not even remember that I was pregnant. So if I bring it up, I'll only risk her being mad at me being the reason we were in the car in the first place."

"You're pathetic."

"Excuse me?"

"You want to be real? Then be real. Don't keep pretending to be something you're not."

I opened my mouth to reply, but I had nothing to say.

"You want to stop being a fake? Start by telling your father who you really are."

"And let him judge me like he judged you?"

"Or let him forgive you like he forgave me."

Daddy forgiving? Judgmental yes, but forgiving? "That sounds funny coming from you."

"You should have stayed around the nursing home a little longer. Daddy said he loved me. He said they didn't care what I'd done, that I'd always have their love."

My head hurt. I got up and found the ibuprofen and dropped four tablets into my hand, then added two Tylenols. I looked at Rene. She was serious. And jealousy was taking a fast escalator in my soul. *Why don't they say that about me? Rene's been off going her own sinful way, and I've been the perfect back-pew Christian daugh-ter.* I swallowed the pills and tried to smile. "That's so sweet."

Rene didn't seem to notice my attempt at honesty was falling short. She seemed to be nestled in the afterglow of reconciliation with our parents.

I squeezed the bridge of my nose and swore I'd never have more than three drinks in a night. Or at least not more than four. Unless it was a very special occasion. Or unless I felt like I did last night. *OK, I'm through with empty promises. I'm trying to be honest with myself again.* I looked up. "I need to talk to Jack Renner. I need to tell him about his fiancée."

"Don't you think he's heard by now?"

"Henry stopped to see him last evening. If Jack knew anything, he kept it from Henry."

Rene clutched her coffee mug with two hands like it might escape. "Be careful, Wendi."

I felt a twinge of guilt. "Careful?"

Rene stared past my façade. "Remember, I fell for a music teacher once, too."

"Jack?" I laughed, but felt a second stab of remorse. "I think your medicine is affecting your mind."

Rene looked away and stayed quiet, but I knew she didn't buy my little charade.

I took a deep breath. I did need to talk to Jack. If for no other reason than to formally say "goodbye." Of course, I wouldn't use those words exactly. It's hard to break up with someone who didn't know about the relationship. But I needed to close the relationship for me.

I was determined not to mess up my second chance as badly as I had the first one.

Sig Eichmann, M.D., was troubled. As a state medical examiner, how many years had he worked with both Henry and Wendi

Stratford? At least six. And yet this investigation was different. It was personal. A death investigation in the home of a friend.

The case of Yolanda Pate was open in front of him. Was it suicide? An accidental overdose? Or something more sinister? A drug screen of her blood revealed high levels of a narcotic. Her alcohol level was above legal limits for intoxication. Certainly, she had ingested enough to suppress her drive to breathe and had died as a consequence. That much was clear to Sig.

What bothered him were the subtle findings. She had a small, fresh cut on the inside of her upper lip, and another on her tongue, likely a laceration from biting her own tongue. *Signs that she was so drunk she bit her own mouth? Or signs of a struggle as someone forced her to swallow more pills than she wanted when she was too drunk to defend herself?*

When I peeked in the door of room 421, Jack set down the book he was reading. "Knock, knock," I said, entering. "Well, look who found a razor."

I set a bouquet of daffodils on a small side dresser beside his hospital bed.

His face brightened. My eyes went from his to the worn leather book on the table. "Hi, Wendi."

I felt a stab of guilt. I was married, thinking about adopting a baby with my husband, but I just couldn't stop my physical and emotional reaction to this man who was thoroughly under my skin. My face must have been transparent.

"Feeling guilty?"

How did this man read my mind? I looked at the Bible, another reminder of my failure as a Christian. I shrugged it off and smiled. "Is that any way to greet a lady?"

His expression softened. "I'm sorry."

I touched the edge of his bed. "May I?"

He smiled and I sat. His eyes narrowed. My face couldn't hide the fact that I had bad news.

"Jack, something's happened." I paused. "It's Yolanda."

"Yolanda," he said slowly, accentuating each syllable as if deciding whether the sounds fit.

"She's dead, Jack. Suicide." I let it out in a rush, not knowing how to deliver such horrible news.

He closed his eyes and began turning his head right to left, back and forth as if grinding away an old memory. His breath escaped across pursed lips. "Oh God. Oh God," he said. "Why?" He opened his eyes to look into my face. I could see pain there. Had he remembered her?

"I'm sorry," I said.

He shifted in his bed, grimacing as he turned. "I don't believe this. She's dead?"

Our eyes met again. He knew it wasn't a topic I'd joke about. "She wasn't dealing with the idea of you two being apart." I touched his hand, snuggling two fingers into his open palm and giving a squeeze. "You could have never known this would happen."

"H-how?" He shook his head, tortured.

"She took some pills."

His voice thickened. "Oh God, oh God. I shouldn't have told her—" his voice halted.

His face paled, and I watched as his lower lip quivered before he sucked it tight against its beautiful mate.

Something in me wanted to crawl right up into his arms and lay my head on his chest and tell him it was going to be alright. But I was trying to remember my second chance, remember I was married, and determined to make it work.

He looked at me again, repeating the word as if the finality of it was still lurking at the edges of his mind. "Dead?"

I nodded, feeling a lump in my own throat as I took his agony as my own. "My sister and I found her in bed."

"I'm sorry."

I shook my head. "I'm glad it was me and not your mother."

He pulled his head back. "Do my parents know?"

"I'm sure the police called her parents. They've probably spread the word by now."

Jack mumbled something under his breath, followed by, "This is a disaster."

I couldn't think of anything to say. I was running on empty myself, and I'd sworn off Christian platitudes. "You couldn't have known."

"She didn't seem like the type to—" He pulled his hand away from mine and covered his mouth. "I mean she seemed upset that I wanted to cancel the wedding, but I never imagined—"

"Don't blame yourself, Jack."

For the first time I saw a flash of something scary in his eyes. "Who should I blame, Wendi?"

"Me?" I said meekly.

As stupid as it was, the comment made him smile. "You're a piece of work, you know that? How long have you been walking around taking the blame for everything?" He paused and picked up my hand again and said softly, "Years?"

I looked at my piano teacher and marveled at what an introspective and discerning man he was ... something I'd completely overlooked in my infatuation with his handsome outward package. Without warning, I felt a tear trickle down my cheek. I was so disarmed by this man who seemed to so easily rock the boat of my soul. I sniffed, unable to confess. The worst thing about it was I knew he was right. And I could pinpoint the day I picked up the weight of the world.

The day I decided to rid myself of the ugly evidence of my passion for a married man.

A few seconds later, he called my name and brought me out of the fog. "Wendi. Whatever it is, forgive yourself." He paused. "God certainly has."

"You presumptuous—" I stopped myself. I just couldn't lash out anymore. I looked down at my hand in his. He'd curled his fingers around mine, not knowing the havoc he wreaked in my soul. I could only mutter the words he'd said. "Forgive yourself."

After a moment, I cleared my throat. "How did this get so backwards? I'm supposed to be comforting you over the loss of someone you loved."

"I'm glad you're the one to tell me."

I leaned over and planted a kiss on his cheek. To me, it wasn't flirtatious. It was a natural response to a moment of heart emotion.

I touched the top of his head, where new, bristly hairs were sprouting and coloring his sandpapery scalp. Our eyes met for a moment, and then I saw a flash. Something had changed. I followed his eyes to the foot of his bed, where a man in a military uniform stood hand in hand with a stocky woman with silver hair. I wondered how much of our tender moment they'd witnessed.

The man spoke with a nod of his head. "Jack." An understood greeting from the military man.

Jack seemed to hesitate. I looked at his eyes. *Recognition?*

The woman stared at me, her expression one of distaste. Suddenly, I felt like looking in the mirror to search for flaws. *Ketchup on my blouse?* "Jack," she said. "We came as soon as we heard."

Jack opened his hand, and I pulled away, feeling heat in my cheeks. He winced as he coughed. "Do I know you?"

The man took a step forward. "Don't be ridiculous, Jack. We're—"

The woman took his arm, interrupting him. "William, Yolanda said he was suffering from amnesia."

Whoever these strangers were, they were intruding into Jack's privacy. I shifted in my position, turning a shoulder to Jack and staying firmly seated between him and the couple. My mother-bear instincts kicked in. There was a cub to protect. "Would you kindly introduce yourselves? This man has been through a serious car accident. Don't be alarmed if he doesn't know you."

The woman clutched the man's arm. "We're Yolanda's parents."

"Yo-lan-da," Jack said, hopping from stone to stone across the stream of syllables.

The officer stepped forward and held out his hand. "Major William Pate," he said.

Jack shook it, and I noted just the hint of a smile tickle the corner of his lips and disappear.

The man held up his hand towards the woman. She was stylish, if a bit overweight. "This is my bride of thirty-five years."

She looked as if she might burst into tears. "Jack, don't you know us? I'm Gloria."

Jack's face remained motionless. He had small wrinkles crossing his forehead, something he had every time I played a piano tune badly. "I'm afraid not."

Gloria stepped up and reattached herself to the major's arm. "Oh William, it's like we've lost them both!"

Jack winced.

The woman looked at me. I felt the ketchup feelings return.

"Oh," I said, clearing my throat. "I'm Wendi Stratford. Yolanda had been staying at my house."

The major nodded. "Yes." Not oh goody. Not how horrible. Just a neutral matter-of-stating-the-facts yes.

Gloria turned. "You!"

I looked at my blouse. One extra button opened but no ketchup.

The woman's voice was etched with irritation. "My baby said Jack had mistaken you for her!"

I clutched at my neckline. "I—uh—"

Jack tried to rescue me. "A mistake," he said, holding up his hand as if hoping the bull wouldn't charge. "My mother told me my fiancée was beautiful. When Wendi walked in, I just assumed …." His voice trailed off weakly.

I liked the memory. I would have cuddled the event in my soul and smiled had the Pates not been grieving their departed daughter. Besides, I was trying to say a soul goodbye to this man, and I wasn't supposed to hug him or the memories he gave me.

Gloria scowled. "And it's not like you're wasting any time trying to convince him otherwise from what I saw a minute ago."

"Now, dear," William said, patting his wife on the shoulder.

She shrugged him off. She might have been the wife of a powerful man, but he wasn't going to stop his tank from aiming straight at me. "Yolanda had a sixth sense about you." She took a step towards me after throwing away her husband's arm. She raised her hand and pointed her index finger towards my face. "She said your husband's an absolute gem, and that you didn't seem to see how blessed you are."

"Gloria," the major said, reaching for her arm. He looked at me as she moved out of his grasp. "She's just upset."

"She was only comforting me, Mrs. Pate," Jack said. "She'd only told me just now how Yolanda had died."

"Suicide, is that what she told you?" Gloria asked.

Jack nodded. "I feel horrible about this. I think I upset her."

The silver tank frowned and moved back onto her husband's arm. A move of solidarity. "We don't think she could have done that." She shook her head. "It was an accident," she said. She looked at me. "Or worse."

That was it. The last straw. I didn't care whether this woman had just lost her daughter. She'd fired one too many shots across my bow for me not to respond. I stood up and faced her. I opened my mouth, prepared to launch a defense of my own, when Henry came in. I held my tongue. After a second of nothing, I huffed. "Mr. and Mrs. Pate, I'd like you to meet my husband, Dr. Henry Stratford." I looked at my husband, the gem, as Yolanda called him, and forced a smile. "These are Yolanda's parents."

Henry nodded compassionately. "We are so sorry for your loss. Yolanda was quite a young woman," he said, as if he'd known her for years. "If there's anything we can do while you're in town. A place to stay," he said, gesturing with an open hand. "There's always room at the Stratfords'."

I looked at him, unable to fix upon a plastic smile. Henry was out of his mind if he thought I would let this woman under my roof.

Mr. Pate shook Henry's hand. "We're staying at the Omni," he said, "but thanks."

My husband nodded. "Oh. Nice place. Great Sunday brunch if you're still around." Henry turned towards Jack. "Well, I won't keep you from the Pates. I was just coming to check on your progress. Are you walking?"

Jack nodded, smiling. He looked relieved to have something else to talk about. "Down to the nurses' station three times this morning."

Henry touched Jack's stomach. "Eating?"

"Some. Not much appetite yet."

Henry looked at the data on a clipboard hanging on the end of the bed. He looked at the Pates. He shook the major's hand for the second time. "Nice to meet you," he said. Then, he turned to leave and added with a solemn tone, "Try not to stress my patient too much."

I was surprised. It was as close to confrontation as Henry came.

The major saluted Henry. "We were just leaving."

"We were? We just got here." The silver tank crossed her arms across her ample bosom.

"We were."

Henry paused and looked at me, and I saw something flicker in his eyes before he followed the Pates out of the room.

I could hear Gloria chatter all the way down the hall. "The nerve of that woman, moving in on that brain-damaged boy. I never ..."

I traded smiles with Jack. He looked at me and mouthed a question, "I'm brain-damaged?"

I shrugged.

"Some comfort you are," he said.

"I'd better go." I looked down at him for a moment and said my mental goodbye. *I'm married, Jack. These moments I've shared with you were never meant to be. Goodbye.*

"Go practice your piano."

Henry's cell phone rang out the theme song from *Rocky*. He looked at the digital readout of the caller and was tempted to curse. *Anders.*

He walked to an isolated corner next to a bank of hospital elevators and pushed the green answer button. He looked around and kept his voice low, but strained. "I told you it's over. Don't call me again."

"Doc, is that any way to talk to an old friend?"

"We're not friends."

"Sorry about your wife."

"My wife?"

"Gorgeous woman. You've got good taste in women. But you needed to understand the consequences of your decision." He paused. "Too bad she had to die."

"Die?" Henry didn't understand.

"Don't tell me you haven't been home." He listened as Anders cursed. "Go home and check your bedroom." He chuckled. "And you'll reconsider backing away from our business relationship."

Suddenly Henry understood. "You fool!" he said, looking around to be sure no one was listening. "That wasn't my wife!"

CHAPTER 20

Chris Black looked up to see a man and woman exit room 421. The man was tall, wearing a military uniform and escorted by a woman with silver hair and a scowl on her face. He listened as they approached. "The nerve of that woman," she said, "moving in on that brain-damaged boy."

"Mr. and Mrs. Pate?" Chris said, flashing his detective badge. "I'm Detective Black with the Charlottesville PD. Can we speak?"

The military man sized him up. "Is there a problem?"

"I'd just like to ask you a few questions about your daughter." He pointed down the hall away from the nurses' station. "There is a small lounge down the hall."

Mr. Pate nodded. "Sure," he said, extending his hand. "I'm Major William Pate." He pointed with a tilt of his head. "This is my bride, Gloria."

The detective nodded and led. There was a grouping of six chairs, all unoccupied. He sat across from the couple. The woman grasped the man by folding her arms around his elbow. She spoke before Chris could ask his first question.

"My daughter wouldn't commit suicide." She shook her big silver hair back and forth. "She was just about to graduate. She had too much to live for." She leaned forward and whispered, "I think that Mrs. Stratford killed her."

"Now, Honey," the major said. "That's a pretty outrageous thing to say. You've only just met her."

"You saw how she kissed Jack just now. She probably saw her chance to cut in."

Chris raised his eyebrows. *She was kissing Jack?*

Mrs. Pate shook her head. "I know what I saw. And I know what I sensed. That woman's — "

"She's the wife of the man who saved Jack's life, dearest. Don't forget that."

She glared at him. "You're gullible, William. You'd believe any pretty face."

Obviously, the major was used to dealing with the silver bullet's fury. "I believe you, Buttercup." Mr. Pate rolled his eyes and looked back at Chris. "We haven't even heard why you wanted to question us."

"It's routine, actually. We investigate all unexpected deaths. Many apparent suicides prove to be just that."

"You must not have heard me," Mrs. Pate snapped. "Our daughter wouldn't have — " She dissolved into tears, and her voice closed around a sob.

"Easy, dearest," the major soothed. "Let the man do his job."

"Did Yolanda ever speak of depression? Of wanting to die?"

The major nodded. "She was pretty upset by Jack's accident. You know about that, I guess." He paused, his lips trembling.

"Yes, sir."

The major was silent for a moment, collecting himself before speaking again. "She called home every night, crying about how Jack didn't remember her or their wedding plans." He spoke slowly, as if trudging through the snow of his daughter's pain. "It was horrible for her. She had her heart set on a life with him."

Mrs. Pate sniffed and unwound herself from her husband's arm in search of a tissue. When she found it, she emptied her nose loudly.

Chris looked away.

Mrs. Pate tucked the Kleenex away and pointed at the detective. "You need to check out that woman in there. Mrs. Stratford. Outside, she may be all innocent, but I think it's a skin over some rottenness, I'll tell you."

"Of course." He made a note. "Did Yolanda ever actually mention Wendi, uh Mrs. Stratford?"

"She went on and on about her and her husband," Mr. Pate said. "She was so impressed at their kindness."

"She said Jack mistook her for Wendi," Mrs. Pate added.

The major shifted in his vinyl chair. "She said Dr. and Mrs. Stratford were the perfect couple."

Mrs. Pate cleared her throat. "What she said was that Mrs. Stratford didn't know the gem she had in her hand."

"I see. Could I have a number where I could reach you?"

The major handed him a card and pointed to a number at the bottom. "I can be reached at this number. Leave a voice mail."

Chris took the card and stood. "Thanks. I'll certainly keep you informed."

The couple thanked him and walked to the elevator.

The detective looked at the notes in his hand. What was up with Wendi? Why was she in the center swirl of so many problems?

He walked to a quiet place and called the chief of police, Mosby.

After two rings, the chief picked up. "Mosby," he barked.

"Chief, it's Black. Look, I just talked to Yolanda Pate's parents." He chuckled. "Boy is her mother a piece of work."

"Get to the point, Black. I've got work to do."

"She's completely convinced that something fishy is going on here. She claims her daughter would never have committed suicide."

The chief sighed. "All mothers would say that."

"She's convinced Wendi Stratford is involved."

"Evidence?"

"Only a grieving mother's suspicions." Chris paced in the lobby talking softly into his cell. "She thinks Wendi Stratford was having an affair with Jack Renner, Yolanda's fiancé."

"It's only a suspicion unless you can give me something solid."

"I've got to watch my bias."

"Trust your gut, Black. You've always had good instincts. Just make sure you have real evidence, not just your disdain for a woman who embarrassed us."

Chris nodded into the phone. "Sure, boss."

"Talk to anyone who might have seen them together. See if there is anything in it. Have you talked to the ME?"

"Just the prelim exam is in. She definitely died of an overdose, but it looks like she may have been forced to take the pills. What Sig has doesn't sound conclusive."

The chief chuckled and talked with his voice quiet. "Be as objective as you can, but for my sake, find something concrete. Nothing would be sweeter than to nail her to the wall."

"Right."

"Keep me informed."

"I'm on it."

Once I was in the comfort of my Mercedes, I inhaled the smell of leather and dialed Chris Black. Although he'd seemed distant since our court clash, I still counted him an ally, one of the few I had within the force. If anyone could be counted on to be fair, I thought it was Chris.

"Detective Black."

"Chris, it's me, Wendi."

"Wendi, Wendi, what is it, dear?"

"Cut the crap, Chris. I need to know what's happening."

"That's something I'd like to know. Maybe you should tell me."

"What's that supposed to mean? I want to know if you've talked to Jesse Anders. Find out why he's lying to you."

"What am I supposed to do? As far as I know, he hasn't committed a crime."

"He's defrauding an insurance company."

"So let them fight it out in court. Bring your evidence in your little leather satchel and have at 'em, Baby. That's what you do best, isn't it?"

"Sarcasm doesn't work for you. I'd like it better if you just told me how you felt."

He forced his breath out into the phone, a sharp distorted sigh. "Why are you calling me?"

"Look, I just wondered if you'd found out anything. Jack is my friend. I'm concerned about this Anders guy and wondered if you might have found out anything that could link him to the hit-and-run."

"Jack is your friend. I've been meaning to ask you about your relationship with him."

"He's—" I halted. I'd made a new commitment to stop covering up. *But my relationship with Jack doesn't have anything to do with this. Does it?* "A friend," I said. "Only a friend." My heart stung with an attack of conscience. I half expected to hear a rooster crow or something.

"A friend?"

Chris was torturing me. Sure, I'd thrown myself at Jack, confessed my adulterous feelings toward him. But nobody knew that, not even brain-damaged Jack. *So it isn't really a lie. He is only a friend now. But we had an affair once. For five minutes.* "We're friends, OK? You've heard of them, right? I used to think you were one of them. Share coffee. Share a laugh. Maybe even a misery or two."

"Friends are loyal."

"Friends tell the truth."

I was getting mad at Chris and getting nowhere.

"Tell me you weren't having an affair with him."

"Tell me what that has to do with anything."

"His fiancée is dead. Love triangles can cause normal people to act in strange ways."

"Are you accusing me of something?"

"I'm just asking questions."

"Get off it, Chris. Why don't you just admit you're out to embarrass me and settle an old score? I thought you were bigger than that."

The silence on the other end of the line told me I'd hit the mark. When he spoke again, it was with forced control, but I could hear the irritation just under the surface. "Answer my question. Were you having an affair with Mr. Renner?"

My sin was buried. Yes, I'd blown it. But no one else knew. Not even Jack could counter my testimony. "Of course not. He was my piano teacher. A friend. Nothing more." I winced and listened for roosters.

He sighed. "OK."

He didn't believe me. Chris always said "OK" at the end of our arguments, but not because he believed anything I said. He was just done arguing.

I tried to sound upbeat. "Call me if you hear anything about Anders." I paused. "I still think that Yolanda may have had some link to him. Why else would she have erased my camera?"

"You're assuming she did."

I knew she did. I just couldn't convince the evidence-prone detective. "Chris, you know me. I'm not a criminal. And you're in the center of the department. Evidence is swirling all around. I have a right to be in the loop."

"OK."

He was putting me off again. I knew when I was in trouble. Chris was the only real inside source I had for information in the PD. If he turned against me, I wouldn't have a prayer. I frowned at my thought. *I'm not sure I believe in praying anymore anyway. What's the point? God—if he cares—sees right through my skin.*

I hesitated, unable to resurrect a positive feeling about ending a conversation on such a downturn.

I didn't have to. He ended it for me. "I've got to run."

I sighed. "Ciao."

Click. The call had been terminated. I felt like crying. My only inside-PD source had just deserted me.

I let loose a curse. It was heartfelt. And I was alone in my Mercedes. But I felt guilty. Funny how that worked. I only felt like God was watching when I messed up.

The thought made me smile. *Then he must be watching me all the time.*

At home, I was greeted by a Charlottesville PD forensics team sitting in my driveway. I begrudgingly let them in and showed them to my bedroom, where a yellow police tape still crossed the doorframe. I knew if I balked, they would bring back a warrant.

Just what they wanted to do in there and why was mysterious to me. Perhaps there was something about Yolanda's autopsy that had pricked their curiosity. I walked back down the hall listening to the clicking of the camera shutters, as the team seemed to be documenting their way into the room. *What reason would they have to go over the room again? Whatever they know may be the reason Chris Black treated me like a criminal.*

I sat at the kitchen table tempted to open a bottle of Virginia wine, but decided to water the willow trees instead. I recognized the familiar emotion as I unwound the garden hose. Guilt. But why should I feel guilty for the death of a woman I didn't kill?

I sighed and pointed the hose at the base of the first tree. Now, with sudden clarity, I knew the answer to my own question. It was as if the hose in my hand had washed away some of the dirt that had obscured my understanding. It was something I called "spillover" for lack of a better word. Ever since my decision to hide my affair with Bob, I'd colored the world's events in the same way as I'd colored that decision. I felt guilty. Guilt from one stupid affair and its consequences now spilled over into every situation. If there was any way I *could* feel responsible or guilty about someone's problem, I'd default to feeling that way. I looked over my shoulder. The sun was too high in the sky to cast that condemning shadow at this time of day.

I found myself wondering if I was responsible for the slow growth of the trees. Maybe I didn't water enough. Maybe I needed to fertilize.

I thought about visiting Mom. *No. She'll probably want to know why I left the way I did the other day, and I don't feel like talking about it. I wonder if she even remembers my pregnancy.*

By indulging in a drink, stuffing in some comfort-carbs, visiting my mom, or watering the willows, I wasn't doing so well at dealing with negative feelings. I shook my head and played with the water stream with my thumb. The more force I applied, the faster the water sprayed through the smaller opening. That's what I felt like. God was pushing his thumb over my life, and everything was rushing forward out of my control.

A few weeks ago, I'd gone to the hospital to deliver Henry's favorite laser pointer. He didn't feel just right talking to a group of medical students without his engraved silver laser pointer.

I slipped into the back of a darkened lecture hall where my husband gave a presentation on the work-up of abdominal pain. He'd flash up a picture of some physical finding and ask the students what they should do next.

"The abdomen is rigid," Henry said.

A woman on the front row raised her hand. "I'd order a CT scan."

The students around her nodded.

"An ultrasound of the abdomen," offered another.

Henry listened patiently as the students offered suggestion after suggestion as to how to manage the problem. He just stayed quiet, shaking his head back and forth as if he and he alone held the keys to unlock the mystery. Finally, when he spoke, he cleared his throat, and smoothed the lapels of his white coat. He lifted his index finger in emphasis and proclaimed, "Never let the skin stand between you and a diagnosis."

The students didn't get it. There was laughter at Henry's antics, but they just didn't catch his drift.

My surgeon husband smiled as recognition dawned on the girl in the front row. He heard her whisper the answer. "Operate!" he said, his voice at a feverish pitch. "Open the skin. Look under the hood!"

The students laughed again. I used the commotion to interrupt and hand Henry his pointer. I heard one of the students repeating the phrase under his breath as I left the room. "Never let the skin stand between you and a diagnosis."

I wasn't sure if it was surgical dogma or if Henry was just making a point, but I took the saying to heart. I went directly from that medical school classroom over to my favorite travel agent and purchased two tickets to Jamaica, one for me and one for Jack. I

was through showing the world a different skin from the inner me.
I was determined not to let my skin stand in the way. I wanted to
show my real colors.

Now, I sniffed back a tear. So much for my vacation plans. *At
least my willows are being watered this week.*

I must have stayed in the yard for a full hour, refusing to let
go of that stupid hose, lost in my own thoughts as I let the water
flow on each of the six trees. I'd bought them. Jack planted them.
Watering them seemed like the decent thing to do, keeping the
trees healthy while Jack was in the hospital.

I sighed, not knowing what to do next. I didn't exactly want to
stay inside and appear overly interested in the forensics team. The
reality was that even though I'd officially closed the book on Jack,
I was afraid to move forward. Jack had made me feel alive. I hadn't
felt that way with Henry in years — until this week. Every time I
watched Henry in action around the hospital, I remembered why
he'd been able to sweep me away in the first place. But unlike Jack,
Henry never wanted to poke much below the surface. Perhaps my
skin scared him.

I looked up as a trio of investigators filed out of my house,
casting furtive glances my way and clutching a half dozen sealed
plastic bags. I waved, but refused to smile. I was too weary to care
if it made me look guilty.

I looked at the stream coming from the garden hose and
thought once about turning it on them, but my frontal lobes provided the appropriate override of my reptile notions, and I kept the
hose pointed at the trees.

When the ground was saturated, I turned the hose on the
driveway, spraying the dirt back into my manicured lawn. *If only
my own sin were so easy to cleanse away*, I thought. *What had Jack
said? "Forgive yourself."* I looked over at the steeple with the cross on
top of the Baptist church and cringed. *How could I forgive sin that
I knew God despised?*

A man of about thirty with freckles and a red goatee approached. "I've taken down the police tape, Mrs. Stratford. You can do whatever you want in there," he said, waving his hand. "Clean away."

I raised my eyebrows. "Hooray."

I wanted to ask what precious evidence was hidden within the bags, but held my tongue. My curiosity wasn't winning me any friends lately.

I watched them leave, noting that the red-goateed leader signaled a left turn before leaving my driveway.

I shook my head and pushed my thumb into the pathway of the cold water. *Maybe Henry isn't as weird as I thought.*

By seven-thirty, Henry was late for dinner and on his way to a confrontation with Cindy. He drummed his fingers on the steering wheel of his Mercedes and sighed. He needed a concrete plan to reorder his life before it unraveled completely. How long had it been since he felt in control? He thought back to the first time that fate had brought Jesse and Linda Anders into his life. A humid summer night party had ended in tragedy when Jesse wrapped his car around a tree. Jesse, perhaps predictably, had escaped with a few bruises. His wife wasn't so fortunate.

Henry read her cervical spine film himself, missing a subtle finding of soft tissue swelling in front of C–7. He'd taken Linda's cervical collar off and told the resident to observe her until she was sober. When he rounded the next morning, she was alert, but paralyzed below the waist. The resident hadn't even picked up on the tenderness over the patient's upper back.

It was a preventable mistake. He should never have trusted the exam of an intoxicated patient. The resident hadn't ordered a T-spine film until he realized that the patient was no longer moving her legs.

His error was the leverage Jesse needed to lure Henry into a web of deceit. It began simply enough. A narcotics prescription for

Jesse's poor wife. Then another. And another. *"My friend sprained his shoulder, Doc." "My sister has migraines." "My neighbor threw out his back."*

"My wife wouldn't be in this wheelchair if it wasn't for you."

What began as innocent favors had ended in hundreds of prescriptions for powerful narcotics and for phenylephrine-containing sinus drugs that could be modified to make crystal meth, the hottest party drug at UVa. Initially, the threat of a lawsuit kept Henry compliant. Later, it was the threat of exposure. Last week, Henry made some tough choices. He told Jesse it was over. Certainly Anders would have the sense not to risk incriminating himself by exposing Henry.

But he'd underestimated Anders. When Henry tried to pull away, Anders threatened him. Now, everything seemed to be spiraling into a violence way beyond Henry's control.

And to top everything off, in the middle of his despair, Cindy Swanson whisked into his life. But the allure of secret intimacy had failed to satisfy. Instead of relief, his brief exhilaration turned into compounding regret.

He slowly chewed the chalky antacid tablets to try and quell the fiery discomfort in his upper abdomen. *Now Wendi wants to adopt a baby. But I'm not the Christian man she thinks I am. I'd always thought I could be the perfect husband, but now I've cheated on the only woman I've ever loved.* He wiped his forehead with the back of his sport-coat sleeve and turned into the drive leading to Cindy's apartment. He wasn't sure how to handle Anders, but he knew what he needed to do to preserve his relationship with Wendi. He needed to put a full stop to his affair. He'd tell Cindy it was over. He'd go back to his wife and never stray from his pretty little brunette again.

He walked up the sidewalk to her door, before knocking quickly. A moment later, the door was open and Cindy reached for his hand, tugging him towards her front room. "I just knew you'd come," she said. She leaned in for a kiss. Henry complied. A kiss of greeting without passion.

She narrowed her eyes and stepped away, her fingers tugging at her collar before coming to rest in a fist in front of her heart. She started shaking her head before he could speak. "You've come to tell me it's over."

"Cindy, I—" he stopped, the words dry in his throat.

"You said things last night. You wanted a new start. You wanted freedom."

"I meant those things. It's just—well, Wendi—"

"You said you didn't love her."

Cindy's eyes began to glisten. This wasn't going the way he'd planned. She stepped forward, falling into his arms. She kissed him, an act of desperation. Once. Twice. He didn't want to respond. But her mouth was open against his, trembling, searching.

One moment she was in his arms. The next, she was on the floor, their kiss interrupted by a powerful hand that grabbed her from behind and tossed her aside. As Cindy screamed, Henry saw him standing in the partially open doorway. *Anders!*

Jesse Anders pointed a gun at Henry's chest. "Seems you have a more interesting life than I imagined."

"How'd you get here?"

Anders sneered. "I followed you from the hospital. It wasn't hard."

He reached over and yanked Cindy to her feet by her hair and looked at Henry. "You're going to be sorry you ever threatened to expose me."

He shoved Cindy forward into Henry's arms and shut the door.

Henry stepped in front of Cindy. "What do you want?"

Anders' hands trembled as he pointed the pistol towards the duo. His forehead glistened with sweat. "It's time you and I came to an understanding. I'm the one in charge and you're going to listen to me."

"What do you want?"

"You just don't get it, do you, Doc?" Anders replied with a redneck drawl. "You have no idea what kind of suffering my Linda goes through every day. And every day, I promise myself that I'm going to make you pay."

"What will it take? Money? You could sue me."

"Sit down!" Anders pointed the gun to the corner of the room. "Over there. Against the wall." He shook his head. "Oh, we're way beyond that, Doc. For just one day, I want you to feel what it's like to lose someone you love."

Cindy sat beside Henry on the floor. "Who is he?" She spoke softly into Henry's ear, but Anders overheard.

"Tell her, Doc," he sneered. "We're business partners, aren't we?"

Henry shook his head, keeping his eyes focused on the gun. Anders appeared to be high, or in withdrawal. "He's the husband of a patient."

"Tell her what you did, Doc." He paused. "My wife is paralyzed. All because of Dr. Stratford."

Henry tried to keep his voice steady. "Your wife is paralyzed because you were driving drunk, Jesse."

Anger flared red in Anders' face. He lurched forward and kicked Cindy in the forehead, snapping her head back against the wall.

Henry gasped, and leaned over Cindy as she slumped to the floor. She moaned and her eyes appeared unfocused. "Cindy?"

She coughed once, splattering Henry with spit before whispering his name. "Henry."

He watched as her pupils disappeared beneath her upper lids. He put his fingers against her carotid artery in her neck. The pulse was steady and strong. "Cindy?"

She didn't respond.

Anders kicked Henry's foot. "Say it!"

Henry stared at the crazed man and shook his head.

Anders lifted his foot, apparently to stomp on Cindy's head.

"Stop," Henry screamed. "It was my fault. I didn't see the break on the X-ray!" The surgeon knelt over Cindy, shielding her from another blow. He started to weep. "I didn't see the abnormality. It was my fault." He looked up at Anders' hardened face. "What do you want from me?" He felt his voice closing around a sob. "Why are you torturing me?"

"You threatened to cut me off."

Henry shook his head. "You killed Yolanda Pate."

"The blonde? What was she doing in your bed, Doc?" He shrugged. "It was dark. I thought she was your wife."

"You would kill my wife and expect me to cooperate with you?"

"Oh, you'll cooperate. How much would you lose if the law finds out about the drugs, Doc?"

Henry felt his gut tighten. "Stay away from my wife."

"Then you'll cooperate?"

He sniffed and wiped his nose with the back of his hand. "Promise me you'll stay away from Wendi."

Anders backed away slowly, smiling while keeping his gun trained on the surgeon. Then, slowly, he pulled out a wrinkled paper that had been folded into his shirt pocket. "Here," he said. "Time to write some new prescriptions." He handed the paper to Henry. "If you do right, Doc, I'll leave Wendi alone."

Henry turned his attention to Cindy. Her face was ashen. He lowered his cheek to graze gently against her nose. "She's not breathing!"

With Henry late for dinner, I entered our bedroom and flipped on the light, feeling a little more than weird about the fact that someone had died in my house and in that very place. The 6000 had been stripped bare to the mattress. I supposed the police must have taken the sheets for evidence. What they were so concerned about frightened and angered me. Chris Black had come just shy of accusing me of murder, something absurd. Yolanda was heartbroken and unstable. Her death was a tragedy, and maybe I'd gotten in her way by falling for her fiancé, but I'd never intended for her to come along and react the way she had.

Unsettled, I spent less than a minute in my bedroom before walking back into the den, where Rene was reading a book about dealing with HIV. "Let's pack up Yolanda's things," I said. "Her parents will be wanting them."

Rene grunted, and I plodded towards the basement to the guest room, where I emptied the dresser of Yolanda's things, placing them neatly into her suitcase. I was holding a picture of Jack when Rene came in.

"She had good taste in men," Rene said, nodding her head towards the photograph.

I let down my guard. "Really." I avoided my sister's gaze and quickly placed the picture facedown on one of Yolanda's wool sweaters.

Rene was more interested in the clothes than the picture anyway. She pulled a sweater out of the suitcase and held it up. It had a weave of grays, purple, and forest green. "Ooh. This girl did have good taste," she said.

I shook my head, thinking about my life. I've never really liked wool sweaters. Oh, I've worn plenty of them, but only for the looks. Wool always seemed to prickle my skin, and I was relieved when I could finally shed the sweater in the privacy of estrogen central and scratch all the places where the wool had offended. *Maybe I'm not supposed to be wearing sheep's clothing if I'm not a sheep.* I shrugged. "I guess so."

"You guess so? Look at this label," Rene said, pointing at the designer insignia.

"I'm going to start shopping at Wal-Mart."

Rene laughed. "And I'm going to date another musician."

I looked at her. She didn't believe me. The problem was, I wasn't sure I did either. So far, my changed life, complete with a new man and romantic heart-communication on the sands of Jamaica, was more talk than walk. I sighed. "OK, maybe I'll start with buying some socks there." I smiled. "I'll work my way in."

Rene started through a stack of underwear. "Whoa," she said. "Look at these."

Red lace and very sexy. I didn't want to think about why she'd bought them or whom she dreamed of showing them to. "Put those down," I scolded. "Have some respect for the dead."

"That's just it, Wendi. She's dead. She wouldn't care."

I plucked the panties from her hand and threw them back in the suitcase. "I'm trying to straighten this place up."

Rene disregarded my advice and kept oohing and ahhing her way through Yolanda's wardrobe.

"Stop it," I said. "Hey, I'll let you go through my closet if you want. I'm sure there's something in there that you'd like."

"You're too fat."

"And you're pregnant. It will fit soon."

She stuck her tongue out at me.

I laid a pair of jeans in the suitcase. "Why do you think the police took my sheets?"

"You didn't strip the bed?"

"Are you kidding? They had a yellow tape across the door until just a few minutes ago. They'd taken over a room in my own house." I put my hands on my hips. "It's like they think it was something other than suicide."

"Don't they do autopsies to show how she died?"

"The medical examiner will give an opinion. But I doubt if Dr. Eichmann has even completed his exam yet."

"Call him. See what all the fuss is about."

"I know him, Rene. He won't like me snooping in his business."

"Who would kill Yolanda?"

I started thinking of a short list. I was on top. I looked at Rene, hoping she couldn't read my guilty conscience.

"OK," she said, plopping down on the bed. "Who are the suspects? The only ones in the house that night were you, me, the Renners, and Henry." She paused. "The Renners did seem like they were in a hurry to leave."

"There's no motive."

"Maybe the Renners didn't want her to marry their son."

I shook my head. "That's no reason to kill her."

"Maybe you did it," Rene said. "You were jealous of the way Henry admired her hair."

"You noticed that too?"

My sister let her mouth fall open and let her tongue flap out like a drooling dog.

"Stop it. He didn't look that bad."

"Stop worrying. Henry's quite normal in that respect, from what I can see. He has an eye for fine women," she said, looking at me. "My sister being the prettiest of all."

I frowned.

"I'm being serious."

"I don't doubt it," I said, lifting my head and glancing at my own reflection in the mirror over the dresser.

I didn't feel pretty. I didn't even want to think about it, so I changed the subject. "I'm not sure I can sleep in my bed again."

"It's a comfortable bed. You're melodramatic."

I wrinkled my nose. "I am not. It's just eerie. I feel like giving it to the Salvation Army or something."

"Give it to me," Rene said. "It's not going to haunt me."

"Are you moving out?"

She nodded. "I need to find a place soon. I can't stay with you and Henry forever."

I softened. "You are my sister. Stay as long as you need."

She laughed. "Maybe I'll stay as long as you need."

Rene helped me lug Yolanda's suitcases upstairs. "What's for dinner?"

"Wednesday. Fish." I stared at my sister. "Is that why you're here? Free food?"

She laughed. "At least you seem to have gotten something positive from Mom. She was an awesome cook."

I didn't want to think positive thoughts about our mother, but her comment launched me into memories of Sunday dinners with pot roast and mashed potatoes, squash casseroles laden with cheese, and fresh baked rolls. "I remember."

Wednesday night meant grilled fish on the obsessive-compulsive Stratford calendar, but as per the normal recent routine, Henry didn't show. Trauma surgery had become the mistress I couldn't compete with.

It was nine-thirty p.m. as Rene and I finished up loading the dishwasher. I looked at her as she handed me the last plate.

"What? Why are you smiling?"

I shouldn't have told her yet. I knew how high Rene's expectations could climb, but I just couldn't resist. I'd allowed my own emotions to begin an ascent of their own. "I asked Henry about adopting your baby."

She stared at me, mouth agape. "Well? What did he say?"

I tried to wear an exterior of calm. "Oh, you know Henry. I wouldn't let him give me a reply." I broke into a grin. "But he didn't say 'no.' He told me I'd be a good mother."

The phone interrupted our excitement. I picked it up in the kitchen. "Hello."

"Wendi, I'm glad I caught you." The voice was strained and easily recognizable to me as Detective Chris Black.

"Chris?"

"We've got a situation here. I'm afraid it's not pleasant news."

My gut tightened. Most of the time when Chris called, I ended up at some complicated, gruesome, multivehicle crash site collecting evidence until the break of dawn. I glanced at Rene and stepped away. "What's up? A crash?"

"Of sorts. It's Henry."

"Henry was in a crash?"

"Easy, babe. He's OK."

I willed my heart to slow down. I didn't tolerate sexist language from too many men, but Chris and I went way back. I knew him to be harmless, so I let him "honey" me, "sugar" me, and "babe" me all he wanted. "What happened?"

"He struck a pedestrian."

I gasped. I knew Henry's makeup well enough to know how much this would torture him.

"He called a paramedic crew, then followed them to the University ER and helped code her himself." He seemed to hesitate. "Wendi, the girl died."

"How horrible." I knew I'd better get to my husband fast. "Is Henry there?"

"He just left. He asked me to call you. He should be home in a few minutes."

"Will there be a police investigation?"

"An officer came to the scene and filed a report."

"Anything out of the ordinary?"

"Are you looking for business?"

"Funny, Chris. I'm on vacation, by the way. I'm just interested. It's my job."

"For the record, everything corroborated with his story, including the brake skid marks in front of the body location and blood on the pavement."

I winced. As much misery as I've witnessed, you'd think I wouldn't mind blood, but I only endure it. "How is Henry?"

"You know Henry. The ever-polished surgeon."

"On the outside." I groaned. "He's going to take this hard. With his obsessive personality, he's going to brood over every little awful detail."

I listened as Chris's breath whistled into the phone. "There's more, Wendi."

I waited, wondering what could be worse. In the few seconds I had to dissect the tension in his voice, I half expected him to say something crazy. Henry was drunk and was being charged with manslaughter or worse.

"The pedestrian was a surgical resident in his program. He killed a surgeon in training."

"Oh no," I said, my hand trembling at the edge of my mouth. "W-wh-who?"

"Cindy Swanson."

CHAPTER 21

Thankfully, by the time Henry came home, Rene had the sense to retreat to her guest room in the basement and let me help my husband through his grief.

He arrived with his suit wrinkled, sans tie, and with bloodstains on his white shirt. He walked to a cabinet where he hid the hard liquor from my father and lifted a bottle of Jack Daniel's to his lips before acknowledging me.

I slipped around behind him as he slumped into a leather recliner in the den to console himself with Jack and a ready glass. "I'm so sorry, Henry," I said, kneading the tension from his shoulders.

He grunted and sipped his drink.

I kept my voice tender. "Tell me what happened."

He shrugged. "Worked until late. Left the hospital about seven and stopped by Cindy Swanson's apartment to pick up a draft of some data she promised."

My guard went up. He was dropping by the blonde's apartment? *Stupid move, trauma chief.* I held my tongue and shifted my position on the couch.

His face was expressionless. He spoke in a mechanical monotone, as if reading a stock report. "She lives in Jefferson Hill. You park underneath in the deck, then walk around to the sidewalk steps leading to the front landings." He pinched the bridge of his nose and closed his eyes. "Anyway, she gave me the stuff I needed, so I walked back out, got in the Mercedes, and started back up the lane towards the street. She must have forgotten something, because the next thing I knew as I sped up the lane was the sudden image of Cindy falling in front of the car." He looked up at me, eyes bloodshot and unfocused, as if he was reliving the horror. "She had run down the sidewalk steps with a few additional papers and slipped just as she got to the bottom. I had just enough time to slam the brakes." He shook his head slowly. "Her face struck the pavement right in front of the wheel."

I felt myself shudder. I stayed quiet, not knowing how to respond. After a few minutes Henry drained his glass, and I slipped around behind him to massage his neck. There was nothing to say. This was a horrible event, and there was only one way to go. Forward. Nothing could change it, erase it, or make it go away. Only time, and I was sure a great deal of it, would ease the memory of this for Henry.

I massaged his scalp, envying the thickness of his hair. One thing I understood about this man was that he would talk about it when he was ready. My job was to try and be there when the story finally bubbled to the surface.

The confrontational me wanted to ask him just what he thought he was doing visiting a beautiful young resident in her apartment. But now wasn't the time for jealousy. Henry needed my support, not my suspicions, so I bottled it and poured him another drink.

I moved around and sat on a couch facing him. "We'll get through this," I promised.

He looked at me with eyes that were glazed over, the alcohol already numbing his pain. Not enough, though, to cover something else, something I'd recognized in others but never in my trauma surgeon husband: fear.

"Sure," he muttered. "No one keeps a Stratford down."

We sat in silence another ten minutes before I stood and walked towards the stairs.

"Where're you going?"

"The guest room. I'm not ready to sleep in our bed yet."

Henry sighed. "But the 6000 is so much more comfortable."

I shrugged. "I know, but I'm still not sleeping there. Not yet. Maybe if I buy a new mattress cover." I looked at the disappointment on Henry's face. *Perhaps it is different for you. You deal with death every day.* "I'm sorry, Henry."

That night, Henry stared at the glowing green lights of his alarm clock as 2:10, 2:11, 2:12 crawled by with unbearable lethargy. He rose, dry-swallowed a sleeping pill, and looked at his reflection in the bathroom mirror. The man in the glass slumped forward, haggard and defeated. He couldn't erase the memory of the night's horror. The image of pain on Cindy's face. Eyes pleading with him to protect her, to intervene, to stop a madman high on drugs and bent on revenge. He shivered as the memory of his helplessness mocked him.

Emotions of fear, anxiety, anger, and revenge all fought for supremacy within his soul.

He studied his sallow complexion in the dim light. A wave of nausea rose and faded with the fresh memory of the barrel of a gun shoved into his face.

"This is what happens when you stop cooperating, Doc."

He splashed water on his face and lifted a thick terry-cloth towel to muffle his cries as shock yielded to an eruption of emotion. He shuddered uncontrollably and gasped, his normal façade of control and professional demeanor flung aside.

After a minute, he lifted his eyes to meet those of his reflection again. He nodded at the image, sensing the hardening of his resolve.

He'd been caught in a riptide once. He was twelve years old, vacationing at Nags Head, North Carolina. The water was fast-flowing and deep, his tiptoes scraping as the sand slipped away and out of reach.

Henry sniffed and smiled at the memory of his battle with a force far more powerful than his adolescent body. His cool head saved him that day. He'd followed the instructions of his own father, who'd warned him of the dangers of the current.

He was in a riptide of sorts again, caught against his will, control yielded to forces far more powerful than his own. And yet he understood his responsibility. He alone had decided to swim in these troubled waters.

There, in the dim light of the bathroom, he began to formulate a plan.

"Anders," he whispered. He looked at the towel in his hand and tossed it on the floor in disgust, as if to rid himself of the evidence of his tears. He was a man. A surgeon. He would not yield himself to displays of weakness again. He sniffed again, swallowed, steadied his voice, and declared to his reflection, as if resolving to take out the trash, "Anders, I'm going to kill you."

The next morning, while Henry performed surgery on his English muffin, I quizzed him about my list of worries. "I think Yolanda erased the pictures from my Nikon."

Henry didn't look up. He mumbled with his mouth half full of bread. "Why would she do that?"

"I can't figure that out. I was closing in on someone I was convinced was the guilty party in Jack's hit-and-run. I'd gone up to Ruckersville on a tip from an insurance agent. I found a truck grille covered with the same blue paint." I shook my head. "But something's going on. Chris Black went up to check out my story and found nothing like I described it. So I took him my camera, but everything had been erased."

"Why would she erase your camera?"

"I have no idea. I've wondered about that quite a bit, even imagining she knew the guy that struck Jack's car, like maybe she planned to have Jack killed."

"Now that's crazy."

I shrugged and sipped at my coffee. "I know. But it seems so many weird things have been happening at the same time, I was searching for a link."

"What do you mean?"

"Maybe she was due an insurance payout if Jack died, so she hires this Anders dude to kill him and make it look like an accident. Then she realizes I'm on to this guy, flips out, and commits suicide."

Henry dropped his butter knife. "Did you say 'Anders'?"

I nodded. "Jesse Anders. Why? You know him?"

Henry wiped his mouth with a napkin and cleared his throat. "I treated his wife." He paused, looking intently at me from across the breakfast table. "Stay away from him, Wendi. This guy is trouble. He could be dangerous."

I could tell from his tone of voice that my husband was dead serious. But now I was more curious than ever. "Dangerous? What do you know about him?"

"My work has provided plenty of opportunity to intersect with the down-and-outers of our fine society, honey. Anders is a druggie. A dealer. If he's covering something up, and you expose him, he seems the type to seek revenge."

"How would you know?"

Henry's voice was quiet, just above a whisper, yet so serious, it seemed melodramatic. "He threatened to sue me, Wendi."

I started to respond, but he interrupted, "Stay away from him."

Again, I opened my mouth in protest, but my words lodged in my throat when I saw Henry's expression. I nodded, but wondered if Henry really expected me to comply. Threats from parties on the opposite side of the law from me had never stopped me before.

Henry squinted in my direction before standing in front of the foyer mirror. He seemed satisfied that I was sufficiently scared not to get myself into trouble. Oh how little my husband really understood about my personality. To Henry, it would be unthinkable for me to cross him. And I suppose, if truth be known, I'd had little reason to do it in the past. But he'd never made demands of my professional behavior before.

I watched his routine. In the end, he checked his zipper once. Patted the fly. Smiled at himself. Turned to go, then back for a second check. Patted his fly a second time. Again, his shoulders shifted, revealing his intent to walk away. He turned back to the mirror a third time, running his finger along his zipper a third time. I watched his face reflect his inner torment as he turned to go again. Then a fourth time, now with a casual glance at me.

OK, I thought, *this is new territory for Henry.* He's never, ever checked more than two times until this week, and now, he'd done a quadruple check. I'm not sure what I expected. Lightning, perhaps? Something was definitely stressing my husband.

I smiled at him, offering him a little wave to send him off, but worrying that the axis in Henry's world had shifted. I stood and carried my coffee to the front room to watch him leave. I guess I shouldn't have been too freaked out about his compulsivity explosion. After all, he'd accidentally run over one of his residents last night. That should be enough to disrupt his routine.

Henry signaled for a left turn as he approached the end of our one-hundred-foot driveway. *OK*, I thought, *it's not the end of the world.*

Rene seemed to be intent on sleeping in, so I tiptoed around sipping Kenyan AA coffee as the events from the last few days filtered and refiltered through my cranium. I bounced from crisis to crisis, from my blowup with my parents to my father's plea that I should try to learn to know my mother again. I thought about Yolanda and Chris Black and his questioning about my relationship to Jack.

I thought about Henry and wondered if we were going to make it. I swung a pendulum from being excited about the possibility of adopting Rene's baby to being upset that he was at the apartment of a gorgeous blonde resident when he should have been home with me. That's when I remembered something that Chris Black told me last night about Henry's pedestrian accident scene and I realized why the whole thing seemed a little funny. *"For the record, everything corroborated with his story, including the brake skid marks in front of the body location and blood on the pavement."*

Brake skid marks? Almost impossible for a Mercedes with antilock brakes.

With my curiosity pricked, I sat down at my kitchen desk and called Sig Eichmann, the medical examiner. As a forensic pathologist, he deciphered the cause of death. As an accident reconstructionist, I looked at the pattern of individual injuries to assist in piecing together just what took place. The collection and interpretation of forensic evidence surrounding death and of postmortem physical evidence were shared arenas for us and had brought Sig and me into collaboration on many cases.

I imagined Sig wearing his green apron over a paper gown and latex gloves as I dialed. A few minutes later, his secretary forwarded my call. "Wendi," he said with his rich German accent, "I'm up to my backside in alligators here. Two homicides, an overdose, and a pedestrian accident." I listened to him sigh. "What do you need?"

"A favor." I hesitated. "I want to know about Cindy Swanson."

He made a clicking sound with his cheek. He was thinking.

"The pedestrian death from Charlottesville last night."

"Ooooh." More clicking sounds. "I've not finished with that one. Dana's looking at it. Crushed skull. Intracranial bleeding. Death from a head injury, I'm sure." He paused. "Who asked you to look into it? Police consult? Insurance?"

I held my breath for a second. Sig probably didn't know Henry was involved. I couldn't lie to Sig. "She was an acquaintance."

"Wendi," he said. "I shouldn't be giving you information. I could get in a lot of trouble if—"

"I know about confidentiality, Sig. I'm not telling a soul," I said.

"Please, Wendi. My office has had too much bad press lately. An uncontrolled information leak could get me fired."

"Sig, relax! I won't tell anyone."

He sighed again, and his breath whistled into the phone.

"Look, I'm sorry," I said. "But I already knew about the case from Chris Black. He called me about it last night. You haven't told me anything I didn't already know."

"Tell me again why you called."

"I just wanted to hear it from you."

"You're suspicious of foul play."

I didn't want to bias him. "You told me what I wanted. She died of a head injury resulting from a pedestrian accident. End of story, right?"

The silence on the line told me he wasn't buying my technically true explanation. I thought about my commitment to cast aside my fake life. "OK," I continued with a sigh. "That's not the whole story. The pedestrian was struck by my husband."

Sig huffed. "Wendi, I'm so sorry." He paused. "But I wish you hadn't called me. Your personal attachment to this case makes it worse that I've offered you information."

"You told me nothing," I countered. "Nothing that I didn't know from my husband or Chris Black."

The clicking noises resumed. Sig's paranoia about protocol violations rivaled the acceleration of my what-iffer. That's what Henry always called it when I started in on an accident reconstruction with a hundred different possible scenarios.

Sig continued, "I'd better go. Violence never sleeps, you know. I'm here, day after day, sorting out the sins of man."

His choice of words made me wince. "OK, Sig. I've got the picture. I'm not trying to interfere."

"Goodbye."

I shook my head and ended the call no closer to an answer than I was before.

Sig Eichmann, M.D., sat down at his desk and picked up a slice of cold cheese pizza. As he ate, he reviewed the gross findings of the Swanson case.

The patient had suffered multiple skull fractures and a severe underlying brain injury. The skull was crushed, eggshell fractured, and the overlying skin held the tell-tale markings of tire tread and ground-in asphalt.

The vaginal swabs indicated recent sexual intercourse, and external inspection failed to reveal any evidence of forced penetration.

The semen sample had diminished sperm motility, indicating sexual contact twenty-four to thirty-six hours before her demise.

In light of the findings, Wendi Stratford's interest in the case bothered him even more. He stripped off his disposable gown and gloves, depositing them in a large red bag labeled "biohazard."

He walked to his office and phoned Detective Chris Black of the Charlottesville Police Department.

The answer was pure business. "Detective Black."

"Detective Black, this is Dr. Eichmann. I'm calling about a case your city forwarded to me this morning, pedestrian accident, Cindy Swanson."

"I know the case."

"I've not concluded my study, but I've got enough here to raise some flags I thought you should know about."

"I'm listening."

"The skull is badly fractured, consistent with the police report I've read. This may be as straightforward as is first apparent, but . . ."

The detective huffed his impatience. "Spit it out, Doc."

"There's more, Chris. I didn't want to tell you." He halted and tried to massage away the growing pain in his temples. "Wendi Stratford is my friend. Yours too, I understand."

Chris huffed. "Damned near embarrassed me out of the department. She cost me a promotion."

Sig frowned. "She called me, trying to get information about my findings. She seemed intent on getting me to say that it was a simple death from head injury due to a pedestrian accident."

The detective cursed again. Sig could hear the squeak of a desk chair. "So what are you saying? You suspect something else is up?"

"I don't know. I just got a funny feeling when talking to Wendi. She's such a straight shooter, but she sounded overly concerned about this case being resolved quickly as a pedestrian death from head injury."

"Her husband was the driver. She should be concerned."

"Maybe it's nothing. Just a gut hunch."

"Stick to the evidence, Doc. Let me follow my own hunches."

"I've got semen sample from the victim. I'm submitting it for a DNA analysis for a fingerprint."

"Wonderful." Eichmann listened to a tapping noise, the detective drumming his fingers on the mouthpiece. "You still haven't told me your final opinion on the Pate autopsy. Straightforward suicide?"

Sig ran his hand through his white hair. "I'm going to officially sign out Yolanda Pate's autopsy as narcotic and alcohol overdose. But straightforward? I'm not sure. She had a few cuts inside the mouth. Could be signs of a struggle before death." He paused. "Overdose victims don't struggle. They just simply quit breathing from lack of a respiratory drive."

"What are you saying?"

"I'm saying that the findings are suspicious for foul play. I suppose she could have bitten the inside of her mouth in her drunken state, then later overdosed on the Oxycontin. But that brings up other issues."

"Issues?" Black sounded irritated.

"The Oxycontin bottle didn't belong to the deceased, and the prescription happens to have been written by Dr. Stratford. Have you talked to this guy, Lanny Bedford? His name is on the bottle."

Black sighed. "Of course. That's my business, OK?"

"Sure."

Chris Black said, "Have a nice day."

The pathologist listened as the detective slammed down the phone. So much for a nice day. He'd seen too much inhumanity today to believe in nice days anymore.

Chris Black wasn't easily intimidated. He looked at Dr. Stratford's ego wall and wondered whether, if he himself had so many diplomas and awards, he would display them in such an arrogant grouping. Ceiling to floor, shoulder to shoulder, like obedient soldiers standing for inspection, all the certificates were bordered by shiny black frames. This morning Chris decided to follow the pathologist's hunch and push on Dr. Stratford a bit, just to see if anything suspicious bubbled to the surface. Besides, he rather enjoyed making perfectionist types like the surgeon sweat.

The detective tapped a silver pen against his cheek and allowed his eyes to bore in on the surgeon's face. "Were you sleeping with your resident?"

Chris watched as the corner of the surgeon's mouth twitched. "Where did that come from? I thought you were here to see how I was doing."

Black leaned back in his chair and forced a laugh. "I am, I am." He paused. "I guess you need to be warned, Henry. They've taken a semen sample from the body," he said, studying the surgeon's face. "It's amazing what our forensics guys can do with trace evidence. Pubic hair, DNA," Chris said, waving his hand in a little circle, before continuing, "and that sort of thing." He chuckled. "They all whisper the truth."

"This has nothing to do with how she died."

Chris raised his eyebrows and stayed silent, letting Henry squirm. The doctor played it pretty cool.

"Do I need to call my lawyer?"

"Do you?"

The surgeon huffed.

"Why don't you tell me the story, Henry? It will save us all a lot of misery. Talk to me."

Henry Stratford adjusted the perfect knot in his tie and lowered his voice. "Look, Chris, you and Wendi are friends. Bringing this up now isn't going to change anything."

"I understand the need to be discreet."

Henry leaned forward over his desk, the fluorescent overhead light reflecting in the sweat on his brow. "We were working on a research paper together." He stared back at the detective. "She came on to me, Chris. I went to her house to tell her it was over."

"Fair enough," the detective responded. "Did Wendi know about her?"

He shook his head. "Only that she was my resident." He paused, looking meaningfully at the detective. "And I'd appreciate it if it could stay that way."

Chris shrugged. "Wendi is perceptive, Henry. I doubt much happens around her that she doesn't see."

"Not this. It was too recent. It happened so fast."

"Too fast for Wendi to threaten Cindy?"

"What are you talking about?"

"I've been asking questions, that's all. A witness says your wife and Cindy had a pretty heated exchange in this hospital a few days ago."

The edge of the surgeon's mouth pulled back again. "Maybe you'd better explain yourself, Mr. Black. Wendi has nothing to do with this."

The detective watched as Henry pulled his hands together in a tight clasp. Even then, he noticed the tremor.

"We had sex," Henry said. "I don't believe that's a crime."

"No." Chris let the silence thicken between them. "But murder is."

"You're out of your mind. It was an accident." Henry shook his head, and Chris noticed a twitch in his jaw. "Maybe she was a bit clumsy. She fell under the car."

"Did Wendi show up, Henry? Was she in a jealous rage?"

"No!"

"You'd cover for your wife, wouldn't you, Henry?"

The surgeon's head snapped back. "Preposterous!"

"Did you know your wife called the medical examiner trying to influence his findings?"

"You're nursing your old wounds, aren't you? You can't believe that Wendi had the guts to testify against your department." He pointed his finger at the police officer. "You leave my wife alone!"

The detective laughed. "Tsk, tsk. You can't believe I'd let something from the past bias me in a professional investigation."

Henry stood up and pointed at the door. "Get out of my office. This is over!"

"Far from it, Dr. Stratford." He smiled, enjoying the reaction he'd gotten out of the starched professional. "This is only the beginning."

CHAPTER 22

Chris had spent two hours talking to anyone who might have light to shed on the reason for Yolanda Pate's untimely demise. He'd looked for anything that might bring him out of the shadows of mystery. Just before he headed back to his office, he stopped in the hospital cafeteria in search of coffee. There, he recognized a nurse who'd been caring for Jack Renner, someone he'd seen when he'd interviewed Jack after his accident.

Chris walked up to the circular table where she sat alone. "Hi," he said, leaning forward so he could read her name tag. "Brenda," he said, "I'm Chris Black with the Charlottesville PD. Do you mind if I ask you a few questions?"

She was nonplussed. "Feel free."

He sat across from her. "I need to ask you about Jack Renner."

He noticed a slight shaking of her head. "I'm not able to give out any medical information."

"I'm not after medical information. I wanted to ask you about his relationship with Wendi Stratford." He paused, studying her face. Her head pulled back, and he saw the muscles around her mouth cinch up. "You cared for Mr. Renner, did you not?"

"While he was in the ICU."

"Did Wendi visit while you were there?"

"Yes."

"How would you characterize her relationship with Jack Renner?"

She seemed to hesitate. "He was her piano teacher."

"Nothing more?"

"Why are you asking me these questions? If you want to know about Jack's relationships, why don't you ask him?"

He shrugged. "Mrs. Stratford is a married woman. He might feel uncomfortable giving an honest answer."

"I'm not sure I am qualified to answer. Jack didn't talk to me about Wendi."

"Did you know Wendi Stratford was having an affair with Jack Renner?"

"How am I supposed to answer that?"

"Is that the same answer you would give under oath?"

"I'm not under oath."

"I could force you to come downtown for a formal interview. Would you be able to answer me there?"

Brenda Lee pushed away the remains of a garden salad. "Look, I don't know any details. Yes," she said. "Wendi indicated that there were ... feelings involved."

"Interesting." He tapped a ballpoint pen against the table. "I guess that must have been awkward for Dr. Stratford, caring for his wife's lover."

Brenda shook her head. "He doesn't know," she whispered. "Now, Mr. Black, would you mind telling me what this is about?"

"I'm afraid I'm not at liberty to tell you that," he said, standing. "You've been most helpful."

By ten-thirty, I was crossing the parking lot at the local police station on my way to see Chris Black. While he wasn't particularly talkative to me lately, our last phone conversation twenty minutes earlier was mysteriously succinct. "Come to the station, Wendi. We need to talk."

When I entered the police station, I walked straight towards Chris Black's office, but was interrupted by a deputy who led me to a small room with a single white table and two chairs. In a moment, another officer, a man with short-cropped silver hair, entered.

"Mrs. Stratford, I hope you don't mind if I ask you a few questions."

My defenses were on alert. "What's this about? Where's Chris Black?" I asked.

"We thought it best that I speak to you instead." He held out his hand. "I'm the chief of police, Ed Mosby."

I offered him a dainty grip, holding my hand palm down like a lady. "You haven't answered my questions."

"I'll get to that, Mrs. Stratford." He sat across from me and rested his clasped hands on the table. "Tell me what you were doing last night between seven and ten o'clock."

I shook my head. "You tell me what this is about. You get nothing from me unless I know what's going on." I folded my hands and returned his stare.

"A young woman is dead, Mrs. Stratford. A young woman we know that you argued with in public just this week." He leaned back in his chair and folded his hands behind his head. "What were your words? 'You'll regret this,' I believe."

"This is insulting. I want to talk to Chris Black."

"He answers to me."

I wanted to curse, but in spite of my new commitment to an honest expression of my heart, my better judgment intervened. I bit my tongue. "Cindy Swanson died of head injuries sustained in a pedestrian accident."

"How would you know that, Mrs. Stratford?"

"My husband had the misfortune of running her over. But you know all that, don't you?" I seethed. "I want to see Chris."

"You knew all about their little love affair didn't you, Mrs. Stratford?"

My jaw slackened. "You insensitive — " I halted and shook my head. "What are you doing? Trying to get me to confess? Confess to what? I have no idea what you're talking about."

"Your husband's lying to you, Wendi," he said, leaning forward again. "But you're a smart woman. You know all about him, don't you?" He paused. "Were you at the Jefferson Hill Apartments that night?"

I snorted. I hated this man. No one had ever talked to me like this before. I twisted so that I didn't need to face him. But maybe this is what he wanted. My anger. Well, he had it. White hot. "No."

"You were jealous. That would be understandable."

"I know nothing of an affair. You're lying!"

"Am I?"

I found myself whispering under my breath. "Son of a — "

"Go ahead, Mrs. Stratford. Get mad. But I'm only telling you the truth." He drummed his fingers on the table. "Painful stuff, huh?"

I stared back at him. The animal in me wanted to fight. But my head told me to sit and see what he would give me.

"If someone came in and started seeing my wife," he said, nodding his head, "he'd have to answer to me." He looked back at me.

I looked back, unflinching.

"So I could understand if you went looking for him last night. And you knew just where to look, didn't you?"

"I don't know what you're talking about. You're telling me Cindy Swanson was murdered?" I shook my head. "Why don't you talk to the medical examiner? Sig Eichmann will set you straight."

The captain smiled. The smile of a cat looking at a mouse backed in a corner. "The good doctor says you called him, trying to influence his findings."

"Ridiculous."

"You called him, didn't you?"

I huffed and crossed my arms across my chest again. "I just wanted to find out the results of the autopsy. I've known Dr. Eichmann for years."

"Professional interest, I suppose?" He tapped his fingers on his desktop as my gut tightened.

I was in complete shock. How this man had come to these preposterous conclusions was way, way beyond me. I studied him for a moment, wondering if another conclusion was possible. Maybe he didn't believe I was capable of murder, but just wanted to bully me to settle an old score. "I want to talk to Detective Black."

"I'm afraid that's impossible. Answer my questions and we'll get this over with in a few minutes."

I thought about calling my lawyer. I thought about slapping this man who sat smugly across from me. I counted to twenty. "I'm listening."

"What were you doing last night?"

"My sister and I fixed and ate dinner. Then we sat around and talked until I heard about this tragedy from Chris Black."

"Names," he said. "I need the names of the people you were with."

I stared him down. "Rene Aldridge, my sister." I paused. "She can verify my whereabouts." I shrugged. "I was with my sister all day."

He stood up. "OK." He opened the door. "I'll be a few minutes."

I stood and took a step towards the door.

He held up his hand. "Sorry, Mrs. Stratford. You'll need to stay here a few minutes."

"Why? Am I under arrest?"

"Not yet," he said as the door closed.

I tried the door. Locked. I slammed my fist against the door. "Ugh!"

I paced the small room. Four large steps from the door to a wall. Three steps side to side. Fifteen minutes later, the door opened again. It was the captain. By the time he entered, my anger and frustration had climbed Kilimanjaro. I was ready to spit. He must have seen it in my eyes. In a quiet voice, he said, "You're free to leave."

I screamed at him, "That's it?"

He retreated back into the hall. "Yes."

I shook my head. "I want to see Chris Black!"

He backed another step, and I followed him into the hall. "You know where his office is." He shrugged. "Feel free."

I huffed and stomped down the hall, up the stairs, and straight into Chris's office. I opened the door without knocking. "What's this all about?"

"Shall I ask you the same question?"

He looked at me. My expression must have warned of my anger. He slid back his chair. "Wendi, have a seat," he said. "I'm sorry," he said, lifting his hands. "I'm sorry this is happening to you."

I took a deep breath and tried to keep my voice level. "Why has this turned into a criminal investigation?"

I watched as his expression tightened. "You know I can't discuss that with you."

"Was it me? Did my call to Sig prompt all of this?"

He sighed. "I'm sorry. You know I'm not at liberty to talk with you about this."

I shook my head. *One, two, three, four, five.* I knew he was right. Chris followed protocol, and I knew he wouldn't give me information because I was Henry's wife. I would have to find out some other way why this accident investigation had turned its focus on finding a sinister motive. "OK, OK." I paused, staring at a man I once called my friend. "Why don't you believe my husband? Have you talked to him?"

He nodded. "This morning."

"Is my husband under arrest?"

"No." He squinted at me. "Should he be?"

I thought about telling him about his officer's mix-up on interpreting the skid marks at Jefferson Hill Apartments, but held my tongue. This investigation had turned weird on me, and I wanted to do a little digging myself. I shook my head. "Of course not."

He held up his hands in surrender. He wanted a truce. "Fine." He softened. "Listen, I'm just being complete."

I was tempted to sneer. His expression had taken on the smugness I'd just seen in his chief.

"I'm sure you've heard of Ockham's razor?"

It was a scientific theory that I'd heard Henry use. In fact, I'd used it myself in accident reconstruction. *An uncomplicated solution is better than a complex one.* I sat back, mirroring his confidence. "Of course."

"So how do you explain all the bodies that are suddenly stacking up around the Stratfords? Two in as many nights, at my last count."

"Am I under arrest?"

"Not yet."

"Then this conversation is over." I stood and stomped out to phone Henry from the solitude of my Mercedes.

"Henry, what's going on? Chris Black said he questioned you."

"You've got me," he said into my ear. "They seem to have a crazy notion that Cindy Swanson was murdered." He seemed to hesitate before continuing. "Did you really try to influence the medical examiner?"

I responded in a forced whisper. "Henry! You know me!"

"Do I?"

"Do I know you?" I shot back. "Maybe you should be telling me about Cindy Swanson."

"I've told you how she died. I don't know why the police are on a witch hunt."

"I'm asking what Cindy meant to you. Were you having an affair?"

"Is that what they told you? They must be playing games with us. Trying to play us off one another."

"What did they ask you?"

"They wanted to know about your relationship with Cindy. They know all about your argument with Cindy in the hospital. Is it true you threatened her?"

I felt my defenses rise. "Yes," I said. "But I only warned her, because I thought she was out of line in disrespecting me. I was referring to her job, not her life."

"They seem to think I'm covering for you."

"That's crazy."

"I would, you know."

"Henry! I've done nothing. Why would you say that?"

"Only because I would. I'd do anything for you. And for the record, I won't let anyone come between us."

I felt my usual guilt. I'd been tempted to believe the allegations about my husband and Cindy, but Henry wouldn't even lower himself to dignify the accusation with a defense. His whole response was so Henry. He was above all the muck. Now, he was assuring me, but I couldn't give him a reassurance in return. I'd had an affair of the heart with Jack, and I couldn't lie to Henry. But I could try not to waste my second chance. I took a deep breath. "Of course not."

"We'll talk at home. This whole thing is an attack on us," he said, emphasizing the "us." "But we can't let this destroy what we have."

I nodded, unsure what I should feel. In spite of my indecision, I was touched by his interpretation of our day. My voice cracked with emotion. "We're still a team, aren't we?"

"Wendi, Wendi," he said softly. "Of course. I've got to run. We'll talk tonight."

Chris Black chewed the end of a cinnamon stick while he paced his small office. He thought about the trouble swirling around the Stratford family and mentally enumerated the things that bothered him. He sighed. Who was he kidding? The whole case was beginning to stink.

He'd obtained a confession from Henry Stratford that he was having an affair with Cindy Swanson. He'd obtained another from Wendi stating that she had threatened Cindy in the hospital earlier that week for Cindy's remark about the way Wendi was treating her husband. In addition, Yolanda Pate was dead and the victim's mother was convinced that Wendi was involved. And now it appeared that Wendi lied to him about an affair with Yolanda's fiancé, a fact he'd confirmed with a witness other than a suspicious mother.

Why would Wendi lie if she wasn't guilty? Was she vindictive against a woman sleeping with her husband? Or did she want to eliminate the fiancée of a man she loved?

The whole thing didn't make much sense. And yet it made perfect sense. He'd known Wendi since college. Yet for years, he'd had the feeling that she'd drifted into living a life of appearances. She seemed to have fallen awake in the American Dream. Outside, the surgeon's wife had everything. Money. A successful career. Respect. A beautiful home. A husband who pampered her. But every time they'd shared more than a superficial chat in the last few years, she'd grown distant. Superficial. Outwardly, she smiled, but he found himself wondering what was hidden on the inside. He was no psychiatrist, but Chris prided himself with a keen ability to dissect below the surface, a quality that kept him at the top of his game as a detective. And now, as he thought about the way Wendi had been acting, it hit him. She'd been acting this way for years. Guilty.

But he must be careful not to let his own bias take over his thinking. Yes, Wendi had been an old college friend. But a year ago, all of that had changed when she decided to testify for a defendant he was sure was guilty. She'd made him and the whole department look bad, and things hadn't been the same in their relationship since.

He looked over both cases, combing every page of evidence. Something didn't add up. Wendi Stratford was lying, covering up. Finally, after an hour, he couldn't convince himself to look another way. If anything, he thought, he was trying hard not to see her as guilty.

He picked up the phone. He needed to talk to the magistrate. He wanted an arrest warrant to pick Wendi Stratford up on the charges of murder.

Henry arrived home at midnight, and I revived because we needed to talk. I opened my eyes and pushed up on one elbow to look at Henry as he brushed his teeth. When he sat on the edge of the bed to pull off his socks, I touched his shoulder. "Tough day?"

He grunted.

I watched as he shed his tee shirt and slid into bed, issued a perfunctory kiss, and turned away from me.

"Night, honey," he said softly. "I'm beat."

"Henry," I said. "We've got to talk. I need to know what's going on."

"Can't we talk tomorrow? I'm exhausted."

"I need to know about Cindy Swanson."

He spoke through a sigh. "I've told you all about it, Wendi. I don't want to go over it again."

"Why did the police think you were having an affair with her?"

"It's their business to see evil. They see an accident and immediately they try to paint it like it was something sinister. Then they need to assign motive. Suddenly both of us are suspects in a murder," he huffed. "It's ridiculous."

I wanted to see Henry's face, but he kept it plastered to the wall.

"Chris Black is vengeful," I responded. "He's still upset about our last court battle."

I wanted Henry to take me in his arms and reassure me that I was the only one in his life, to tell me how I was everything to him, so I could shove aside my nagging doubts, but he responded to my comments with a grunt or two, and a minute later his breathing fell into the regularity of slumber.

Sleep remained elusive to me. Images of the blonde women floated past, Yolanda and Cindy haunting me with memories of our last few days.

I stared into the darkness towards the ceiling. It seemed my entire ordeal had begun with my jailbreak attempt from my plastic life. But I'd been trying to fix that. *Is my life unraveling because*

I'm still running away from God? The thought startled me, partly because it came uninvited, and partly because I believed it. Though I was far from the straight and narrow in my heart, I had talked the talk for most of my life, and I certainly understood what I thought was the chief characteristic of the Christian life: guilt.

How can Rene of all people talk of believing in God's love? And how did Jack dare to presume that I needed to forgive myself?

I sniffed back the first tears, then let them flow as I understood that Jack was right. My relationships and my life weren't going anywhere until I decided to let myself off the hook for hurting my mother. Jack's words came back to me. *Whatever it is, forgive yourself. God certainly has.*

He wouldn't have said that if he knew what I'd done.

It's not like I can just bring it up to Mom after all these years. She may have forgotten everything. It would be unroofing old pain for nothing.

Sometime after two in the morning, I must have drifted into that dreamy state between alertness and full slumber. All I remember was Henry nudging me and asking if I was OK. I touched my cheeks. They were wet with tears.

This time it was my turn to face away. I didn't feel like talking now. I couldn't explain my tears, and I didn't want the surgeon-fix-it solution. I just needed acceptance, the reassuring presence of someone comfortable with my tears.

"It will be OK, Wendi," he mumbled. "I'm taking care of everything."

CHAPTER 23

Ed Mosby's face was stern beneath his silver military haircut. The chief of police shook his head. "Nothing will embarrass this department more than to make a sensational arrest that ends up being wrong."

Chris Black leaned forward on his chair and felt his cheeks reddening. "You told me to trust my gut," he huffed. "And my gut says that Wendi Stratford is hiding something."

The chief sighed. "I agree with you, Chris, and I've heard it all, believe me. So find the evidence we need."

"You've seen the medical examiner's report."

"So Cindy Swanson's death looks suspicious. Bring Wendi back in. Press her. Break her. Make her talk."

"The magistrate talked to you, didn't he?"

"He's only doing what I instructed. I'm to be included on all decisions to issue arrest warrants for murder charges." He stood up, a sign that the conversation was over. "Go out and get Mrs. Stratford. Bring in her surgeon husband for all I care. If you find something concrete, you'll get your warrant."

Thursday morning was to have been my last day combing the beaches in Jamaica with Jack. We would stroll hand in hand discussing our transition back into life in Charlottesville and how to deal with the aftershock wave that would certainly rip through our church and community. Jack would stop and bargain with a peddler, and purchase a small necklace or bracelet for me to wear. Something small, but heartfelt. Something precious that would promise our future together.

Instead, I sipped Ethiopian java with a rising knot in my gut that said I'd better soon figure out what was going on inside the Charlottesville PD or face some serious consequences. And since no one in the department seemed to have a clue about the truth, I got up that morning with a determination to put my own detective skills to work.

I sat quietly while Henry read the *Wall Street Journal* and ate an English muffin, both of us pretending it was a routine morning with nothing extraordinary to talk about. I found myself feeling guilty for suspecting Henry had been unfaithful to me, especially when the splinter in my husband's eye was difficult to see because of the beam in my own. It seemed that my desire to probe Henry's private life had run off in the stream of last night's tears.

I waited an hour after Henry left, told Rene I loved her, but to get a job and pay me rent if she was going to stay for life.

Then, I slipped out, driving right through the shadow of the cross and to the bottom of Azalea Drive, where it intersected with Route 29. I pulled off the road, stopping in the same location I had a week ago when looking at Jack's demolished Accord. I walked the roadside hoping to see something, anything that would speak to me. I wasn't sure what I thought I would see, but felt that somehow events in the last week were linked in a way I couldn't understand. Jack's accident. Yolanda erasing my camera. Yolanda's suicide. Cindy Swanson's death. Jesse Anders' attempt at insurance fraud. It all smelled of something less than fresh, and without an ally in the PD, I was on my own, trusting my instinct. Fortunately, being a woman, I was heavy in the gut-instinct department.

But today, other than what I'd seen the week before, nothing stood out. Most of the glass had been swept away. Other than a disturbance in the grass on the shoulder, and the charring of a few trees and underbrush, the accident was on its way to memory.

I decided it was time for another trip to see Jesse and Linda Anders. As I pulled out onto 29 North, a police cruiser turned right on Azalea, lights flashing. Without thinking, I felt myself shrinking behind the wheel. *Why am I hiding? I'm not guilty of anything. Except trying to escape my life of appearances.*

As I drove, I contemplated my approach to the Anderses'. *"Hi, I was just in the neighborhood and just thought I'd ask you what you're covering up."*

"So, what'd you do with the blue grille?"

"Were you asleep at the wheel? On drugs? Drunk? Why didn't you stop?"

I was halfway to Ruckersville when my phone sounded. I'd downloaded a new ring tone. The chorus to "Skin" by Breaking Benjamin broke the silence. I picked it up and used the phone as a pretend microphone for a few seconds to sing along before answering. "Hello."

"Wendi, it's me." Rene's voice was breathless.

I felt immediate alarm. "What's up?"

"The police are looking for you. Remember the two officers here with Chris Black the other day? They just left."

My gut tightened. "What did they want?"

"How should I know? They wanted you. They wanted to know where you were. How long you'd be gone. What I knew about your relationship with Jack Renner. How you acted around Yolanda. If you acted remorseful over Cindy Swanson's accident. How—"

"Whoa, slow down, sister," I said, shifting my phone to the other ear and looking in the rearview mirror for flashing lights. The way my conversation with Chris Black had gone, this wasn't entirely a surprise. "What did you tell them?"

"Nothing," she huffed. "Wendi, what's going on?"

"I'm not sure. The PD has it in their mind that I've got something to do with these girls who are dropping like flies around me."

An uncomfortable silence hung between us. I listened as she cleared her throat and fell silent again.

"Hey," I said, "Don't you start believin' I had anything to do with this craziness."

"Why do they care about your relationship to Jack?"

I shook my head. I wasn't anxious to talk about Jack to Rene. Especially since Jack had forgotten about the five minutes when there was an "us" to talk about. Especially since I'd turned the page in that book and was determined to forge ahead with Henry. And especially since Rene wanted Henry and me to adopt her baby. I hesitated. "I have no idea." It was the truth. Sort of.

"You were having an affair with him, weren't you?"

"No, I—" I halted. I couldn't lie anymore. I needed to be honest. I took a deep breath. "I liked him, but we never—"

Rene's voice cracked. "Wendi, I think they're going to arrest you."

I felt like cursing. This whole thing was crazy.

"Where are you?"

"Maybe it's best if you didn't know. That way if the police come back, you won't have to tell them."

Rene sniffed. "Wendi, you've got to talk to me. Let me help you figure this out."

"Did they tell you they wanted to arrest me?"

"No, but one of them was carrying some papers." She paused again. "What aren't you telling me?"

"Look, Rene, I'm tired of being a fake, OK? But things are complicated right now. I'll explain everything tonight."

"Wendi, you're not guilty of anything. You don't need to hide."

"I need to find out the truth. And the police don't seem to see anything except their own prejudices against me."

"But you're—"

"I made the wrong people mad a few months ago, Sis. And people who used to be my friends, well, let's just say they aren't acting like my friends anymore."

"You're scaring me."

"I'll be OK. I just need to check on a few things for myself."

"I heard them talking, Wendi. The police are looking for your Mercedes."

"I just need some time."

"Let me help you. I'll bring you my Saturn."

I reflexively checked my rearview mirror and sighed. "OK," I said. "You know where the airport road exits off 29 North? There's a small strip mall on the left just beyond the turnoff to the airport. Meet me in the bakery in the strip mall. I'll be there in fifteen minutes."

"OK."

John Aldridge entered his wife's room after a gentle knock. She lifted her face so her eyes could meet his and accepted a kiss on the cheek. She had a tissue crumpled in her left hand.

"What's wrong, dear?" she asked. "You look tired."

"Wendi."

She sighed.

"Rene just called. She asked us to pray. She thinks Wendi may be in trouble. The police just left the house. They seem to think Wendi had something to do with the women who died."

"Women?"

"Yolanda, the woman who was staying in Wendi's house. I told you about her, the one who committed suicide."

Ruth struggled forward. "You sssaid women."

"The police were asking questions about this Cindy Swanson, the woman who was killed when Henry's car struck her."

"Ridiculous. Wendi didn't have anything to do with those women dying."

"I think I failed her, Ruth."

She shook her head. "She's a good girl."

"Exactly." He slumped forward. "I've raised a good girl. But somehow she's missed out on grace."

Ruth grunted. The way she always did when she was upset.

He nodded slowly. "So how have I failed to pass it on to Wendi?" He sat on the edge of the bed opposite Ruth's wheelchair.

Tears began to flow down Ruth's cheeks.

John handed her a Kleenex and frowned. She'd always been so emotional since her head injury.

"You still don't get it," she said.

John felt his defenses rise. "I don't get what?"

"Do you remember the verse that hung on our refrigerator?"

He nodded, aware of the verse, but unsure how this had anything to do with Wendi.

"Be ye perfect, for I am perfect," she quoted.

"It's the standard of the law. The only ones who can approach a perfect God are those with a perfect record."

"Which is impossible."

"Of course. But with Christ's sacrifice, his record has become our record."

"So true, but that wasn't on the refrigerator, was it?"

"What are you saying?"

"I'm saying you paraded your girls around in front of the church, always had them singing special numbers, always performing." Her eyes bore in on his. "And we looked just like the perfect little pastor's family."

"Perfect family? We've never been that. What with Rene running off with her boyfriend, and—"

"Oh, and you don't think Wendi was paying attention? She saw how devastated you were when Rene left. So she worked all the harder to please you." Ruth dabbed at her chin with the Kleenex. "And I was determined not to lose another daughter."

"Another daughter? Wendi's always been a princess."

Ruth's face broke into an uneven smile. "Of course." The sarcasm was thick in her voice. "You just saw what you wanted to see."

John wasn't sure how to respond. He paced the small room, trying to process his wife's accusation.

"But me, I was the worst of all. I played my part the best. But until the accident, I never really understood it myself."

"Understood?"

"Grace," she said. "This chair." She pounded her fist on the arm of the wheelchair. "I never understood what God's grace was about until I sat in this chair."

John shook his head. "What do you mean?"

"It wasn't until I was so helpless that I realized that God loved me because of who he is, not because of who I am."

"I didn't intend to put pressure on Wendi." He paused. "Or you. I never expected a perfect family."

John sighed before continuing. "I was too busy with the congregation to see." His wife looked blurry through his tears. "So many were converted, but I've failed my own family."

"Sss-stop it," she slurred.

He wiped his eyes as his wife became even more emphatic. "Stop it," she said. "It's not all your fault." Her knuckles whitened against the arm of her wheelchair. "It's mine, too."

"But you were so gracious," he said, reaching for her hand, "the perfect pastor's wife."

"No," she said, pulling her hand away. "I only wanted you to believe it, for everyone to see how perfect our family was, how perfect your ministry was."

"But why? You knew we weren't perfect."

Ruth pushed her chair around with her good foot so that she would face the window. "You want to know what's going on with your daughter, Wendi?"

"Sure," he said.

"You're not going to like what I say."

Rene noticed the blue sedan pull out behind her when she turned on 29 North off of Azalea Drive. It stayed two cars back for three miles, so Rene turned right onto a residential street and watched the sedan follow.

Her heart quickened. She reached for her phone and dialed Wendi.

She picked up after one ring. "What is it?"

"I'm being followed."

Rene listened to her sister sigh. "Lose 'em."

She made a sudden U-turn. "How?"

"Pull into a store. Wait a few minutes. Anything. Make some turns."

"Wendi!"

"Just chill, Rene, it's probably the police. They don't want you. They just want you to lead them to me."

"OK." Rene flipped off her phone and turned back onto 29. After two blocks, she made a right turn into a large Toys-R-Us parking lot. She waited a few seconds before grabbing her phone and heading into the store. She spent ten minutes wandering the aisles and purchased a deck of cards so as not to appear suspicious.

She drove the remaining ten minutes watching her rearview mirror, convincing herself that she had given her company the slip. She pulled in beside her sister's Mercedes and found herself wondering how Wendi, the one who had seemed to have everything, had managed to find herself in such a mess.

Henry looked around the operating room and sighed. This was his domain, a world where he captained the ship, where his words were implicitly obeyed and his work admired. He watched quietly as his intern, Michael Ulrich, helped move their patient off the operating table and onto a stretcher.

"Keep him on an IV cephalosporin for twenty-four hours, Mike," he instructed. "And make sure he has on a pair of pneumatic venous compression sleeves."

The intern nodded. "Yes sir," he responded, smiling through a two-day beard.

Henry glanced at the open top drawer of the anesthesiologist's cart and waited for him to turn his attention to their patient. Then, Henry backed towards the cart and dropped his hand into the drawer and closed his palm around two small glass vials. Swiftly, he withdrew his hand, dropped the medicine into the pocket of his scrubs, and smiled at the scrub nurse as he walked out.

With her good hand, Ruth gripped the arm of her wheelchair. "There was so much more," she said. "Wendi—" she said, as a sob erupted from her lips. "Wendi got pregnant."

John felt his heart quicken. "What? When?"

"John, I didn't want you to know. She was young. Only fourteen. I was afraid the elders who asked Rene to leave would remove you from the pulpit." She looked up. "You know, if you couldn't rule those of your own house, how could you lead the people of God?"

His mouth was suddenly dry. He couldn't find a response.

"So I covered it up. I wanted her to have an abortion. We were on our way to the clinic when our accident occurred."

"Ruth!" he said. "How could you?"

She turned to face him. "I didn't want to lose another daughter." She began to sob. "Oh John, it was so wrong, but I panicked. Something took over, and it was as though someone else was sitting there, talking about abortion as though it was nothing. And I couldn't stop it, couldn't stop myself." She wept a moment, grieving the decision that had cost so much — not least the loss of their grandchild. "Later I realized that I was just playing a game all along. I'd become a professional Christian. I acted like the perfect pastor's wife, but inside, I was dark." She slumped, her shoulders thrown forward in defeat. "I've passed it on to Wendi. She knows only the rules, but has missed out on grace."

John stared at the woman he loved, aching for the pain that flowed out of her. "So that's why she expected us to react differently when Rene told us she was pregnant."

Ruth cried and looked up again. "It is my fault."

"Why didn't you tell me?" He leaned towards his wife, trying to understand.

"I wanted to protect you." She halted. "I wanted to protect me. You see — "

"But Ruth, abortion — "

She held up her hand. "She never went through with it. She lost the baby after the accident. The surgeon took the baby out with her uterus when he couldn't control the bleeding." Ruth stared at him. "I never wanted to you to know." She sniffed. "I wanted to be the woman you thought I was."

John nodded. "Just like Wendi."

"So don't blame yourself. If anyone's to blame, it's me."

Bitterness and compassion stood opposed in his mind. He wanted to love, to understand, but this trickery seemed too much. He looked away, rubbing the back of his neck. "You sat on the front pew. You said 'amen' when I talked of the rights of the unborn."

Ruth spoke slowly, each syllable thick with emotion. "I know it was wrong, John." She paused. "Look at me."

He stood at the window and looked out over the manicured lawn leading down towards the lake. He turned to stare at his wife.

"After Rene left, Wendi was all we had. I was afraid, John." She halted, a sob catching in her throat. "Can you ever forgive me?"

He took his wife's hand. "This is also my responsibility. My family was under pressure to perform because of me." He hesitated. "So Wendi has lived with this secret most of her life."

Ruth nodded and stayed quiet. After a minute, she began again, "We've never spoken of it since the accident. At first I expected her to blame me, to hold it against me that she couldn't have children." Ruth pushed her wheelchair back with her one good foot. "The longer it's been, the more I think she must have amnesia from the accident. Maybe she doesn't remember at all."

John began to pace the small room as he processed the news. "But the accident—" he began. "Wendi was just a child. What was she, fourteen?"

"She was a young woman, John."

He continued to pace, finally stopping and letting his hand rest on the bookshelves. "It all makes sense, Ruth. I think she remembers." He nodded. "So she's lived a perfect life trying to make up for her sin."

"She probably blames me for her inability to have children."

"No," John said, looking down on his wife. "I think she blames herself for putting you in the chair."

"That's ridiculous."

"That's Wendi."

I chatted nervously with Sophia Rodriquez, the owner of Sophia's Bakery, and watched the front window for Rene. Sophia's husband was another one of Henry's triumphant trauma-saves, and the Rodriquezes had returned the favor for countless special occasions, providing fresh breads for dinner parties or a cake for Henry's birthday.

When I finally saw Rene, I was choking back emotions. I was through with the games, through with lying, and in spite of the fact that I'd told myself that this week was going to be the new week of honesty, I'd spent most of it smiling in front of a heart of pain.

We retreated to the back of the store, where Sophia ran a small coffee bar, selling fresh muffins and hot java. We sat in the only booth in the corner, and Sophia immediately brought two mocha lattes.

Rene's eyes bore in on mine. "OK, Wendi, why don't you just tell your sister all about it?"

I sniffed and pinched the bridge of my nose. "You just had to come home to see me during the worst week of my life."

Rene teased at the thick foam that bulged from the top of a tall mug. I could read her ambivalence about accepting it. She was pregnant, and I had chastened her about drinking my java stash. She shook her head. "You still can't compete with me. I'm the queen of messed up."

I smirked. "Thanks." I looked up after inhaling the aroma rising from my latte. "But you haven't heard my story."

She sipped her drink and licked away a small curl of foam from her upper lip. "So spill it. I'm not sitting here to judge you."

"Jack Renner and I were going to run off to Jamaica together this past week. I had it all planned."

I watched Rene's jaw slacken.

I paused. "You said you wouldn't judge me."

She surrendered with her hands lifted, palms facing me, and said nothing.

"OK, there were a few glitches in my little escape plan. I'd never told Jack about my juvenile crush or the fact that I bought the tickets that were supposed to purchase my freedom from my perfect life."

A smile threatened the corner of Rene's straight face.

"Don't you dare laugh!" I said. "God is wreaking havoc in my life for just thinking about leaving my husband."

Rene leaned forward and matched my whispered tone. "What?"

"Well, that's my theory anyway. I asked Jack to run away with me on Thursday."

"What did he say?"

"What could he say? He was shocked. I could tell he liked me, but he was totally unbalanced by my invitation. As far as he and the rest of the world knew, I was the perfect little Christian, happily married to the perfect surgeon with the perfect house and the perfect life." I shook my head. "But for once in my life, I decided to take down the mask. Poor guy fled down the hill and pulled out in front of a truck who decided to run a red light."

Rene leaned forward. "That wasn't your fault."

"You don't get it, do you?" I whispered. "Every time I make a deviation from the straight and narrow, someone I love gets hurt."

Rene started shaking her head, but I didn't wait for her to voice her protest before I continued. "I was on my way to have an abortion." I smacked my hands together. "Mom ends up in a wheelchair." I stared at my sister, daring her to contradict my theory. "And this week, everything around me has gone bust." I sighed. "And it all followed my little departure from my righteous life."

"You've carried the guilt of putting Mom in a chair all these years?"

I nodded. "Who else?"

"Mom, that's who. If anyone is responsible, it was Mom."

"She's not the one who had an affair with the youth director."

"Hey, that wasn't your fault, Sis. He was a married man, a leader with responsibility to keep his hands off. A fourteen-year-old, as mature as you felt, isn't ready to fight off the advances of a man she trusts."

"Tell that to my heart."

Rene sat quietly and reached her hand across to mine. "If it's any consolation, you and Henry seem perfect together."

"Exactly," I moaned. "Too perfect." I sipped my drink. "It's hard to explain. Before I got involved with Bob Seaton, I'd always been a good girl. Since Mom's and my accident, I've never walked away from the path again. At least not in everyone's eyes. But inside, I don't think I've ever really been on board with God. I walk around thinking he's upset with me all the time. I've tried to live up to his expectations, but I just can't do it anymore. I felt like my whole life was a big fake." I wiped a tear from my cheek. "I just wanted to be honest, even if that meant doing something crazy."

"Did you ever feel like an actress on stage?"

I nodded. "All the time." I squinted at my sister. "Why?"

"Because that's exactly the way I felt. Until I ran off with Ray."

"What about now?"

"Since I left, I've never been shy about trying to be real." She seemed to be staring straight through me. "I'm not into pretending to be something I'm not because of guilt."

"Oh, and now you're qualified to be my psychologist, too." My biting words hung between us. We both knew my defense was weak.

"Hey, I'm just echoing what I hear from you." She held up her index finger. "You feel guilty." She held up a second finger next to the first. "So you try to be perfect to overcome your guilt."

I felt a tightening knot in my stomach. My sister had me pegged. My phone sounded. I silenced it and looked at the readout.

Chris Black. There was no way I was going to talk to him. Better let my voice mail pick up than talk to him.

Rene spoke again. "Does Henry know about this?"

"Are you insane?" I sipped my latte. "No one knows. Not even Jack."

"But I thought you said he—"

"He's got amnesia. He doesn't remember a thing."

Rene stayed quiet for a minute and stared towards the front of the store. "OK," she finally responded. "How does all of this tie in with you being wanted by the police?"

I shrugged. "I don't know." I paused and continued in a whisper. "Cindy Swanson had an attitude. She mouthed off to me when I went in to see how Jack was doing after his accident. I told her she'd regret it." I looked up at my sister. "How would I know she would end up dead the same week I threatened her? The police chief claims Henry was having an affair with Cindy. That makes me the jealous wife, and therefore, a suspect, I guess."

"I thought Cindy died from a pedestrian accident."

"Me too," I said. "I need to find out if there is something suspicious about her autopsy. Something that made Chris Black focus on foul play instead of accidental death."

"Maybe your argument with her means you suffer from incredibly bad timing." Rene sipped her latte. "You can't just run from the police."

"Rene, I just can't let them arrest me. The PD is biased against me because I embarrassed them in court last fall."

"And what about Yolanda Pate? The police asked me about your relationship with her." Rene cradled her hands around the steaming mug. "Another coincidence? The fiancée of the man you wanted ends up dead in your bed."

"Rene, you can't believe that I could—"

We looked up to see Sophia. She set down two fresh muffins. "Lemon poppy seed," she said.

When she headed back towards the kitchen, Rene took my hand. "I know you didn't have anything to do with her death. I'm just trying to understand how any of this could be related."

"Like you said," I responded, wrinkling my nose, "incredibly bad timing?"

She nodded. "You need to be honest with Henry."

It was my turn for the jaw drop. I jumped on my defense bandwagon. "Why should I tell him about Jack if no one, not even Jack, remembers my insanity?" I couldn't meet her gaze. Looking down at my coffee, I continued, "The irony of this whole week is that I've started remembering what I liked about Henry in the first place. Watching him care for Jack, seeing his willingness to consider even talking about adopting your baby—" I stopped and choked back the lump in my throat. "Well, let's just say I've discovered my love for Henry may just be enough to carry us forward."

Rene's expression changed, and I followed her gaze to the front of the store where a man had just entered the bakery. She grabbed a menu and whispered from behind it. "That's the man who was following me!"

I glanced over my shoulder. I recognized the man as one of the two young officers who'd been at my house with Chris Black. I looked at Rene, keeping my back towards the officer and the front of the store, and lifted my hand to shield the side of my face.

I watched as Rene lowered the menu just enough for me to see her eyes widen. Her voice was urgent.

"Wendi! What are we going to do?"

ChaPteR 24

"Follow me," I whispered, casting a glance over my shoulder. Then, dropping to the floor, I crawled to an opening in the counter bordering the opposite wall.

Rene obeyed, and in a moment I found myself in the kitchen staring at Sophia's knees. I looked up to see her wearing a red apron dusted with flour. I jumped to my feet and covered her mouth just as she burst out laughing.

"Shhh." I lifted my hand from her face. I looked over my shoulder to see Rene peeking out into the store from behind a curtain.

Rene turned and whispered, "He's coming this way!"

"Is there another way out of this place?"

Sophia pointed towards the back, across a large vat of bagels. "But what—?"

"I'll explain later. Can I borrow your car?"

Sophia shrugged and fished a set of keys from a large leather purse.

"Could you go out there and occupy that man for a few minutes? We'll bring back your car in an hour."

"It's by the dumpster behind the shop." Sophia's gaze turned stern. "Are you in trouble?"

"Nothing I deserve." I smiled and mouthed "thank you."

I ran for the door with Rene trailing. Once in the parking lot, I scrambled for a red Camaro parked by a large green dumpster.

"What was that all about?"

"Some of our most loyal friends owe Henry their lives," I said, nestling in behind the wheel. "Let's get out of here."

Fifteen minutes later, I turned off of Route 29 and onto Azalea Drive and reflexively ducked down when I saw the parked police cruiser beside the road. A pair of Charlottesville police officers seemed to be watching every car entering my neighborhood. Were they waiting for me?

They didn't seem to pay any attention to the red Camaro. I sighed.

Rene didn't like my plan.

"Change with me," I said, pulling to the curb. "Drop me off at the Letchfords' house. I'll cut across their backyard and into the woods behind my house. I can get in the back door to the garage."

"You're impossible." Rene reluctantly jumped out and got behind the wheel. "The police are watching your house."

"Exactly. So just do as I asked and everything will be OK."

Rene rolled her eyes. "Explain to me again why you have to do this."

"It's what I do," I said. "Somewhere in this mess there are some clues to unravel this whole mystery. And if the police are convinced I'm the guilty party, then I'm having a bit of a problem trusting their judgment right now."

Rene pulled away from the curb, lurching us forward as she pushed the accelerator. "I'll be back in thirty minutes in your car. I'll slow down at your driveway, then do a U-turn in the church parking lot to draw the police away."

"Perfect," I said, immediately wishing I'd chosen a different word. I was done with my perfect life. "Here," I said, pointing to the side of the road. "Just drop me here. I can get into the house without anyone seeing from the front."

"I hope you know what you're doing."

She didn't wait for my reply. In a moment, she was speeding back towards Sophia's Bakery. Now all I could do was pray my little plan would work.

The Camaro disappeared down the hill, and I dashed through my neighbor's side yard and into the woods. When I was at my yard's edge, I paused to study the house. Everything seemed normal. *Oh how deceiving the looks of suburbia can be.*

Thirty minutes later Rene slowly drove Wendi's Mercedes up Azalea Drive. She felt like she was trolling for bluefish in the Chesapeake Bay. She hooked what she was looking for when the First Baptist Church was just coming into view. She braked hard and made a U-turn.

Perfect, she thought. *Catch me if you can.*

She punched redial on her cell phone.

After one ring, she heard Wendi's voice. "It's about time."

"I'm on Azalea. Our friends have just picked up the trail."

"Great. Head north on 29."

"I thought you'd be going this way."

"Change of plans."

"Be safe. Oh," Rene said, "flashing lights in the rearview mirror."

"Pretend you don't see them. Try to take them north."

"I'm on it."

I flipped off my cell and pulled the full-coverage helmet over my head. As the garage door rose, I fired up Henry's Triumph Rocket III. It was heavier than I'd imagined, but seemed to balance well between my legs. I'd ridden this thing a dozen times, but always behind Henry. Thankfully, in his completeness, he explained every detail to me before each of our excursions. It was a bit like his preflight check in front of the mirror. *Key. On. Clutch. In. Press the starter. Shift downward to find the first gear.*

I twisted the throttle and slowly released the clutch. I was moving! And no one would ever expect me to be on this baby.

I kept it in first gear all the way down the hill on Azalea. When I saw a car in front of me, I hung back, and snuck through the light, turning south on 29 without stopping. So far, so good. Riding was easy enough.

Once I was in town, I took a right to head for the university.

I'd decided to first head over to Jefferson Hill Apartments to see where Cindy Swanson had died. When I arrived five minutes later, something that Chris Black said was tugging at the back of my mind. He referred to brake skid marks. I'd let the phrase pass without thinking, but now I realized I needed to take a look. New Mercedes with antilock brakes don't leave skid marks.

I motored in the lot beneath the apartments and managed to bring the Triumph behemoth to rest with surprising ease. I was starting to understand why Henry loved this bike so. Behind the darkened visor, I was in my own little world, just a throttle-twist away from freedom. I leaned the bike carefully onto its kickstand

and dismounted. I removed my helmet, lifted my camera from the saddlebag, and retraced the path that I presumed Henry had driven. He'd described traveling back up the lane and hitting Cindy as she fell beneath the front wheels. A sidewalk met the driveway twenty yards from the deck beneath the apartments. The asphalt was clean and dry, a sure sign that the apartment's owner had scrubbed away gruesome evidence. There were no bloodstains and little proof that anything had taken place at all, but true to the detective's report, skid marks were present. A double row of tire marks three yards long ended right at the intersection with the sidewalk.

I photographed the marks from four angles and knelt down to study the pattern. *A typical error*, I thought. The skids were acceleration marks, not brake marks. Brake marks start light and end heavy. Acceleration tire marks start heavy as the wheel spins and lighten as the tire grips the road.

I puzzled over the meaning. Perhaps the skid marks were not left by Henry's Mercedes at all. Perhaps they were there before the accident. Yet Henry's Mercedes was certainly capable of leaving acceleration skids.

I pulled a measuring tape from the pocket of my leather jacket. I measured the distance between the tire marks. I couldn't be sure, but my closest guess was that they belonged to Henry's Mercedes. I'd do a measurement on Henry's car later and make a comparison. Perhaps he wasn't braking at all. Maybe he was leaving in a hurry and hit Cindy Swanson as he accelerated down the drive.

I felt ill at ease leaving the scene. My job lent itself to magnifying my baseline paranoia, and evidence that didn't match up revved my what-iffer into high gear.

Another thought troubled me. Was this the evidence that convinced the police that something was amiss? *No*, I thought, *Chris wouldn't have tried to mislead me by telling me there were brake marks present. There must be some other evidence that makes them think Cindy's death was no accident.*

I decided to pay Sig Eichmann a visit. It was time I knew first-hand what the results of Cindy's autopsy showed.

In a few minutes, I was on Interstate 81 heading south to Roanoke, glad for a long stretch of straight road that wouldn't challenge my novice abilities on the bike. As I drove, I thought about the implications of my findings at the Jefferson Hill Apartments. *Is Henry lying? If he set up Cindy's death to look like an accidental hit-and-run, what was he covering up?* I shook my head. Henry may have been able to fool the PD, but he would have known that I would eventually look at the evidence and pick up the inconsistencies.

Was Henry sending a message that only I could read?

CHAPTER 25

Sig Eichmann and I had been on friendly terms since I spent a three-month period doing an externship with him after graduating from UVa. My focus had been the patterns of injury seen in automobile crashes and how a reconstructionist could work backwards from the human injuries to the type of impact and speed responsible for the specific injury pattern. Although Sig was typically professional and a bit distant, I thought I'd gotten beneath his German skin and was one he counted as a confidante.

Today, I approached his office with a bit of consternation, knowing he seemed a bit suspicious of my motives.

But I had to talk to someone. And I knew Chris Black wouldn't give me an inch. Most likely, he had sent his drones to arrest me. I needed to know the autopsy data to know how to defend myself against it.

His secretary let me in and led me to his door, which was wide open, as usual. His desk was stacked with folders, communication, books, and the evidence of too many takeout pizzas. I knocked on the doorframe. He looked up over half glasses. His white hair was uncombed, in character with his Einstein brilliance. "Hi, Sig," I said.

He frowned. Seeing me was a surprise, evidently not a pleasant one. "Wendi, you're the last person I expected here."

I sat down uninvited. "I'm in trouble, Sig. I need your help."

He lifted his glasses away from his face and sighed. "What have you done?"

"I'm not confessing to a crime," I said. "Unless curiosity and ignorance are punishable now."

I saw the first hint of a smile form at the edges of a face that seemed permanently etched by a constant exposure to some of humanity's worst cruelties.

"I'm a suspect in a murder," I began. "Maybe two." I paused, my voice almost pleading. "Sig, you know me. I couldn't hurt someone like that." I hesitated. "I need to know what the autopsies showed. Why are the police asking questions of me like I'm a common criminal?"

"Wendi, information like that has to come only to and through the proper channels. You know I can't—"

I leaned forward, interrupting him. My voice was quiet, but tense. "Sig! I'm asking you to look the other way. You are my friend. I'm not asking you as a professional consultant. I'm asking you as my friend. You know I'm not capable of murder."

"Is that what the police really think?"

"They seem to." I paused. "It didn't help for you to tell them I'd called you."

"I wasn't trying to cast suspicion on you," he said, wrinkles filling his forehead. "If anything," he added, looking away from my gaze, "I was concerned about your husband."

"But why? Did your investigations find evidence of foul play?"

Sig let his chin sag into his cupped hand. I was putting him in a hard place. He might have to testify that he showed me the evidence.

"The police came to my house this morning to arrest me. I'm here only because my sister tipped me off."

Sig shook his head. "Be careful of Chris Black. He's unable to look at you with any kind of objectivity."

"So, help me," I pleaded. "Put the files on your desk and walk away. You won't see anything."

I saw the conflict behind his blue eyes. He wanted to help me, but what I was asking was a clear deviation from protocol. "Maybe you should be calling a lawyer."

"And sit in jail until they've figured this all out? Sig, this is what I'm trained to do. Let me reconstruct the accident and see if it all fits. I don't need an attorney for—"

He stood up, waving his hand to interrupt me. "I'm dying for a cup of coffee," he said. "I've got so much blasted work to do, it will take all the caffeine I can pump into me just to keep going." He pointed to his desk. "Look at this mess. I try to keep up with my work, filing each completed case by the last name here," he added, touching a wall of filing cabinets. "You know I can't show you about these cases, Wendi." He turned to go. "I'm off in search of coffee." He shut his door behind him.

I was alone, with specific instructions about how Sig filed his cases. The unspoken message was clear. *I can't give you information, but I won't know what you do when I'm gone.*

I scampered to my feet and opened first one filing drawer, then another and another, thumbing through the files until I came to "Swanson, Cynthia."

I opened the folder and scanned the document for conclusions. The injuries were listed from lethal to trivial.

CAUSE OF DEATH: Severe brain contusion, epidural hematoma beneath occipital skull fracture, non-displaced. Other injuries: depressed parietal skull fracture, C2–3 cervical spine fracture with spinal cord transection. Of note, the parietal skull fracture is suspected to have occurred after death, as there is no bleeding around the fracture site as would be expected if it occurred when the heart was beating. Incidental findings: Evidence of recent ethanol ingestion below legal intoxication limit, blood alcohol level 0.3, nonforced sexual intercourse (active motile sperm percentage in sample indicating time of sexual activity twenty-four to thirty-six hours prior to death).

I felt sick. Maybe this was why my mentor was so reluctant to share the findings with me. I read and reread the passage, committing it to memory. *Why would she have a significant skull fracture that occurred after death? And if she'd had recent intercourse, does that mean that Henry . . . ?*

The implications of the report were damning. And scary. *But why do they think that I had anything to do with it? Just because I "threatened" her the week she died.*

I glanced at my watch. I quickly filed away the Cynthia Swanson case and began my search for the file of Yolanda Pate. In a minute, I had it in my hand.

I wiped sweat from my brow and opened the file, again turning pages to the conclusion:

CAUSE OF DEATH: Narcotic overdose. Incidental findings: Ethanol intoxication. Minor lacerations inside lips and on the tip of the tongue, premortem. These could be evidence of a premortem struggle with force applied from the outside of the mouth, as if the deceased may have been forced to swallow, or could merely represent self-inflicted trauma.

I returned the file to the cabinet, not wanting to go where the data was pushing me. *This is why the police are suspicious.* I clenched my fist. *They think I had something to do with these girls' deaths?*

I thought of the next option. *What if they are right to be suspicious? But if it wasn't me, then who?*

The next thought took my breath. *Henry?* He was a lot of things. Arrogant. Hypocritical. But a murderer?

I opened the door into the hall, wanting to be anywhere but Sig's office, which suddenly seemed too small. I passed him next to a coffee pot in a small kitchen. I couldn't talk about what I'd seen, even if Sig would have allowed it. Something in my heart was breaking. Had Henry been unfaithful to me? Was he now trying to cover it up? How could Henry . . . ?

I stumbled forward through the front doors into the sunshine. I squinted and dabbed at my eyes.

I walked numbly towards the Triumph, trying to extract some sense out of the information. I straddled the behemoth and pulled on my helmet, thankful for the tinted visor that shielded me from the world. Inside my full-coverage Shoey helmet, I could cry, talk, and even scream, and the rumble of the Rocket covered it all.

I drove north on I–81, skirting the valley between the Blue Ridge and the Allegheny Mountains. I overtook and passed the interstate truck traffic. I'd known Henry for seven and a half years. I knew he was a poser, always concerned about his appearance. But unless he was a lot bigger fake than I, there was no way Henry was guilty of murder. I couldn't believe that. Pride, yes. An affair with a resident . . . well, Henry could have fallen into that trap, but murder?

I settled into the right half of the slow lane and tried to understand the pieces to the puzzle. The police wanted to arrest me. Cindy Swanson's autopsy suggested foul play. If her skull fracture occurred after death, what had killed the blonde beauty? And if she hadn't died in the accident as Henry reported, why would he lie? What did Henry have to cover up?

I drove another thirty miles, as green hillside scenery passed in a blur. With my thoughts about the mysterious deaths simmering on a back burner, the only other thing cooking in my brain was the craziness of my week. My prodigal sister shows up, HIV-positive, pregnant, and on her own, reunites with our parents and encourages me to mend broken family fences. My piano-teacher-almost-clandestine-lover ends up with a head injury in the hospital with no memory of my seduction.

The next thing I knew, I was fighting back tears and asking God why my life had ended up in such a mess. The problem with my rhetorical-question prayer was that every time I asked it, I sensed the same feeling of condemnation, and the memory of my love affair with a married man smacked me in the face with frightening clarity.

What do you want from me? I've tried to be a good wife, at least until recently. I attend church. I give to the United Way. I raised money for the medical auxiliary to buy new monitors. I even took in my prodigal sister with HIV, didn't I?

I listened, straining to hear anything above the roar of the Triumph Rocket III, the wind, or the sound of my own voice, but the heavens remained closed.

I squinted through my tears. I knew what God wanted. Perfection. But that was the intolerable goal that had driven me to the brink of the crazy plan that I'd initiated and failed.

I drove ahead, conscious of little except my turmoil. Instead of heading north to confront Anders, I knew I needed to see Henry. He knew more than what he was saying. And if he was going to hide all day in his work, I'd go straight back to the hospital and talk to him there.

Something somewhere was very wrong. And I was determined to get to the bottom and clear my own name.

If only my past was as easy to clear.

CHAPTER 26

I wrestled the Triumph into an open space in the doctors' parking area across from the hospital, scaring myself in the process. At highway speed, the cycle was easy to drive; in a parking lot, the weight of the beast was almost intolerable. I shut off the engine, immediately aware that the bike wanted to drift forward because of a slight grade encouraging the cycle deeper into the parking space. I arrested the forward movement by squeezing my front brake, but I wanted to curse my stupidity. I wasn't tall enough or strong enough to roll the bike out of the space by myself. I'd either need help or have to take Henry's Benz and leave him the Rocket.

I carried my helmet and crossed the street to the hospital, enjoying the stares of two male residents. I swaggered and stared back from beneath my killer shades. Wrapped in my leather jacket, I was one bad biker chick. I couldn't keep from smiling. My little excursion on the Triumph gave me new insight into Henry's psyche. Riding the bike had little to do with the fuel economy or reliability of transportation. Riding this bad boy was all about image and power.

I passed Henry's secretary and entered his office without knocking. It was empty. I set my helmet on his desk and sighed. Should I wait?

I looked up as Henry's secretary appeared in the doorway. "He's in the operating room." She frowned. "He asked me to take messages. He said he'd make return calls tomorrow, which means he thinks he'll be a long time."

I looked at Grace. She was young and blonde. Why did she have to be so pretty? "Thanks," I mumbled. "Maybe I'll see if he can see me between cases."

Grace smiled. "Good luck. You're a brave woman."

I walked away, whispering under my breath. "Maybe just a little desperate today."

I searched the OR lounge and the front desk area, places I could travel without scrub attire. No luck. Henry was safely squirreled away in the protection of his surgical haven.

I peered through the double doors leading down the OR corridor.

"Mrs. Stratford?"

I turned in response to the voice of a man. He was large and appeared too young to be sporting a physician's white coat. "Yes," I said, reading his name tag. "Ulrich." I saw him on the day of Jack's accident.

The doctor shoved a pack of Nabs into the pocket of a white coat overladen with supplies. "Are you looking for your husband?"

I wanted to ask him if he ever ironed his coat. "Yes."

"He's in room three, draining a pancreatic pseudocyst with Dr. Myers. He'll be a few hours."

I nodded, feigning knowledge. "Of course." I had no idea what a pseudocyst was. I looked back into the hallway, thankful that the young physician moved on. I studied the room numbers. It looked like room three was only two doors down on the right. Maybe if I snuck into the hall, I could get Henry's attention through the window.

I knew the rules. No one passed the double doors without surgical scrubs. Henry would die of embarrassment if I dared enter his domain without authorization or proper clothing.

I looked back at the resident, who was now leaning over a chart at the OR nursing station.

"Could you go back there and let Dr. Stratford know that I need to speak to him?" I smiled. "It's an emergency."

I could see the conflict on the intern's face. He wasn't supposed to bother the boss.

"An emergency," I repeated.

He took a deep breath and peeled off his white coat. Underneath, he wore a pair of green scrubs that appeared a size too small. "OK," he said. "I'll ask him if he can scrub out and talk to you."

I watched through the doorway as he schlepped down the hall. He hesitated at the door and retrieved a mask from a box above the scrub sink before disappearing through a door on the right side of the corridor.

A minute later, a nurse appeared, holding open the door, making way for Henry. He was in scrubs, covered with a sterile gown that was splattered with blood. His hands were covered by a green towel, and he held them in the air away from his body. His eyes met mine. He traveled halfway down the hall towards me before speaking in a hushed voice behind his mask. "This had better be important."

I suddenly felt very stupid, very childish for interrupting this important god of surgery for my mundane mystery. I cleared my throat. "We need to talk, Henry. I examined the accident scene at Jefferson Hill Apartments."

I studied him for a reaction. He flinched, but only for a second before he regained his regal composure. "OK?" he said, drawing out his words as if to say, "so what?"

"You didn't kill that girl, did you, Henry?"

Henry's eyes bolted open. I could see white above his iris, even from this distance. He stepped forward, alarm apparent on his face. He stopped ten feet from me, apparently conflicted. I wasn't sterile, and I wasn't talking through a mask. He mustn't get too close.

"Talk to me," I pleaded.

His eyes darted around. He couldn't talk to me here. "Later!"

I stood my ground. "Now."

He shook his head. "My patient," he said, looking back towards the operating room.

"Later never comes for us," I said. "Talk to me, Henry." I put my hands on my hips. "Do I need to talk to Chris Black about my suspicions?"

He sighed. "No," he whispered. "I'm taking care of this, OK? You need to trust me, Wendi. Do not talk to Chris about this."

"Honey, what's going on? Let me help you." I waited. "You expect me to shut my eyes to this?"

"No. Everything is the way it's meant to be," he said. "Of course I knew you'd look at the scene." He seemed to hesitate. "We'll talk tonight."

I glared at my husband and spoke with a quiet urgency. "You shouldn't even be working. After what you've been through this week, you could take a little time—"

The door to room three popped open behind him. A nurse in green scrubs spoke sharply. "Dr. Stratford, Dr. Newton needs you. The pressure's down."

Henry glanced over his shoulder. I could read the conflict in his eyes. He took one look back at me, and raised his voice. "I'll explain everything." He turned and walked towards the OR. "Tonight, Wendi," he said.

Our eyes met for a moment before he disappeared into the operating room, but in that second, I understood. Henry winked. He intended for *me* to know something that he was hiding from the police.

But what? What message was he sending me?

He knew I couldn't walk away from this. He knew me. We had talked through accident scenarios a hundred times in the past. He seemed as fascinated with the subtleties of my work as he was with his own. And now Henry was setting something up *for my eyes only.*

As frustrated as I was with everything, a part of me felt buoyed by Henry's subtle communication. He trusted me to understand where he thought others would look with uninitiated eyes and see nothing.

I walked back to his office, pondering his statement. *Everything is the way it's meant to be.*

Once in the haven of Henry's office, I closed the door and sat at his desk, trying to get into the mind of the man I married. I wiggled deeper into his leather swivel chair and closed my eyes, attempting to probe the surgeon's mind. *What is Henry doing?*

The ambiance of the office did little to stimulate new understanding. I knew Henry to be meticulous, thorough to a fault, and forever interested in the patient's well-being. Today, I'd understood a little more about the testosterone swagger that bled from the exhaust of his Triumph. But this week had brought more revelation than just a new appreciation for his love of two-wheeled travel. Something else was going on beneath my husband's skin. Perhaps Henry was as capable as I in the mastery of false appearances.

I looked over his ego wall, the diplomas, awards, and pictures that defined him. What was I missing? Henry the surgeon, the professor, I understood. I studied a little photograph on his desk, Henry and I together at the Wintergreen Ski Lodge. Our heads were tilted towards each other, my blonde hair falling on his shoulder. He had a gleam in his eye and a smile on his face.

Without warning, my eyes were tearing, and my soul bubbling with fresh emotion. *Yes, I'd been arm candy to Henry, but he really loved me, didn't he?* I sniffed. *Is it possible that I've misjudged him? Was he having an affair? Were his subtle clues leading me to find out what he couldn't find the strength to confess outright?*

I thought about my own wayward heart. If Henry was having an affair, how could I point a finger of accusation? Perhaps I'd driven him to it by my own lack of love.

I ran my finger over the top of the picture frame and sniffed. Henry had his idiosyncrasies, but didn't we all? And apparently, Henry still trusted me enough to be playing a subtle game. In a funny sort of way, I felt warmed by our last communication. I looked at a second picture on his desk. It was one I shot. Henry in a leather jacket, sitting on his Triumph Rocket III. I sniffed and smiled. *That's my tiger.*

I decided to write him a note.

"I left you the Triumph. It's in the parking lot, level two. I'm taking your Mercedes. It's a long story. We'll talk tonight, won't we, Henry?" I hesitated, then wrote "I love you" and signed my name.

I opened his desk drawer looking for his keys. I knew that Henry was a creature of extreme habit and that he always kept his keys in the same small drawer divider in the front right. I grabbed the keys as my eyes fell on the edge of a folder barely visible beneath a stack of papers. The name on the folder's edge made me shiver:

Anders.

Rene pushed open the door to her mother's room. John Aldridge looked up from the Bible in his lap.

"Hi, Daddy. Hi, Mom," she said, touching her shoulder.

"Rene, what's wrong?"

"Wendi." She hesitated. "She's in some kind of trouble with the law."

John leaned forward. "The law?"

"Two police officers were at the house this morning. They were asking about Cindy Swanson and Yolanda Pate. It's like they have suspicions that Wendi had something to do with their deaths. Later when I was driving her car, the police stopped me again, looking for her."

"I talked with an officer who was watching the house earlier this morning. Where is she now?"

"I don't know. She's out looking for evidence that can clear her."

Her father nodded. "That's our Wendi. Always trying to find a way to clear her guilt." He sighed. "And the running makes her look even more guilty."

"Guilt?"

Ruth pushed her chair around to face her daughter. "She can't forgive herself."

Rene tilted her head in a question.

Her father explained. "She feels responsible for putting her mother in that chair."

"You know that?"

"Of course."

"Then you knew about her baby?"

John nodded. "Not at the time." He took Ruth's hand. Rene watched as her parents' eyes met. "Mother told me later."

"But why didn't you tell Wendi?"

"It's not for me to tell." He paused. "Wendi needs to confront this herself."

"She thinks you'll judge her."

He shook his head. "She only hears half the message."

Rene understood. "Judgment." She looked at her parents. "What's the other half?"

Her mother spoke the word that warmed Rene's soul: "Forgiveness." Then she asked, "Have you tried calling her?"

"All day. I think her phone is off. She took off on Henry's motorcycle. She thought the police would be looking for her car."

"That's crazy," Ruth said. "That bike's too big for her."

Rene shrugged. "I'm beginning to understand that Wendi is willing to do just about anything to protect her reputation."

Ruth frowned. "Go after her, John."

"Where would I go?"

Rene folded her arms across her chest and looked out the window down the hill towards the lake. "Wendi wouldn't say where she was going. She didn't want me to be in a place of having to lie to cover for her."

"So what do we do?" Ruth asked her husband.

"What I should've done all along with Wendi — put it into God's hands and trust him."

Rene nodded and bowed her head in response. *If only Wendi believed that.*

She hardly knew how to pray. In her mind, she formulated words from her heart. *Show her, Father. Help her to believe in your love.*

I opened the folder and placed it on the top of Henry's desk. At first glance, the contents seemed mundane. Closer inspection quickened my heart. Copies of prescriptions, hundreds of them, all for the drug Oxycontin, were arranged by date. I leafed through the contents. *Why would Henry make copies of prescriptions? And why so many for one drug?*

I recognized the drug name from listening to Henry. I knew only that Henry liked to prescribe it for patients in pain.

Why is the folder titled "Anders"?

I thought back to my breakfast chat with Henry the previous morning. When I'd brought up Anders' name, Henry blanched. The image of my iceman dropping his butter knife played over in my mind. *"Anders is a druggie. A dealer. If he's covering something up, and you expose him, he seems the type to seek revenge."* I remembered the fear that flashed across my husband's face. *"Stay away from him."*

I paged through the paper, searching for anything that might clue me in. Two names stood out. Henry had written prescriptions for Linda Anders on four occasions, each time dispensing another fifty tablets of the drug. I recognized only one other name: Lanny Bedford. His name had been on the prescription for Oxycontin that was on my bedside stand the night Yolanda Pate died. It was another puzzle piece from my crazy week that I didn't understand and Henry hadn't been able to explain away.

I shoved the folder back into the top drawer and grabbed Henry's Mercedes keys. I checked my watch. Five o'clock. I had just enough time to take a look around the Anderses' place in Ruckersville and get back to make supper for Henry.

Despite my husband's warnings, I drove north on 29, determined to unravel the connection of Anders to the mystery swirling around me. I needed to examine Anders' truck and the grille. I needed to understand why Anders' name was on a folder in my husband's desk. *Anders is a drug dealer. Henry wrote hundreds of narcotics prescriptions and keeps them in a folder labeled "Anders."* The next logical connection tightened a knot in my stomach. *Was Henry helping Anders get drugs?*

That made no sense. The Henry I married would never participate in something like this. *Or would he?*

Thirty minutes later, I passed the Anderses' small ranch homestead twice, moving slowly down the winding country road wondering about the best approach. I really only wanted to look at the truck again, and maybe take a look around the garage to see where

Jesse might have stashed away the protective grille. Unfortunately, the house stood on a little knoll, so approaching on foot or by car was out unless I wanted to be spotted right away.

The Anderses' place was just past a small Exxon station that housed a convenience store. I decided to park there and cut across a field to the edge of their property, then approach from the edge of the woods. At least there I'd have a better chance of reaching the truck to take a few new pictures before I aroused any suspicions. I thought about going straight to the front door and knocking, but figured if Jesse was really hiding something, I'd have a better chance of getting information by coming in under the radar, so to speak.

I remembered the dogs just as I reached the edge of the property. It looked like a one-hundred-meter dash to the back of the house. The truck cab was in the driveway. I made it halfway to the free-standing garage behind the house when I was joined by a large Doberman Pinscher. I froze, standing still as the dog growled, sniffed my outstretched hand, and then rolled over to let me scratch his brown belly. From that spot on, he seemed content to walk along with me until I reached the garage and he was distracted by a rabbit. I studied the house. There were lights on and the faint sounds of a familiar country music band drifting towards me.

Hoping Jesse Anders was occupied, I decided to look at the truck first and get a few new photographs. I began by inspecting the front end. I ran my hand along the creased fender and frowned. Chris Black was right. The fender had been scrubbed clean. There was no sign of blue paint, not even the dime-size chip I'd seen before. I took pictures from ten angles and glanced toward the house. *So far, so good.*

Emboldened by the lack of any interference, I decided to test my theory about the way Anders had set up the accident by seeing whether the vehicle would coast if I could get it into neutral with the emergency brake off. I opened the driver's door and slipped in. I knocked the gearshift into neutral and released the parking brake. The vehicle edged forward towards the edge of the driveway and the sloping field beyond. I jerked back up on the handbrake to arrest the movement. That didn't prove anything to me except that the vehicle could have run away if the brake hadn't been set, something I think Anders should have noticed right away if he always parked the cab in the same place.

I looked around the inside of the cab. There was an empty Burger King cup on the floor and an ashtray overflowing with cigarette butts. In the glove box, I found something more interesting. Behind a pair of mirror sunglasses were two pharmacy pill bottles. I read the labels slowly. Both were Oxycontin. Prescriptions to a Mary B. Smith and a Brent Somers. And both written by my husband.

I closed my hand around one of the bottles and shoved it into my camera bag and threw the other one back into the glove box. I didn't like this at all. I slipped from the truck and tried to close the door quietly. Inside I was fuming. I thought about the narcotics in my possession. *Henry is going to answer all my questions tonight. What is he going to say about this?*

I turned my attention to the garage, moving quickly, with a glance over my shoulder towards the house. I tried the door handle. Locked. I rubbed a smudge from the window with my hand and squinted through the glass into the darkness.

I sighed, seeing only my own face in reflection. I waited a moment for my eyes to adjust and shifted to cup my hands around my eyes to block out the light. As I lifted my hands, I caught sight of a man reflected in the window. He wore blue jeans and a flannel shirt and held a pipe lifted above his head like a man about to swing an axe.

I gasped and felt a sharp pain in the back of my head as everything went black.

CHAPTER 27

After his case, Henry retreated to his office and locked the door. He opened the lowest drawer of his filing cabinet and retrieved a small box. Inside were ten vials of Fentanyl, a powerful narcotic, enough to keep an addict like Anders happy for a long time.

From the pocket of his white coat, Henry lifted another vial, tilting it upside down so that he could access it from the bottom. He plunged the tip of a needle and withdrew three milliliters of the clear fluid. Then, he carefully distributed the fluid into the vials of narcotic.

That ought to be just enough.

He placed the box in his briefcase and hung up his white coat. That's when he saw the note. He stared at the paper. *I left you the Triumph. It's in the parking lot, level two. I'm taking your Mercedes. It's a long story. We'll talk tonight, won't we, Henry? I love you. Wendi.*

He folded the paper into perfect quarters and slid it into his shirt pocket, picked up his briefcase, and headed for the freedom of his Triumph, wondering if he was man enough to follow through with his plan.

I awoke slowly, inventorying my body parts. I opened my eyes. *Where am I?* I explored a painful goose egg on the top of my head and looked around. It appeared I'd been placed in a small bedroom. Tan ceiling with a water spot from an old leak. Worn curtains. I put my hands to my side. I'd been placed on a bed. I started to rise up when my neck sent out a screaming pain message. "Ugh."

"Well, look who's waking up." The voice was female and came from the foot of the bed.

I struggled up on one elbow and squinted towards a woman. She appeared midthirties, perhaps my age. She sat in a wheelchair holding my camera bag in her lap. She turned over the picture ID badge I had attached to the handle. It was something I'd had made to identify me as an accident reconstructionist. She reached forward and dropped the bag on the foot of the bed. "You were blonde, huh?"

I rubbed the back of my head. "Where am I?"

"Maybe you should let me ask the questions. What are you, some sort of photographer?"

I strained to focus. "Some sort. I do accident investigation." I paused. "What happened to me?"

"Let's just say you were caught trespassing."

I started to remember. I'd come to the Anderses' house to see how Jesse might be connected to Yolanda's and Cindy's deaths.

The lady in the chair huffed. "My husband's such a fool. He thought he knew all about you."

A man came in behind her and pointed a handgun at me. "I told you to tell me when she came to."

"She just woke up." The woman backed up her wheelchair by using a small joystick. "How rude of me," she said. "I haven't even made introductions. Mrs. Henry Stratford, I'm Linda Anders." She pointed to her husband. "And this is Jesse, my husband."

"Would you mind telling me what's going on?"

"Maybe you should tell me why you were snooping around!"

"I was asked by your insurance agent to investigate your truck accident."

Jesse smirked. "And I suppose your investigation included helping yourself to my medications."

I followed his eyes to the top of a nearby dresser to the bottle of Oxycontin I'd placed in my camera bag. My mind raced ahead trying to connect with a rational thought. "I — I saw my husband's name on the bottles." I struggled to a sitting position.

"You shouldn't have come here," the lady said.

"So I'll leave. Pardon me for the intrusion." I started to stand, but immediately felt dizzy.

Jesse shoved me back onto the bed. "Not so fast."

The sound of an engine revving in the driveway caught the Anderses' attention. I recognized it immediately as the sound of Henry's Triumph motorcycle.

Linda backed her wheelchair to the window and lifted the curtain. I caught a glimpse of the cycle just as my husband dismounted.

"Henry!" I said.

Jesse cursed. "What's he doing here?" He pointed the gun at me. "Did you tell him you were going to be here?"

I shook my head. "No!"

"Give me the gun." Linda held up her hand towards Jesse. It wasn't a request.

He sighed and handed it to her.

"Go see what he wants," she ordered. "I'll stay with snoopy here and make sure she doesn't make a sound." She glared at me. "Not a peep, you understand? We have nothing to lose by killing you." I watched as she sneered at her husband. "You told me she was already dead."

He returned a smirk. "Can I help it if another blonde was sleeping in her bed?"

I gasped.

Jesse left us alone, and Linda moved her wheelchair to position herself between the bed and the door.

"What's going on? Did he kill Yolanda? What business does my husband have here?"

Linda rolled her eyes and kept her voice just above a whisper. "You are naïve, aren't you?"

I whispered back. "I don't understand."

"Listen," she said as a pounding on the front door commenced. She pointed the gun at my face. "Lie down. Face down. And not another sound."

I tried to hear the conversation between Jesse and Henry, but only heard muffled voices. Two minutes later, I heard Henry's Triumph fire to life again. *He was leaving me!*

"Get up," Linda hissed.

I sat, rubbing the back of my head and fighting a wave of nausea. "Jesse told me you were pretty." She seemed to be staring at my face. "Girl, you're flat gorgeous."

I wasn't sure it was a compliment. "How would Jesse have known anything about me? I'd never met him before today."

"You'd never met *him*," she said. "But he knows all about you."

"I don't understand."

She smirked. "You wouldn't. He told me you were self-absorbed."

I didn't know how to respond. I decided if I was going to get any helpful information, I might as well plunge straight ahead. "Is my husband helping your husband get drugs?"

"Maybe you're not as naïve as you seem."

"Is your husband blackmailing Henry? Henry wouldn't do something like this on his own."

The corner of her mouth teased upward. "And why not?"

I shrugged. "It's wrong. Henry wouldn't do it."

"It's wrong?" She forced a laugh. "As if you would know about that."

"Excuse me?"

"You're in no position to judge my Jesse. He's only looking out for me."

"By selling drugs? Do you know how many lives he's ruining?"

"Shut up," she said. "You're no better. In fact, you're worse."

"I'm not dealing drugs."

"OK, so that's not your particular sin. What about adultery?"

My mouth dropped open. "You know nothing about me."

She cursed me. "I know all about Jack, Wendi," she said, emphasizing my name.

What? Now I was completely baffled.

It must have shown on my expression, because Linda started to laugh. "I know you have a piano lesson every week and go sit at Starbucks for an hour together before Jack goes to his next lesson. You giggle," she said, wrinkling her nose. "You allow your hand to rest on his. You're teasing him, aren't you?" Her expression hardened. "Your daddy's a preacher. You disgust me."

I forced my mouth to close. "How do you know these things?"

"Jesse," she said. "He's observant."

"He's been following me?" I squinted at my captor. "Why?"

She offered a plastic smile. "He feels guilty."

"I don't get it."

She glanced over her shoulder towards the door. "Jesse was driving drunk the night he wrapped our car around a telephone pole. He got out with bruises. I ended up paralyzed from the waist down." She paused. "He blames your husband, 'cause he didn't pick up the fracture and no one protected my spinal cord when I had a fractured back."

"Sounds more like anger than guilt."

"You don't know my Jesse. He feels responsible for putting me in this chair. But he can't admit it. His guilt just bubbles out as anger." She paused. "And your husband just happens to be the natural target."

"So why does he know so much about me?"

"Because he dreams of getting even, of making your husband suffer the same loss as he has had." She shrugged as if it was a natural way to do business. "I suffered because of your husband. So he wants you to suffer."

"He killed Yolanda Pate."

"Was that the blonde in your bed? You're quick."

"He tried to kill me to get back at my husband?"

"Guilt makes you do all sorts of strange things."

My mind tried to close around this new information.

Jesse tried to kill me?

If he knew all about my routine with Jack, and his truck was the one that was involved in the hit-and-run, did Jesse intentionally run into Jack's car because he thought I would be with him? The way I'd been every week for the last two months?

A growing dread gripped my gut. *It's really true, then. Jack's accident was my fault.*

The door opened. Jesse held a small box in his hand and a broad grin on his face. "Looks like Dr. Stratford and I are back on speaking terms."

"What's that?" Linda asked.

Jesse lifted a small clear vial from the box. "Something new. A narcotic about ten times the potency of morphine."

I studied Linda for a moment. When I saw needle tracks in her arm, I began to understand her smile.

He opened the top drawer and removed a syringe.

"What are you doing?" Linda asked.

"Hey," he said, "You don't expect me to unleash this on UVa's campus without trying it myself, do you?"

"Not yet. What about her?" She pointed the gun at me.

"Let her go. She won't talk. We've got too much on her husband."

"You're insane," Linda said. "She'll sacrifice you, me, and Dr. Stratford without a second thought."

He shook his head. "I promised Dr. Stratford that I would keep my hands off of her."

"You told him she was here?"

"No!" Jesse stared at me. "It was when I visited him at his girlfriend's place," he said. He smiled, revealing a missing tooth right next to his front two top incisors. "He begged me to leave you alone. He said he wouldn't cooperate unless I promised." He laughed. "So I promised."

"It's too late for that," she said. "Kill her. He'll never know."

Linda looked out the window again. "How'd you get here? Where's your car?"

"Down the hill. Parked in the Exxon's parking lot."

"Give Jesse the keys." She kept the pistol leveled at my chest.

Jesse began to protest, but Linda shook her head. "Just go get her car."

"But Stratford will cut me off if he thinks we—"

"So make it look like an accident."

Jesse set down the little box of narcotics and nodded. He disappeared from the door only to return with a pair of handcuffs. "Hold out your hand!"

He forced my obedience and snapped the cuff around my right wrist and the other end around the metal bed frame.

With that, Jesse left the room and Linda followed. The door shut. I strained against the cuff and stared at its polished surface. It looked just like the ones that Chris Black carried. My mind raced ahead, and I wondered if the Anderses had friends within the PD that helped him do business.

I lay on the bed with my right hand above my head. *If Henry is helping this jerk get narcotics, how does it work? How does Anders end up with prescriptions that Henry writes for other people?*

Was this why the pill bottle was next to Yolanda Pate's body—Jesse was sending Henry a message?

In the other room, I could hear Linda giving Jesse instructions. "Wear gloves. Don't leave any prints in her car. You can drug her, and run her car into the reservoir up above Rebert's Dam."

God, help me. I stopped, my conscience assaulting me. *God, do you really care enough to help me? Do you really love messed up people like me?*

I sniffed, feeling helpless and afraid.

Yes, I felt like a hypocrite, but the urge to pray persisted. And that's when I realized that I did believe. I believed God was there. I did believe, at least I wanted to believe, that he loved me. And just then, thinking I was going to die, I understood that I needed him in my life.

It's not that I don't believe in you, God. I do believe. It's that I know I'm a disappointment to you. I know I've been a fake.

It was wrong of me to want to run away from you. What I really want is to stop feeling so guilty.

I thought about Jesse Anders. *Has he destroyed his life because of guilt?*

It's ironic, huh, God? Both Jesse and I feel the same kind of guilt. He put his wife in a wheelchair driving drunk. I feel responsible for my mother's condition.

Guilt had allowed Jesse to be manipulated by a bitter wife. Guilt had driven me into a plastic life that I hated.

Help me, God. I sniffed. *Help me to believe.*

I spent the next ten minutes alone, wondering if this was going to be my last hour. And that terrified me. I'd listened to enough of my father's sermons to know that death was only the beginning, and I knew I wasn't ready to meet God face to face. I had fences to mend. With Mom. With Dad. With Henry.

My prayers got shorter and more desperate. *Please, God, I'm not ready!*

When Jesse returned, I strained to hear their conversation through the closed door. It sounded as if I was going to get my first taste of illicit narcotic use, and not the good stuff that Henry had just delivered.

A minute later, Jesse appeared with what appeared to be a giant syringe. He emptied the entire thing into my thigh, right through my jeans, but not before I gave him a good kick in the chest and he dropped right down on top of me with his full body weight. I felt a sharp sting, then the sensation that my right leg was on fire.

Within a minute, my forehead started buzzing. My vision blurred. My eyelids felt as if they'd suddenly tripled in size. I felt warm. Euphoric.

Hey, this isn't so bad.

I felt tired. So tired, like I hadn't slept in a week and I just couldn't resist. *Goodbye, Henry. There'sss ssso much I would do differently ifff I only had...*

By the time Henry got home, Rene had tried Wendi's cell phone a dozen times. Rene was sitting at the kitchen table with her phone in her hand when Henry walked in.

"Is Wendi in the bedroom?" he asked.

"She's not here. She's been gone most of the day. Have you talked with her?"

"Only briefly. She came by the operating theatre." He shook his head. "Can you believe she took my Triumph out?"

"I'm afraid for her, Henry. It's like she's on a mission to prove her innocence or something."

"What?" Henry placed his helmet on the table and sat down. He seemed to be studying his hands or something.

Rene found herself wondering just where Henry's hands had been that day. *Inside a few bodies, most likely*, she thought.

When he looked up, she could see fear in his eyes. "The police left messages at my office. They are looking for her. They wanted to know where she was."

"What do we do?"

"Wendi will figure everything out. She always does," he said. He stood and retrieved an imported beer from the refrigerator. "What's for supper?"

Rene stood up and held up her hands in frustration. She put down her phone. "Have you been listening to me? Wendi has been missing all day. She isn't answering her phone. She's wanted by the police."

"Have you called them? Maybe they have her." He casually sipped from the green bottle.

"Aren't you worried?"

He shook his head. "No." He walked towards the back deck. "Wendi's not guilty of anything," he said, "except trusting me."

Rene followed him onto the deck. "Henry, what's going on? Talk to me."

He sipped his beer and looked out over the wooded hill leading down to Route 29. He didn't look at Rene when he answered. "Wendi is the best thing that ever happened to me. She rescued me when I was bound for a boring academic life."

Rene touched his arm. "Henry, you should tell her. I think she's forgotten how wonderful she is."

He turned to face his sister-in-law. "The funny thing is, she's so good at putting on a happy face, that she's forgotten how beautiful she is without it."

Henry tilted his head back and drained the bottle before heaving it off the deck into the woods.

Rene stepped back. "Henry!"

Henry walked back into the house, pausing as he passed her to rest his hand on her shoulder. "I'm off on an errand."

Rene stood on the deck, confused by his demeanor, and equally concerned about his apparent lack of distress over Wendi's disappearance.

He stopped at the front closet and put on his leather jacket. Then he left, helmet in hand, and whistling the theme to *Rocky*.

My first conscious thought was that I was already dead. I was in my casket. But it was cold, and there wasn't any padding. My head hurt, and I had the vague sensation that I was floating. For a few moments, I collected my wits and lifted my hand into the darkness above me. I rubbed my wrists. The cuffs were gone. I was in a small area covered by stiff carpeting. *The trunk of Henry's Mercedes.*

I listened to the road noise, aware of how much louder the ride was from the trunk. In another moment, I started repeating my desperation prayers. *Please, God. I don't want to die.*

It occurred to me that Jesse Anders must be taking me to stage my own suicide. I'd heard his wife giving him instructions. *If anyone is going to believe I drove into the reservoir, he's going to have to take me out of the trunk. And that will be my chance to escape.*

I felt the car turning and listened to the sound of gravel beneath the tires. *He's turned onto Reservoir Road. He's heading up towards Rebert's Dam.*

We drove for another five minutes before Jesse slowed. Then I heard the crunch of gravel and felt the lurch of the car as it crawled forward over some sort of low barrier. *A curb? Is there a curb bordering the water?*

Then everything became still. The engine was still running. In a moment, I heard the clink of the electronic trunk release. I was just thinking that I should run when I heard Jesse's voice and I froze, feigning unconsciousness.

"OK, Wendi. Time for you to drive."

He pulled me into his arms and over his shoulder. My limbs felt clumsy and uncoordinated, so staying limp in his arms came naturally. He dropped me in the front seat and buckled my seatbelt. He didn't bother to position my hands on the wheel. He merely threw the car into drive and slammed the door.

I opened my eyes to experience the last light of day. I had little time to react. I wanted to grab the wheel and try to steer back up the bank, but the water's edge was rapidly approaching and the bank was too steep. The Mercedes picked up speed and rushed down the grassy slope, bouncing as the incline steepened. I flailed for the window control and tried one last prayer. *Help!*

I lunged forward as the front end of the Mercedes plunged into the water. Momentarily stunned, I realized the airbag had deployed. The car bobbed. We were floating! Water started pouring into my window. Cold water.

And then the car tilted, tipping forward. I took a deep breath and hoped Jesse Anders wouldn't wait around long after the car disappeared. With my lungs full, I braced myself against the cold and felt my head slipping under the water.

ChaPteR 28

I squirmed through the open window into the cool water, swimming beneath the surface with strong kicks back towards the shore, but on a diagonal trajectory. I wanted the cover of the marsh grass, which grew just to the right of where the Mercedes had entered. When I thought my lungs would burst, I made two more strokes and closed my fist around wet cattails. I allowed my head to surface just so my eyes and nose were exposed. My breathing seemed to me a siren, so I tilted my head to allow my mouth above the surface, gulping air with abandon. Night was fast approaching, with the sun nestled well below the tall pines that rimmed the reservoir to the west. The air seemed to hang cool and close to my face, delivering a marshy fragrance that reminded me of mold. I silently peered back to the location where the Mercedes had disappeared, swallowed by the murky water. A circle of light highlighted the appearance of a stream of bubbles. I stared back at the source of the light and saw only a bright spot that scanned from side to side, Jesse Anders, no doubt, scanning the surface to document my departure.

I sunk deeper into the reeds to hide from view. Anders watched from shore until the bubbling stopped, and then, apparently satisfied that I had drowned, turned his flashlight beam away and moved on.

It was only after Anders had moved on that I began to feel cold. Bone-chilling cold. But I was determined to stay hidden for a few minutes before exiting the water and figuring out my next step.

Inwardly, I felt strangely invigorated. Alive. Grateful. I had called out to God and he had answered me. "Thank you, Father," I whispered. "Thank you."

H enry downshifted the Triumph and leaned low through a sweeping left turn, before rolling on the throttle and watching his headlight dance across the guardrail posts. A right turn followed. He rolled with the cycle, enjoying a new sense of freedom. *Careful*, he chided himself, *everything has to go according to the plan.*

Just a few more miles.

Henry lifted his left hand and felt in the pocket of his leather jacket, closing his hand around a small pocket watch. "Wendi," he whispered into his full-face helmet, "I love you."

He slowed and loosened the helmet strap.

He passed a yellow sign bearing a black U-shaped arrow, a warning to slow down.

Henry took a deep breath and twisted the throttle, rocketing the cycle onward into the night.

Jesse Anders waved his flashlight towards the oncoming headlights of his wife's van. The vehicle pulled to a stop beside him as the driver's window lowered. His wife wasn't smiling. "Get in," she said.

"It's done," he said. "What took you so long?"

"Shut up," she said. "I knew you'd feel like celebrating, so I prepared a sample of Dr. Stratford's newest." She tossed a small paper bag towards her husband as he climbed into the captain's chair beside her.

"There's a deserted cul-de-sac just beyond the dam." He looked in the bag, which contained the syringes and two stretchy rubber tourniquets, and smiled. "Let's party."

He watched as Linda maneuvered the van, a specially equipped handicapped one with hand controls. She amazed him. Although she hadn't let her injury keep her from driving, he knew it had robbed her of so much. He quieted the urge to apologize. Again.

"Let's go home. It's safer there."

"It's a beautiful night, baby. We can start in the van and move our party out onto the grass by the reservoir. The stars are going to be awesome."

"I don't want to drive after I've taken a hit."

"So we'll wait. Nothing says we can't stay all night out here if we have to." He lifted a syringe and turned on the overhead light. "Besides, I don't think we should use this all at once. If this stuff is half as potent as the doc says, we'd better take it slow."

"Turn off that light. I don't want anyone to see."

"There is no one else around."

She huffed, but cooperated, slowing to a stop at the end of a deserted cul-de-sac. She seemed anxious to relax. As soon as they were stopped, even before shutting off the engine or headlights, she grabbed a tourniquet and stretched it around her arm, holding it tight in her teeth to distend the vein near the elbow. She felt the bulge of the vein one time before plunging the needle into her arm and slowly pushing in one cc.

Jesse hurried to join his wife in a bit of private celebration and wrapped the rubber tourniquet tight around his upper arm.

Shivering, I dragged myself through the mud and soggy cattail grass at the edge of the reservoir. I needed to get to a phone. Step, squish, step, squish, I slogged onto the slippery mud along the bank. I watched as a set of headlights approached and passed. I yelled, but I was too far down the bank to signal or be heard.

I crawled up the steep slope to the road's edge and looked back towards the water. Henry's Mercedes was gone. *Hopefully, he'll be so glad to see me that he won't care about his car.*

I looked up and down the road, pausing to watch a vehicle turn at the end of the road and face its headlights back in my direction. I decided to ask for help. Perhaps the occupants would have a cell phone and I could call Henry. I walked towards the headlights, feeling the water slosh between my toes within my Nike running shoes.

Jesse was just beginning to feel a delightful warmth and a buzzing sensation in his forehead when Linda's arms jerked forward. He watched as she had some sort of seizure and then slumped forward against the steering column. The horn began to sound.

He looked forward to see a figure walking towards them. It was a woman, shielding her eyes from the headlights. After a moment, Jesse realized it was Wendi Stratford. His head was spinning. The drug was wonderful, but he needed to fight its effect for a moment and take care of business.

He nudged his wife. *I hope it's a good trip, darling.*

Jesse grabbed a handgun from beneath the seat and opened the door.

I approached the car by walking in the road. I was soaked, but I didn't care. I was alive and determined to get back to my family for a second chance at getting relationships right.

From thirty feet, I could see that it was a van. *Great, probably some teens out here parking.* I walked forward. "Hello?"

The horn began to blare. I startled. *Goofy kids!*

Just then the passenger door swung open and I recognized Jesse Anders as he raised a pistol in my direction. I gasped and sprinted sideways to the corner of the van.

The pistol fired, missing wide to my left. Jesse took one step toward me, then dropped to the ground, where his arms and legs seemed to quiver for a few seconds before he was still. I peered into the car. Linda was slumped over the steering wheel, depressing the horn. I opened the door and grabbed the shoulder of her denim jacket, pulling her to the side. She tilted out of the captain's chair and hung suspended in the shoulder-and-waist harness. Her eyes were open but unseeing.

I quickly turned my attention back to Jesse. His body was still, the handgun lying on the pavement beside him. I scurried to his side and lifted the gun. "Get up!" I shouted, pointing the gun at his head.

His body remained motionless. I nudged him with my foot. "Get up!"

I knelt and rolled him over and felt for a pulse. I shook my head. I didn't understand. I walked back to the van and reexamined Linda. She too was pulseless, her face hanging from her neck at an odd angle and her eyes open and staring into eternity.

Whatever had killed Jesse and Linda had done so rapidly. I backed out of the van and studied Jesse's form, spread eagle on the pavement. In a moment, I saw myself. This was the end of a life of guilt. His guilt had pushed him into a tireless pursuit of revenge, ultimately taking a bitter turn into drug abuse and crime. Where would my life of guilt lead me?

CHAPTER 29

Thirty minutes later, I was huddled in the back of a county sheriff's car, sipping lukewarm coffee and listening to the drone of the police radio.

When Chris Black from Charlottesville PD showed up, his demeanor was less than comforting. He sat on the seat beside me. "Tell me your theory."

"I've been all over this with the county deputy over there," I said, tilting my head towards the van.

"Tell me."

"Overdose," I answered. "There was drug paraphernalia in the car beside Linda. Her arm is bleeding from a recent needle stick. She must have come up here to pick up Jesse after he sent me off into the reservoir in Henry's Mercedes."

Chris nodded and put in a call to the medical examiner.

I sat quietly, and purposefully didn't disclose where the Anderses had received their most recent supply of narcotics. I needed to talk to Henry before I said anything about that.

When Chris got off the phone, I cradled the Styrofoam cup beneath my chin. "Have you gotten through to Henry?"

He shook his head. "I'm going to need to have your blood drawn for some tests. We need a sample to figure out exactly what Anders injected you with." He paused. "You talked to your sister?"

I nodded. "She's coming to get me."

The detective looked away. "Charlottesville PD has been looking for you all day."

I shrugged.

He touched my arm, and I instinctively pulled away. "Don't play games with me, Wendi. What'd you do, have your sister drive your car to lead my men off scent?"

"She warned me that your boys were looking for me." My eyes bore in on his face, which was dimly lit by the dome light in the cruiser. "I've done nothing illegal, Chris. I had to do something, if only to clear my name. So I spent the day looking at the evidence for myself."

His voice sliced with sarcasm. "And?"

I decided to tell the truth. I knew I wasn't guilty. If Henry was hiding something, I suspected that Anders was involved. "Cindy Swanson was dead before Henry hit her, wasn't she?"

"You tell me."

"Your investigators misinterpreted the accident scene. The skid marks on the driveway were acceleration marks, not brake marks. Cindy's autopsy showed evidence of a neck fracture in addition to multiple skull fractures, but there was a problem: the skull fractures appeared to be postmortem."

"So Henry's story was a cover-up?"

"That's my theory." I sipped my coffee. "So if I was guilty, why would I tell you these things?"

The detective stayed quiet. My instinct had paid off. Chris didn't know what to make of my honesty.

When he spoke again, I could hear the suspicion in his voice. "When I called you that night and told you of Henry's accident, you already knew, didn't you?"

"That's ridiculous."

"He was having an affair. You were jealous."

"If I was covering up an accident, I would know how to do it."

"And I'm to assume Henry wouldn't?"

I shook my head. "Henry should have known." I had a private theory about that, one I wasn't ready to share with Chris. Henry and I had talked through so many accident scenarios that I knew he would know how to set it up. My only conclusion was that Henry intentionally left me a subtle clue, something no one else would recognize. Henry was sending a message he knew I would receive and interpret, even when the police got it wrong. *I know Henry. He's not capable of murder, so why would he disguise Cindy's death to make it look like an accident?*

I remembered something Anders said. "Wait," I said. "Jesse Anders may have had something to do with this."

"You think you can pin this on the dead guy?"

I nodded. "He said something to me today, something about visiting Henry at his girlfriend's house. I'm willing to concede that Henry may have been having an affair, so perhaps Anders had something to do with Cindy's death."

Chris grunted. This was obviously a new thought for him. "I'll need to talk to Henry."

Chris left me alone until the ME arrived and drew my blood. "Look," I said, as he let me out of the patrol car. "I've got to get changed. Come by the house tonight if you need anything else from me."

He paused. "Don't run, Wendi. We'll have more questions for you tomorrow."

I looked up to see my sister, grateful for the excuse to ignore Chris. Rene hugged me, enveloping me into a bear hug that helped squeeze the water from my shirt into hers. She laughed. "Thank God you're OK."

I sniffed. "Let's go home. Where's Henry?"

"Don't know. He left home on his cycle, saying he had an errand to do." She hesitated as we got into her Saturn. "I'm scared for him, Wendi. Henry was acting strange."

My chest tightened. If facing death had done anything, it had made me take a hard look at the path I'd chosen. "I need to talk with him." I looked out the window. "I'm going to tell him everything."

I could see Rene nod her approval from the corner of my eye. She'd started down a reconciliation sidewalk this week herself. I was determined to follow. I was going to shed my fakery regardless of the cost.

"Only Henry?"

I took a deep breath. "No. Mom and Dad, too."

"What happened to you tonight?"

"I told you on the phone. Jesse Anders tried to kill me. He intentionally drugged me and strapped me into Henry's car and sent me bon voyage into the water."

"I'm not looking for the facts. What happened to you?"

I sighed and kept staring out the window. "Maybe running away isn't the best way to solve my problems."

That night, I stayed up waiting for Henry and rehearsed my repentance. *It's all my fault, Henry. Things will be different. I want to be a real Christian. I can't sit in the back row and smile like I'm a saint when inside I'm not a Christian at all.*

Henry, I'm seeing now that I was wrong in pushing God away. In pushing you away. Pretending to be something I'm not—and for what? I want things to be different.

I fell asleep on the couch hugging a throw pillow and whispering Henry's name until sometime after two in the morning.

I awoke at three and four, convinced I'd heard the Triumph, then looked at a calendar held by a magnet on our refrigerator. I'd checked it before, but wanted to be sure. I traced my finger down the days. Henry wasn't supposed to be on call, but it would be just like him to have traded call days and forgotten to tell me.

I tried paging him, but he wouldn't reply.

It wouldn't be the first time he spent the night operating and failed to tell me.

I called the UVa Hospital operating rooms. "No," a cheery female voice responded, "Dr. Stratford hasn't been here all night."

I fought back a rising tide of panic. I paced the front room and lifted the curtain back from the window, staring into the blackness. A few minutes later, I brushed back my tears and washed my face in the kitchen sink, paced some more, and dripped strong Ethiopian coffee. I felt helpless. I wanted to do something, anything, but without knowing what was wrong, I could only pace and pray. I walked back to the living room and traced my hand along the piano. Suddenly I wanted to sell it, give it away. It reminded me of my foray into unfaithfulness.

My mind ran ahead of me. Was Henry in an accident? Did his disappearance have anything to do with Jesse Anders? With a bit of trepidation, I picked up the phone and called Chris Black.

Chris picked up after four rings, his voice heavy with sleep. "Black."

"Chris, it's Wendi," I began, trying not to sound too alarmed. "Henry is missing. He didn't come home last night."

"It's still night, Wendi," he huffed. "I'm sure he's alright. You know Henry. He's probably in the theatre."

I groaned. "I'm not joking, Chris. Henry isn't in the OR. I've called. Rene said he left last night on his Triumph. Something's up. I want a search."

"He hasn't been missing long enough," he said, exhaling sharply into the phone. "But I tell you what, I'll tell the patrol boys to look out for him, OK?"

I hesitated. "Chris."

He waited while I thought. "What is it, Wendi?"

"It's just, well, I think Henry might have been mixed up with this Anders guy."

"What makes you say that?"

"When I started investigating Anders' truck wreck, Henry told me to stay away from him. He told me Anders was a druggie." I paused again before plunging ahead. "Look, Henry showed up at the Anderses' place when they were holding me there."

"Henry? He was there? You didn't tell me—"

"I wanted to talk to Henry first. Look, I'm sorry, but I was scared about what it might mean for Henry. He showed up and gave Jesse Anders some narcotics. Linda held a gun on me the entire time, so I wouldn't alert Henry to the fact that I was there."

"Hmmm. I wonder if the drug Henry gave them was what they used in the van."

The thought had occurred to me, too. I suspect that the Anderses were pushing Henry beyond the limits. Maybe he knew that Anders had tried to kill me and he was trying to protect me. Maybe Henry was exacting his own quiet revenge. "Can't you get your men to look for him?"

I listened to him sigh. "We'll find him. Sounds like we need to ask Henry a few questions."

"Thanks."

I set the phone down in its cradle. Maybe I should look for Henry myself. But where would he have gone?

After all that's happened, could Henry be leaving me?

Minutes followed and turned into hours. The sun came up. The police began to search, but Henry wasn't to be found. Henry didn't report to give his scheduled medical school lecture, didn't show up for hospital rounds, and left his operative cases untouched. A night out operating without calling me was one thing, but this was something else entirely.

I spent from ten until two in Chris Black's office, going over every detail of my week. He still seemed fixated on whether I had something to do with Cindy Swanson's death. He leaned forward and lifted a burger out of a McDonald's paper bag on his desk. He unwrapped it with meticulous care. An image of Henry unwrapping a sterile instrument flashed through my mind.

He slurped his Pepsi through a long straw and spoke through a quiet belch. "This whole disappearance of Henry is quite convenient for you, isn't it?"

I wanted to dab the ketchup from his cheek. Either that or slap him, but the latter didn't seem like what I should do, given that he seemed so suspicious of everything I did. I picked up a paper napkin from his desk and handed it to him. "Convenient?"

He swiped at the ketchup. "Mmm. Thanks. Sure," he said. "Henry's probably the only one around who knows exactly how Cindy Swanson died. Last night, you tell me Henry dropped by Anders' place, so you know I'm anxious to talk to him. What'd you do, warn him to leave town, then call me and tell me he never came home?"

I was flabbergasted. "Why you—"

I stopped when I looked up at the chief of police, Ed Mosby, who'd just entered Chris's office. Mosby tipped his head towards me, a gesture of hello, and addressed his detective. "Anything new on Dr. Stratford?"

"Nope. Seems like he's vanished," Chris said, looking at me. "And that leaves us without anyone to corroborate your story that Jesse Anders told you that he went to Cindy Swanson's house."

"I had nothing to do with Henry's disappearance. You can ask Rene. Henry left home while I was still being held by the Anderses. He never came home last night. Rene can vouch for that as well."

I shifted in my seat, feeling anxious and angry. How could he continue to accuse me of wrongdoing?

"Send a forensics team to Cindy's apartment. And this time, assume she died somewhere other than under the wheel of Henry's Mercedes. There has to be some evidence somewhere."

"Proving she died before Henry struck her won't tell us who killed her, will it?"

I looked at Ed Mosby. "Will you listen to another theory?"

The chief sat. "Sure."

"According to Linda Anders, Jesse blamed Henry for Linda's being in the wheelchair. They claim Henry misread an X-ray of her spine and she was paralyzed as a result."

The duo looked at me, feigning interest.

"Linda said Jesse was out to harm me in order to make Henry suffer like Jesse did." I paused, making sure I made eye contact with Chris. "Remember the blue paint on the truck grille of Jesse's?"

"Go on."

"Jesse had been stalking me, watching everything I did. He knew I always went to Starbucks with Jack Renner after our piano lesson. Jesse knew exactly when I'd be on the road and ran the red light in order to T-bone the car just where I'd be."

Ed touched the top of his silver hair as if checking to see if each bristle stood appropriately upright. Apparently satisfied, he looked at me. "But you weren't there."

"But by routine, I usually was."

"What's this have to do with Cindy Swanson?"

"Jesse was trying to injure me, kill me perhaps. When he learned his plan had failed, he got even more desperate and killed Yolanda Pate in my bed, thinking it was me. He even left Henry a calling card, a bottle of narcotics that Henry had prescribed."

"How is that a calling card?"

"Henry must have been helping Anders get narcotics for personal use and distribution. I think Anders was blackmailing Henry, making him cooperate."

"So where does Cindy Swanson come in?"

"Eventually, Jesse realizes his mistake and gets even more desperate to show Henry that he means business, that he can control the lives of those Henry apparently loved. He shows up at Swanson's apartment, kills her, and forces Henry to cover it up."

"Why would Henry do that?"

I shrugged. "Blackmail? Perhaps Henry was convinced it was the only way to protect me from this madman. I heard Jesse tell his wife that he promised Henry that he wouldn't hurt me when he was at Henry's girlfriend's place." I paused, letting my theory hang in the air. It all made sense. In fact, it was the simple solution that Ockham's razor demanded. All the crazy events of the week could be explained by Jesse's desire to get back at Henry and control him.

I watched as Ed and Chris exchanged looks. After a minute, Chris wiped his mouth with a napkin and stood up from his desk. "Why don't you go home, Wendi? We'll find you if we have any other questions. Or a need for any more of your crazy theories."

I stayed quiet, but let my eyes search the face of the chief of police. Maybe, just maybe, I'd found another ally in the department.

Ed Mosby nodded. "You need to stay at home by the phone. We'll keep looking for Henry. Let us know if he shows up or calls."

"Sure," I mumbled. "Sure."

As I was leaving, Ed called out, "Wendi, how did you ever come up with that theory?"

I smiled. "It's what I do."

Days passed. Evidence trickled in. A search of Henry's office turned up a definite link with Jesse Anders. State pharmacy records revealed hundreds of extra narcotics prescriptions turned in at dozens of different drugstores across the state. Early interviews supported the idea that Henry wrote the prescriptions for real people, who then turned the drugs over to Anders for a small percentage of the profit. Anders, in turn, provided narcotics to the University of Virginia campus and fattened his wallet.

A forensics team spent hours in Cindy Swanson's apartment, discovering evidence of Cindy's blood on the floor in the front room close to the door. It was likely that Cindy died right there, possibly from a violent kick or punch that fractured her cervical spine, ending her ability to breathe. The autopsy reports on Linda and Jesse Anders confirmed they died of a narcotics overdose, but another substance had also been found: succinylcholine, a powerful neuromuscular blocker used to paralyze patients for surgery. Examination of the remaining vials of Fentanyl that Henry delivered to the Anderses revealed that each one was tainted with the paralyzing drug. My suspicion was that Henry acted outside of the law out of fear for my life. Perhaps he knew that the Anderses couldn't resist using the drug on themselves before they distributed it to the university students.

Day by day I waited for word on Henry, paced, and drank too much Ethiopian java. By Sunday afternoon, knowing I'd find my parents together at the nursing home, I whispered a prayer and decided it was time for transparency. I was ready to show my parents my real self and accept their judgment.

I found Mom in her wheelchair and Dad reading to her from the book of Galatians.

"Knock, knock," I said, gently rapping on the door.

They looked up together, their faces bright. "Wendi."

I sat on Mom's bed and sniffed. My eyes were brimming with tears before I got out the first words of my confession. "I've been such a phony. I've been nothing but a fake since I was a teenager. I've acted like a Christian, but that's all I was: an actress."

I brushed away a tear and looked at my mom. "I have to tell Daddy, Mom." I looked at my father and then at the floor. "I'm the reason Mom is in this chair. I was pregnant and Mom was taking me to get an abortion when we had the accident. We would have never been in the car that day if it weren't for me. It's all my fault," I sobbed.

I felt my father's hand on my shoulder. "I know all about it, Wendi."

I jerked upright. "You knew?"

He nodded his head. "Wendi, you were young. We share your guilt, honey. Your mother was involved in covering your affair and I was guilty of not being there for my family. I paraded you around in front of the church, my perfect little girls." My dad's shoulders were pitched forward in defeat. I looked at the lines in his face, pain etched in each one. "I failed you. You missed out on the gospel of grace. You tried to be perfect without the cross."

My mom's hand joined my father's on my back as I leaned forward, letting his words wash over my soul. "I was so wrong, Wendi," she said. "But you're not responsible for putting me in this chair. This chair has taught me so much. It was God's toughest grace to me, a way for me to understand that he loves me regardless of my abilities." She patted my back. "Do you understand? Here in this chair, there is little I can do but *receive*. Undeservedly. Without merit. That's grace," she whispered, now crying with me.

After a minute, I collected myself, gathering my runaway emotions beneath a pseudocalm. "Something's happened to me. Last week, I was convinced the answer to the disconnect between my skin and my heart was to change the part of me that the world couldn't see: I was determined to escape my hypocrisy by acting out the careless passions that I felt inside." I took my father's hand. "Now I know the real answer to my discontent was to find the reality of what my lips were confessing, instead of following my heart."

My mother prompted. "And?"

"I discovered faith."

My father smiled. "Tell us."

"When I was facing death, locked up in the Anderses' bedroom, I marveled over how naturally I cried to God for help. It was as if suddenly I just knew he was there, waiting for me to believe in him." I halted, feeling my voice threatening to close. "Suddenly I just knew everything I'd heard was true. I believed he loved me."

I listened to my mother's quiet sobs and watched as my father embraced her. After another minute, I realized they were both staring off through the window. I stood and followed their gaze. They seemed to be looking down the hill at the little chapel. The light was falling, illuminating the cross.

"That's it, isn't it?" I said, placing my hands on my parents' shoulders. "The cross. That's what I missed all along."

My mother's voice was just above a whisper. "It changes everything."

I smiled. A real smile. It was something that bubbled out of me as natural as rain and sun causing tulips to bloom. I was forgiven. I'd looked at the cross and seen something other than condemnation for the first time: *Grace!*

I touched my cheeks, feeling the muscles that scrunched up the corners of my mouth into a wide grin, and marveled at the reality of it all. This was the real deal. Out with condemnation. In with things too wonderful to understand. Down with artificial sweeteners and plastic expressions. In with chocolate and forgiveness.

CHAPTER 30

Trevor Anderson had been on the Appalachian Trail for eighteen days. He was running low on Snickers bars and in need of a shower. He unfolded his map and took out his compass. He knew there was a lodge at Big Meadows, but that was more than a day's walk. He sighed and looked at his compass. "There," he muttered to his black Labrador Retriever, "Skyline Drive should be just over that rise. Let's hitchhike down to the lodge, grab some grub and a shower, and catch another ride back." He scratched the dog behind the ears and smiled. It was a good plan.

He folded the trail map and stuffed it in the outer zip pocket of his backpack, lifted the pack, and started off the path towards the road. After a half mile, he heard the sounds of traffic drifting down what appeared to be a series of rugged cliffs. *Crud*, he thought, *I'm going to have to find another way up. The approach here is too steep.* He looked up at the light as it came through the canopy of pines far above his head and sighed. "Come on, Sicily, let's try a bit further down."

But Sicily, his black Lab, had other plans. Up the embankment towards the base of the cliffs she ran, ignoring his pleas for her to return.

That's odd. It's like she's on the scent of something.

Trevor hiked on behind her, stepping from boulder to boulder. That's when he saw a glint of light. There was something shiny at the base of a tree. He picked up what looked like a twisted piece of chrome, a broken mirror of some sort.

As he puzzled over the mirror, Sicily barked incessantly, as a hound bays at a coon up a tree. Trevor jumped up onto a nearby boulder to see what the commotion was about. And that's when he saw the crumpled red motorcycle.

He rushed forward. And knelt by the cycle, a massive metal rhinoceros of red and chrome. Trevor looked up. Sicily was on point, her gaze away from him, in a thicket of blackberry bramble.

Trevor gasped. There was a body in the woods.

When I arrived home, a Charlottesville PD patrol car was in the driveway. Inside, I found a young officer talking with Rene. Their expressions told me more than I wanted to know. I felt my gut tighten.

"Wendi," Rene began timidly. "They've found Henry."

I didn't want to ask. But I needed to ask. I put my hand on the back of Henry's leather easy chair. "Is he—well, is he—" the words clumped in my throat—"dead?"

I watched as Rene traded glances with the officer. I knew from the look they gave me.

The officer nodded. "I'm awfully sorry, ma'am."

I felt weak. Seven days ago, I wanted nothing but escape from my marriage, my husband, and my perfect life. Now, I just wanted a chance to tell Henry everything. "No," I whispered, finding my way into the leather chair. "No."

Rene moved to my side, but I wanted none of her comfort. I shook my head. "Where? Where did they find him?"

"Skyline Drive. Apparently, a car crossed the midline into his path. His cycle struck a guardrail. He and his bike were found seventy-five feet down the side of a steep drop-off." His voice was steady. "There was no way to see him from the road. A hiker saw his red motorcycle this afternoon and investigated."

"Henry," I said, trying not to cry. I looked at Rene. "He loved that motorcycle. I guess he just wanted some space. He used to ride up there after demanding cases to clear his mind."

I cried, not caring that the officer was watching. After a minute, I blew my nose and stood up. "I want to know exactly where they found him."

The next day, I spent two and a half hours examining and photographing the site of Henry's accident.

Rene stood by me patiently, occasionally asking questions about my findings, items I preferred not to share with her.

From the position of the bike and the location where they'd found Henry's body, I could calculate his speed.

I studied the skid marks on the road. A set of car tire marks indeed crossed the midline. In fact, the car skid ran all the way across the road and dug up the patch of clover off the shoulder on Henry's side of the road. A second set of skid marks, apparently made by the Triumph, ran right up to and stopped at the guardrail.

The guardrail was dented, and a bit of red paint documented the impact.

Apparently, and according to the police report, Henry had made an evasive action to avoid collision with the driver of an unnamed car, slammed his brakes, struck the guardrail and launched himself and the Triumph off the road, down the embankment.

Apparently. But by the time I finished my site investigation, I was convinced that Henry was again talking to me.

I thought back to the way he'd set up Cindy Swanson's "accident." He knew I'd pick up the subtle clues there, even if his efforts were sophomoric and simple. Here, after looking around, I realized Henry was after a deception at a whole new level. This was premeditated, pure and simple, and way out of the league of the on-the-spot thinking Henry had done on the night of Cindy Swanson's death.

The motorcycle skid marks leading to the guardrail were heaviest just in front of the railing, evidence that this too was an acceleration skid, made with the cycle throttling away from the guardrail, not a braking skid heading into the railing.

I confirmed my suspicions later that day, when I went to the impound lot where they'd put Henry's Mercedes after retrieving it from the reservoir up above Rebert's Dam. I took out a large flathead screwdriver and ran it between the wheel and the edge of the tire. As I suspected, there were fragments of clover, evidence of a significant lateral torque applied to the wheels, just as one might see if the car was forced into a sideways skid through a clover patch. The lateral torque opens up the space between the wheel and the tire, allowing the trapping of grass or other material in the gap. I measured the distance between the wheels. It matched the skid marks left in the road by the car that had supposedly run dear Henry off into the guardrail. My husband had committed suicide and set it up to look like an accident.

What I didn't understand completely was why. I suspected that Henry had gotten roped into a deception by the Anderses, and when Jesse went off and tried to kill me, Henry took the law into his own hands. I suspected he was protecting me when he laced the Anderses' narcotics with a paralyzing agent. I supposed Henry didn't feel like he could turn in the Anderses to the law without implicating himself. And Henry was way too proud for that.

But I wouldn't share my findings with anyone. I owed my silence to Henry. He deserved to be remembered as the fine surgeon he was, a man who was killed by the carelessness of another driver. But I knew better.

It wasn't until a week later that I understood a bit more about the complexity of the man I called my husband, and had to swallow another clue that Henry intended one way for the world and another entirely for me. It was a clue that told the world that all was happy between us. This was his final goodbye. To the world, he died a hero, a man with one love, his precious bride. To me, well, Henry was a wonderful guy. I owed him so much more than I gave him, and I bear responsibility for sending him over the edge.

I was reading the mail on a Saturday afternoon when the doorbell rang. It had become a routine. Coffee, a mountain of Kleenex, and a date with Henry's fan mail. "He saved my life." "He gave us back our daughter." "I was never so grateful to anyone as to your husband for the compassion he showed."

I brushed a tear from my cheek and set aside a letter, cradling it gently for a moment because of the treasure it was to me. I walked to the foyer and opened the door to an old friend, Sig Eichmann.

He tipped his hat. In spite of his lifelong analysis of some of humanity's most gruesome horrors, Sig remained a consummate gentleman. "Good afternoon, Wendi."

I smiled, happy to see my old mentor. "What brings you here?"

A soberness came to his face, bumping his smile away. "I'm so sorry about Henry."

I nodded. It had been a week. I still didn't know how to respond.

"I thought you'd be curious about my findings."

"You know me."

He opened his briefcase, a worn leather satchel that documented evil and injury. "I've made you a copy of my report. Read it if you like. Burn it if you need to. It's all routine, nothing surprising really."

I set the report on the kitchen table. Sig followed me in. "Coffee?"

"No thanks," he said. "I really can't stay. I've left Carol at the international grocery store."

"Sure."

He cleared his throat and reached into his pocket. "I've brought you something else." He held up something that glinted in the light. A pocket watch. Etched with a heart. "Henry was carrying this when he died. I thought you should have it."

My hand trembled as I received it. *Oh, Henry.* I turned it over in my hand and pressed a little release button on the side, popping the lid and looking inside. A small photograph of my face had been pressed into the little chamber. I recognized it immediately. It was the pocket watch I'd given Jack.

"Where did you get this?" My voice carried an accusatory tone I wished to disguise.

He looked confused. "Henry," he said. "I examined his body and his clothing. This was in his pocket."

I swallowed hard. I couldn't process this in front of Sig. "Th-thanks," I stammered.

We stood quietly for a moment as my fingers whitened around the metal object in my hand.

The moment was awkward for me, but Sig seemed to let it pass as evidence of my grief. He stepped back to the front door, excusing himself.

"Sig," I called to him. "Thank you for this."

"Sure," he said, letting himself out the front door.

I paced the house, wondering how I'd forgotten the silly little watch. I'd given it to Jack. I'd seen him put it carefully away and promise it would be our secret.

So what happened to it?

I knew what happened to you when you hit the emergency room after a trauma. I had been on the receiving end of the work-up. Most people know the ABC's, the Airway, Breathing, and Circulation of resuscitation, but few people know about D and E, Disability and Exposure. Henry must have found it during the exam. Perhaps he took it off and was going to give it to Jack when he recovered. *But then he must have looked inside and seen me.* I felt a rush of shame. *Henry knew all along. He knew about my relationship with Jack, and yet he went on caring for both of us just the same.*

Was it my unfaithfulness that drove him to seek solace in the arms of his resident?

"Henry," I whispered, clutching the watch. "Forgive me."

The revelation hit me hard. I may have thought I was fooling everyone, but Henry had read me like an open book. My plastic smiles may have satisfied the curiosity of others, but my husband knew the truth.

He carried the watch, knowing that anyone who saw would know that I was his love. Leave it to Henry to preserve my dignity in the public eye. He knew me so well.

"I've changed, Henry," I spoke softly. "I'm not the same girl who wanted to run away."

That's when the irony struck me in force. Rather than expose me as unfaithful, he allowed everyone else to see something on the surface that would look right to the world, knowing all along that on the inside, I was hiding a life of sin. Ultimately, Henry had died to cover our shame. Right as I was coming to grips with my façade, Henry had used it one more time to protect me.

I was tempted to despair, drawn to wallow in the guilt that had become my copilot. But I knew this was the way of the old Wendi. I knew I was guilty. But I also believed that someone had paid the price for my sin in the ultimate sacrifice. Because of the cross, I would never again look upon my failures as a stimulus to run away from God. Because of the cross, I could face my sin, and run to the source of grace.

I took a deep breath and started to pray.

CHAPTER 31

A month later, my life had fallen back into a predictable hum. Rene decided to stay at my urging, at least until her baby was born, *and then*, I thought, *who knows?* I'd begun to consult again. Chris Black even seemed to be interested in my opinion, and I let the memory of his accusations drift away, covered by the miles we'd traveled as friends before my fateful week of misery.

I was about to leave the house, on my way to investigate an accident near Harrisonburg on I–81. A truck carrying a kabillion Rocco turkeys had overturned on an entry ramp. My doorbell rang just as I reached the front door.

I opened it to see Jack Renner. His hair had begun to grow out, leaving him looking younger, a military recruit with a sheepish grin. "Hi."

My surprise must have shown. I hardly knew what to say. There was too much personal history with Jack, the down-and-dirty stuff I knew about my behavior towards him that had been blotted out in his accident. I cleared my throat.

He held up his hands and blurted, "Surprise," as if it might be a question.

I shook my head. "Oh, I wasn't expecting anyone. I was just on my way out and there you were." My words tumbled out in a rush, one on top of the other, like the words of a schoolgirl when she stumbles into the captain of the football team.

"I don't mean to interrupt."

"No, no," I said, feeling heat in my cheeks. "Don't be silly. Come in."

He came in and walked to the piano, taking a seat on the bench. I sat on the couch and folded my hands in my lap.

"I heard about Henry," he said. "I'm sorry." He paused. "He saved my life."

I nodded. According to the mail, apparently Henry had saved half of Charlottesville.

Jack swung around and faced the keyboard and began playing something I'd heard him play a dozen times. It was jazz. Or something Jack called jazzoid. It was a term I think he made up himself, meaning jazzlike music that he felt free to embellish with his own soul. His music always lifted me. I sat beside him on the bench and immediately flashed back to a day I'd love to forget.

He looked at me, smiled, and kept playing, letting his song rise and fall, doing the communicating for him. It was a happy tune, a frolicking melody with lots of little trills around the edges of the chords. "I've been thinking," he said, stopping suddenly by collapsing his hands with a crash on the keys.

"Thinking," he said slowly. "Of going to Jamaica."

"J-Jamaica?"

He looked at me and I felt my stomach tighten.

"W-why Jamaica?"

He shrugged. "White sand. Warm sun. Cool water. I've never been. A friend invited me once, but something came up." His eyes bore in on mine. "So I never went."

"Don't play games with me, Jack. Tell me what you remember."

"Everything," he said.

I looked down, ashamed. "Everything."

"Well I didn't exactly remember everything. To remember implies that there was a time when certain events were forgotten, or at least set aside."

"I don't understand."

"I remember our last piano lesson," he said. "There hasn't been a day when I haven't held your words in my heart."

"But you said you didn't remember."

"I said a lot of things. Stupid stuff. Stuff like not knowing my fiancée. I'd been trying for weeks to break up with Yolanda without knowing how. I didn't want to hurt her. Amnesia was a convenient way to drop her softly, without her feeling like I didn't love her."

"Why didn't you tell me that you remembered what I had done?"

"I didn't think it was too reasonable for me to remember that and not remember Yolanda."

I wanted to slap him. He must have seen it in my face. He held up his hands. "I'm not proud of what I did." He paused. "Perhaps it was the craziness that came with the head injury. Perhaps it was the zany idea that my fantasy of being with you could come true." He stood up, backed away, putting distance between us. "I'm ashamed, Wendi. What I did was wrong."

I started pacing. I hadn't anticipated this. I had confessed my unfaithfulness to God, but not to Jack, as I thought he had no memory of it. I started to speak twice, but both times the words lodged in my throat. I started again after clearing my throat.

"What is it, Wendi?"

"I was so wrong to treat you the way I did. I was a married woman. I owe you an apology. I should never have behaved the way I did."

He nodded. After an awkward silence, he spoke again. "You stopped coming to see me."

"I had to. Once I thought you knew nothing about my crazy proposal, I decided that God had given me another chance to get things right with Henry. Continuing to see you was too painful."

A smile teased at the corner of his mouth. "I saw you in church on Sunday." He chuckled. "But you weren't sitting in your normal spot."

"You noticed? I decided the back row wasn't the place for me anymore."

"What's happened?"

"Everything." I sat back down on the piano bench and clasped my hands in my lap. "For the longest time I acted my way through life, pretending to be a Christian, but never really believing. Everything that has happened to me, your accident, being suspected in a murder, almost being killed, losing my husband . . . well God used all of it to make me take a hard look at the fake life I was living. The bottom line," I said, "is that I've come to understand God's love for me just as I am. I don't have to pretend to be something I'm not." I held up my hands. "That's it." I squinted at him. "So is this why you came, to tell me you faked the whole amnesia thing?"

"Pretty much."

"Ugh!" I said, covering my face. "And all along, I thought my disgraceful behavior was only known to me."

He laughed at me.

I smiled in return. Getting my secret out in the air felt better than I'd thought.

"Now that I'm on my feet again, shall we resume your piano lessons?"

Now I laughed. "I don't think so, Jack. I think we both know I'm hopeless in that area."

He shuffled his feet. "I, well, I'd like to grab a Starbucks with you sometime."

I looked at his face. That perfect face with the perfect smile. "Jack, I—" I halted. "I can't."

His smile faded.

"I've got another new relationship I need to work on just now," I said, picking up a leather-bound book from the coffee table.

His eyes lit up before he nodded in understanding, perhaps with a little regret. "I'd better go."

I walked him to the door. He was halfway to his car when I called after him. "Jack."

He turned.

"Are you up for any landscaping jobs yet?" I hesitated as he shrugged. "I want you to move those golden willows. They're going to block my view of that steeple soon, and I won't have that."

He smiled with me. "I'll check my calendar."

All I'll Ever Need

Harry Kraus, MD,
Bestselling Author of
Could I Have This Dance?

The grueling past months finally seem
about to blossom into a happy future
together for Dr. Claire McCall and her
fiancé, John Cerelli. But their wedding
plans are interrupted by circumstances
so devastating they threaten everything Claire holds dear: her
medical career, her relationship with John, and quite possibly
her freedom.

Working through the turmoil caused by a near rape, Claire
has sought a counselor to help her untangle her emotions.
What the counselor uncovers is shattering, but things are about
to get worse. The man who assaulted her escapes from jail—and
then, to top it off, Claire is accused of euthanizing a terminally
ill patient.

But the next death is the one that could shake Claire's world
to its foundation.

How can so much be happening so fast—unless someone is
choreographing this lethal nightmare? In this exciting sequel to
Could I Have This Dance? and *For the Rest of My Life*, nothing
may be as it seems. Not the present. And not the past.

Softcover: 978-0-310-27283-0

Pick up a copy today at your favorite bookstore!

Could I Have This Dance?

Harry Kraus, M D

You can't dance this dance unless it's in your blood. Claire McCall is praying it's not in hers.

Claire McCall is used to fighting back against the odds. Hard work, aptitude, and sheer determination have helped her rise from adverse circumstances to an internship in one of the nation's most competitive surgical residencies. But talent and tenacity mean nothing in the face of the discovery that is about to rock her world.

It's called the "Stoney Creek Curse" by folks in the small mountain town where Claire grew up. Behind the superstition lies a reality that could destroy her career. But getting to the truth is far from easy in a community with secrets to hide. As a web of relationships becomes increasingly tangled, two things become apparent. One is that more than one person doesn't want Claire to probe too deeply into the "Stoney Creek Curse." The other is that someone has reasons other than the curse for wanting Claire out of the picture permanently.

Somewhere in the course of pursuing her career as a surgeon, Claire lost touch with the God who called her to it. Now she realizes how desperately she needs him. But can she reclaim a faith strong enough to see her through this deadly dance of circumstances?

Softcover: 978-0-310-24089-1

Pick up a copy today at your favorite bookstore!

For the Rest of My Life

Harry Kraus, M D

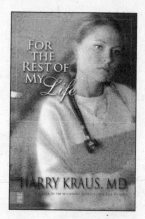

The riveting, emotional sequel to the best-selling *Could I Have This Dance?*

Claire McCall, MD, is haunted by the question: Does she have the gene for Huntington's Disease, the disease that disabled her father? This exciting sequel picks up with Claire moving back to Stoney Creek to work as a family physician and help her mother care for her disabled father. She rekindles her relationship with John Cerelli and—just before she's going to find out if she carries the HD gene—discovers an engagement ring hidden in his car. When John fails to "pop the question" before learning the results of the test, Claire believes he is only interested in marrying her if she does not have the HD gene. She runs away from him without learning the results of the test, or the strength of his love.

Claire copes with her romantic disappointment by plunging into her work. But a brutal rapist attacks three of Claire's patients, just as each young woman is recovering from a recent accident or surgery. When Claire has surgery for appendicitis, she herself is attacked. Only her trust in God can keep Claire safe.

Softcover: 978-0-310-24978-8

Pick up a copy today at your favorite bookstore!

Share Your Thoughts

With the Author: Your comments will be forwarded to
the author when you send them to *zauthor@zondervan.com*.

With Zondervan: Submit your review of this book
by writing to *zreview@zondervan.com*.

Free Online Resources at
www.zondervan.com/hello

 Zondervan AuthorTracker: Be notified whenever your favorite authors publish new books, go on tour, or post an update about what's happening in their lives.

 Daily Bible Verses and Devotions: Enrich your life with daily Bible verses or devotions that help you start every morning focused on God.

 Free Email Publications: Sign up for newsletters on fiction, Christian living, church ministry, parenting, and more.

 Zondervan Bible Search: Find and compare Bible passages in a variety of translations at www.zondervanbiblesearch.com.

 Other Benefits: Register yourself to receive online benefits like coupons and special offers, or to participate in research.